The Fire at Netherfield Park

by

Renata McMann

&

Summer Hanford

Cover photo by Mark McCullough
Cover by Summer Hanford

ISBN-13: 978-1532789267
ISBN-10: 1532789262

Dear Reader,

After enjoying our story, consider signing up for our mailing list, where you will have the opportunity for free gifts, information about new releases and in person events, and more. Join us by visiting **www.renatamcmann.com/news/**

Acknowledgments

With special thanks to our editor, Joanne Girard

"Renata McMann" and Summer Hanford met in an online course at AllWriters.org. Both feel that working with Kathie Giorgio and Michael Giorgio considerably improved their writing skills. Thus, we give a long overdue dedication to AllWriters' Workplace & Workshop, LLC. at **www.allwritersworkshop.com**.

By Renata McMann and Summer Hanford

After Anne
Their Secret Love
*A Duel in Meryton**
Love, Letters and Lies
The Long Road to Longbourn
*Hypothetically Married**
The Forgiving Season
The Widow Elizabeth
Foiled Elopement
Believing in Darcy
Her Final Wish
Miss Bingley's Christmas
Epiphany with Tea
Courting Elizabeth
The Fire at Netherfield Park
*From Ashes to Heiresses**
Entanglements of Honor
Lady Catherine Regrets
A Death at Rosings
Mary Younge
Poor Mr. Darcy
Mr. Collins' Deception
The Scandalous Stepmother
Caroline and the Footman
Elizabeth's Plight (The Wickham Coin Book II)
Georgiana's Folly (The Wickham Coin Book I)
The Second Mrs. Darcy

*available as an audio book

Collections:

***A Dollop of Pride and a Dash of Prejudice*:**
Includes from above: *Their Secret Love*, *Miss Bingley's Christmas*, *Epiphany with Tea* and *From Ashes to Heiresses.*

***Pride and Prejudice Villains Revisited – Redeemed – Reimagined A Collection of Six Short Stories*.**
Includes from above: *Lady Catherine Regrets*, *Mary Younge*, *Mr. Collins' Deception* and *Caroline and the Footman,* along with two the additional flash fiction pieces, *Mrs. Bennet's Triumph* and *Wickham's Journal.*

Georgiana's Folly & Elizabeth's Plight: Wickham Coin Series, Volumes I & II
Includes from above: *Elizabeth's Plight* and *Georgiana's Folly.*

Other Pride and Prejudice variations by Renata McMann

Heiress to Longbourn
Pemberley Weddings
The Inconsistency of Caroline Bingley
Three Daughters Married
Anne de Bourgh Manages
The above five works are collected in the book:
Five Pride and Prejudice Variations

Also by Renata McMann

Journey Towards a Preordained Time

Books by Renata McMann writing as Teresa McCullough

Enhancer Novels: Stand-alone novels in the same universe

Enhancers Campaign
The First Enhancer
The Pirates of Fainting Goat Island
The Enhancer with Meg Baxter

Bengt/Tian stories:

The Secret of Sanctua A Bengt/Tian novel
Kidnapped by Fae: a Bengt/Tian Short Story

Other stories:

The Slave of Duty with Meg Baxter
Lost Past

Thrice Born Series by Summer Hanford

Thrice Born Novels

Gift of the Aluien
Hawks of Sorga
Throne of Wheylia
The Plains of Tybrunn
Shores of K'Orge

Songs of Rebellion Series

Ballad of Discord

Under the Shadow of the Marquess Series

*The Archaeologist's Daughter**
*The Duke's Widow**
The False Lady

Ladies Always Shoot First Half Hour Reads Series*

Captured by a Duke
To Save a Lord
One Shot for a Gentleman
Anything for a Lord

A Lord's Kiss Half Hour Reads Series*

Last Chance for a Lord
To Know a Lord's Kiss
A Lord's Dream
Deceived by a Lord

Installments in Scarsdale Publishing's Marriage Maker Series

One Good Gentleman
My Lady of Danger
Rake Ruiner
Dreaming of a Gentleman
My Lady, My Siren
The Runaway Baroness
His Imaginary Courtship

The Fire at Netherfield Park

Chapter One

~ Fire ~

Sally Smith

Her second day working at Netherfield Park found Sally Smith peeking through the thick panes, straining to see Mr. Bingley's guests arriving. Mrs. Nicholls, the head cook, had permitted Sally this singular indulgence, allowing her to leave the kitchen for a short time. Sally was both frightened and excited to be working at Netherfield Park. She was frightened because she worried over making a mistake and being sent home. She was excited because Mr. Bingley, whom she hadn't yet seen in her short time in his employ, was holding a ball.

Sally strained upward on her tiptoes, peering through the top of the glass, where it was thinner. There wasn't as much to see as she could wish, for the women had cloaks covering their ball gowns. Still, their hair was splendid; gloriously curled and topped with feathers, gems and ribbons. For their part, the gentlemen were ever so gallant looking. They had on capes and grand hats, and some carried walking sticks. Sally wished most to see Mr. Darcy. She'd overheard some of the older girls whispering about his excessive handsomeness. She supposed he wouldn't be arriving by carriage, though, residing in Netherfield as he was.

The display of carriages was as grand as the gentlemen and ladies. As she watched, there was a line of six discharging their occupants. Sally had never seen so many carriages lined up at once. It seemed every time the line got shorter, another arrived. After discharging their passengers, the carriages trundled away. She knew they were off to Meryton, or even the homes of the owners, since there was no point in waiting at Netherfield. The ball, Mrs. Nicholls had said, would last well into the small hours of the morning. She'd also said Sally might be allowed to go to sleep before it ended, but she was too excited to sleep.

"Sally?" a voice said behind her. "You're to go back to the kitchen now."

Dropping her heels to the floor, Sally turned. It was one of the other new girls, Jenny Parks. Mr. Bingley had requested the staff be increased, and not simply for the ball. Rumor said he wished to stay in the area because someone had caught his fancy. Wagers were being made, of course. Sally knew her brother had put a ha'penny on Miss Jane Bennet. She privately agreed. She'd never seen Miss Bennet, but everyone knew she was the loveliest miss in all of Hertfordshire.

"Do you remember your way?" Jenny asked.

"Course I do," Sally said, a touch offended. "It's not that big a house."

"Good, because Mrs. Nicholls said I may stay a bit and watch for a turn. She said you're to report to the undercook."

Sally cast one last look through the pane before hurrying away. She didn't want to be known for being idle. Maybe, if she worked diligently enough, they would permit her a peek into the ballroom. What splendid things she should see then.

When she reached the kitchen, Mrs. Nicholls was busily stirring a sauce, her wide red face serene. The undercook put Sally to work chopping vegetables. Sally handled the knife with care, aware it was far better and sharper than the one she used at home. She smiled as she chopped, knowing they'd sent for her because she'd demonstrated her skill the previous day. Sally had been doing the cooking in her cottage since her mother died more than a year ago. Mrs. Nicholls would never let Jenny Parks use such a fine knife.

Sally's smile disappeared, her wariness of mistakes returning. Her skills weren't needed at home any longer. Not since her father remarried, getting two new sons in the bargain. Her father's new wife was a much better cook and housekeeper than Sally, no matter how much she tried, and her brothers were better workers in the fields. Father had made it plain he couldn't afford an idle girl. If Sally didn't keep her place at Netherfield Park, she would have to work in the mill. The mill terrified her. She'd heard, and sometimes seen evidence of, the horrible things that happened there. If she could marry, she would have a place again, but she was only twelve. It would be years before she could be a wife. She would be a good worker for Mrs. Nicholls, though, so she would be able to stay in Netherfield Park until she was old enough to marry.

A shriek cut through Sally's musing and she nearly nicked her fingers. Turning, she saw Mrs. Nicholls bearing down on her, arms flung out wide. Sally's mouth gaped open in surprise. Mrs. Nicholls was usually so calm.

"We can put it out," someone called from deeper in the kitchen.

"Sally, get outside. Out the kitchen door. Now," Mrs. Nicholls yelled, waving her arms in a shooing gesture.

"Out?" Sally stumbled back from Mrs. Nicholls' mad charge.

"Run home, girl! Go!"

Sally dropped the knife. Turning, she scrambled across the room to the garden door and yanked it open. Shoving it closed with all her might, she ran home, crying all the way. What had she done to excite their anger?

Elizabeth

Elizabeth arrived at Netherfield Park with little eye for the splendor. Her gaze searched the room instead for Mr. Wickham, for what good was such a lavish affair if she hadn't anyone with whom to banter? With Mr. Wickham, she could expound on Miss Bingley's selection of draperies, or hear his opinion of their host's choice of punch. The topic mattered little, for Mr. Wickham was sure to make any detail into entertainment for them both.

By the time the first dance was beginning, she still hadn't seen him. Adding to her annoyance, she was engaged to stand up with her cousin, Mr. Collins, for the first two dances. Mr. Collins made no secret of his reason for being in Hertfordshire. Her father's estate was entailed to him and he'd come to visit in an odd attempt to atone for the entailment by marrying one of her father's five daughters. To Elizabeth's dismay, it was obvious he'd decided on her. She wished she could let him know there was no way she would marry him. She didn't understand how he could be so oblivious to her lack of interest, though she'd quickly grasped understanding his fellow man was not Mr. Collins' strength.

Mr. Collins, apparently summoned by her thoughts, appeared along with the music. Elizabeth tried to put on a good face, but her cousin's dancing mirrored his social interaction. He danced poorly, yet thought he danced well. He strove to please, but only succeeded in calling attention to himself and offending. The entire experience, including his attempts to converse, was as awkward and unpleasant as Elizabeth had dreaded. The moment of her release from him was ecstasy.

She danced next with an officer, and had the refreshment of

talking of Wickham, and of hearing that he was universally liked. When those dances were over, she returned to Charlotte Lucas, and was in conversation with her, when she found herself suddenly addressed by Mr. Darcy who took her so much by surprise in his application for her hand, that, without knowing what she did, she accepted him. He walked away again immediately.

Elizabeth turned from Mr. Darcy's retreating form to regard Charlotte with wide eyes. "What have I done?"

"I can hardly say, or account for it," Charlotte said. "You seem to have agreed to stand up with Mr. Darcy."

"That is how it seemed to me as well," Elizabeth said. She smiled, though little amused. "First I must cater to my odious cousin, and now to a man who abhors me. Where will it end?"

"Oh, Lizzy, I daresay you make it out to be worse than it is."

"I assure you I do not," Elizabeth said. "I would rather stay beside you than dance with either gentleman. You cannot convince me you would accept them."

"I confess I would accept any man here," Charlotte said. "Some of us have not the luxuries of youth and comeliness you have."

Elizabeth, realizing she'd plunged into a source of discontent, turned the topic away. They talked pleasantly thereafter until Mr. Darcy appeared to collect her.

"Miss Elizabeth, Miss Lucas," Mr. Darcy greeted with a slight bow. Straightening, he held out his hand to Elizabeth.

Her face composed, Elizabeth placed her fingers lightly in his. She was surprised at the strength and warmth of his hand, discernable even through their gloves. She'd expected Mr. Darcy to have hands as cold as his demeanor. She glanced back once as he escorted her to their position, surprised to see a flicker of envy on Charlotte's face.

The music started and Elizabeth turned her attention to the dance. For all his reluctance to display his skills in the past, she was forced to admit Mr. Darcy kept a fine step. He seemed disinclined to friendly discourse, however, and she wondered again that he'd pursued standing up with her. It was painfully obvious he took no pleasure in her company, nor could she in his.

As his silence drew out, Elizabeth permitted her gaze to wander the room. Finally, it alighted on Mr. Wickham, likely newly arrived, who was dancing with her youngest sister, Lydia. Mr. Darcy must have seen Elizabeth's smile, for, at the turn, he followed the direction of her gaze. His expression firmed into the one of displeasure he wore so well.

Mr. Darcy's dislike of seeing Mr. Wickham could not have been plainer. Knowing how infamously he'd treated Mr. Wickham, as Wickham himself had informed her, Elizabeth felt Mr. Darcy's reaction to be dreadfully unfair. What right did Mr. Darcy have to scowl at a man he'd injured? How dare he act as the wounded party when he was the one who'd denied Mr. Wickham the living meant for him?

Unable to quell her anger, Elizabeth said, "When you met us there the other day, we had just been forming a new acquaintance." She directed her gaze to Mr. Wickham as she spoke, hoping to wound Mr. Darcy's conscience, assuming he had one.

The effect was immediate. A deeper shade of hauteur overspread his features, but he said not a word, and Elizabeth, though blaming herself for her own weakness, could not go on. At length Darcy spoke, and in a constrained manner said, "Mr. Wickham is blessed with such happy manners as may ensure his making friends—whether he may be equally capable of retaining them, is less certain."

Elizabeth opened her mouth, defense of Mr. Wickham on her lips, but Mr. Darcy halted in his steps. Before she could quite grasp his defection, her feet carried her several paces away. Seeing Mr. Darcy looking about the ballroom, Elizabeth hurried back to his side.

This time, her retort was halted by the concern on his face. He looked upward, seeming to scrutinize the ceiling. Other's had stopped dancing as well, impeded by the obstruction she and Mr. Darcy made.

"What are you doing?" Elizabeth kept her voice low, though there was no hope of not making a spectacle now.

He took her hand, drawing a gasp from her and several onlookers, and led her almost forcibly to Mr. Wickham. Elizabeth looked between the two men, wondering what sort of confrontation Mr. Darcy was planning. Mr. Wickham eyed Mr. Darcy with what Elizabeth felt to be excessive trepidation, Lydia glaring at his side.

"Whistle," Mr. Darcy said to Mr. Wickham with some urgency. "Now."

Surprise flickered across Mr. Wickham's face but he pulled off his gloves. Handing them to Mr. Darcy, Mr. Wickham put his fingers to his lips and whistled. It was the loudest whistle Elizabeth had ever heard. Beside him, Lydia put her hands over her ears.

"I hope you know what you're about," Mr. Wickham said to Mr.

Darcy.

"I hope so, too," Mr. Darcy said quietly.

Elizabeth looked between the two in confusion. Mr. Darcy's behavior was strange, but Mr. Wickham's was at least as much so. After what Mr. Darcy had done to him, why would Mr. Wickham trust Mr. Darcy when asked to call attention to himself in this rude way? People near them were staring, but much of the room hadn't yet noticed their odd display. Mr. Wickham whistled twice more without prompting. Lydia winced at each shrill note.

Now, everyone seemed to be staring at them. Belatedly, Elizabeth realized Mr. Darcy still held her hand in his. He let go at the same moment she pulled away.

Mr. Darcy cupped his hands around his mouth. "Everyone please go outside," he shouted. "There appears to be a fire. Do not stop for your cloaks. If the fire is nothing, you can come back for them."

The room was a sea of startled eyes.

"Now," Mr. Darcy roared.

Wickham whistled again, gesturing toward the entrance hall. People started moving, but their pace was slow and accompanied by speculation. Elizabeth could hear a range of sentiments, from twittering laughter to mild annoyance. Looking up, she took in the layer of smoke accumulating against the high ceiling.

"Lydia, you should get Mother and the others and leave," she said.

"But what if something interesting happens? I want to see it."

"Enough to risk being caught in a fire? Don't be silly."

Lydia rolled her eyes. "I'll get Kitty. I know where she is. I daresay Mary and Jane already left. They always do as they're told."

Elizabeth nodded, taking her sister by the shoulders and giving her a push to get her started. She noticed Lydia looked back, her gaze lingering on Mr. Wickham. Mr. Bingley came hurrying past her sister then, charging up to Mr. Darcy.

"Is this necessary? It could be a smoky chimney," Mr. Bingley demanded of Mr. Darcy before glancing at Elizabeth. "Miss Elizabeth," he said, adding a distracted bow to his greeting.

"I hope it is only a chimney, and then you may have a laugh at my expense," Mr. Darcy said. "I'll go upstairs to warn the servants there. Try to get everyone outside." He looked to Mr. Wickham when he said the last.

Mr. Wickham nodded. Turning away, he began calling for people to leave, all but herding them toward the door.

"I'll check the kitchen. The smoke seems to be coming from that direction," Bingley said, leaving as quickly as he'd come.

Mr. Darcy turned to face her. To Elizabeth's surprise, he recaptured her hand, pressing it for a moment. She was too stunned to pull away, and he released her almost immediately. "I'm relying on you to set a good example by going directly outside. In spite of what I said, I expect a mob in the cloak room."

He looked at her with an intensity that struck her as odd. She nodded, deciding to follow his order.

Jane

Jane Bennet was dancing with her cousin, Mr. Collins, when a piercing whistle cut across the room. She halted in the steps, turning in the direction of the sound. She was aware of Mr. Collins beside her, babbling questions or apologies, she didn't know which, as two more whistles cut through the ballroom. Through the crowd, Jane could see Mr. Darcy standing with her sister Lizzy, holding her hand no less, and with Lydia and Mr. Wickham. She realized it was Mr. Wickham doing the whistling.

Mr. Darcy let go of Lizzy's hand, cupping his to his mouth. "Everyone please go outside," he shouted. "There appears to be a fire. Do not stop for your cloaks. If the fire is nothing, you can come back for them."

The room filled with whispers.

"Now," Mr. Darcy roared.

With a startled yelp, Mr. Collins left her side, running toward the door. Jane watched him for a moment before turning back to see Lizzy push Lydia off in the same direction. She knew she should leave as well, but she remained rooted where she stood by a French door. She simply couldn't leave until she knew Mr. Bingley was safe. Her eyes roamed the room. All she wanted was to be sure he—

Mr. Bingley hurried up to Mr. Darcy and Lizzy. Jane let out her breath. He appeared unharmed, but agitated. Well, he would be, of course, as his home was afire. She started toward them, but Mr. Bingley left Mr. Darcy and Lizzy, heading toward the kitchen.

Jane gathered her skirts a bit higher, changing course to follow him. She pushed through people going the other way. Whatever was Mr. Bingley thinking, heading away from the exits? Now that Mr.

Darcy had pointed it out, she was keenly aware of the smell of smoke. The prudent thing would be to leave. She would have to catch up to Mr. Bingley and inform him so.

She reached the doorway he'd exited the ballroom through, finding the smoke much denser there, a state emphasized by the lower ceiling. Of all the brave things to do, Mr. Bingley was going toward the source of the fire. Likely, he wished to contain it. Well, she couldn't let him go alone. What if he sustained an injury? She hurried after him, though she'd lost sight of him now, her pace quickening.

Jane turned a corner to find Mr. Bingley in the act of opening a door. Black smoke billowed out, seeming almost to have a physical force as it slammed into him. She screamed, something she hadn't done since she was a small girl. Rushing forward, she could hardly see him, but she could hear his coughing and sputtering, and feel heat pouring out in the smoke's wake.

"Get down," she cried. "Oh, Mr. Bingley, do get down."

"Miss Bennet," he called, coughing.

Jane reached out her arms, feeling for him in the smoke. He was a dense blur in her already swimming vision. She grabbed his arm, yanking him toward the floor. "Please, Mr. Bingley, we must get down," she repeated, toppling him toward her.

He let out a muffled exclamation as they both fell, splaying out his arms to catch himself, so as not to crush her. In spite of his efforts, they still landed in a heap of limbs. He made to jump up, but she caught his arm.

"The air is clearer down here," she said. "We must crawl if we're to make it."

His eyes darted around, lingering longest on her. "I daresay you're correct, Miss Bennet." He quickly, but with care, untangled himself from her.

Fighting not to blush, Jane pulled up her heavy skirt and tied it into a knot above her knees, knowing she couldn't crawl with it in the way. When she was finished, she raised her eyes to find Mr. Bingley's face suffused with red. She didn't think it was due entirely to the smoke billowing around them. "I can't crawl otherwise."

He nodded. "Given the circumstance . . ." His eyes went to her bundled skirt and he coughed. "That is, I believe I should precede you, as ungallant as it seems."

Jane's heart fluttered, making it even more difficult to breath. She realized she and Mr. Bingley were completely alone. She couldn't concentrate on the smoke, or the crackling heat she could feel advancing on them. All she could think of was the gaping sense of loss that had shot threw her when he'd opened the kitchen door and been engulfed in smoke. She tilted up her chin, something she'd seen Lizzy do often enough. "No," she said. "We will go side by side." And they did.

Darcy

Darcy stood for a moment, watching Elizabeth walk away. He was pleased to see her disappear from view in the direction of the entrance hall. Spurring himself into motion, he made his way toward the staircase, taking in the people still milling about. He shook his head at their lack of haste, glancing up at the ever-thickening smoke. Wickham, to his credit, had managed to get a great number of Bingley's guests to leave, but now he was nowhere to be seen. He'd probably made a hasty retreat, taking himself away from danger.

Darcy took the stairs two at a time, wishing Netherfield were smaller. Reaching the top, long strides carried him down the hall. "Fire," he called as he went, loudly but calmly. Inspiring panic would do no good. Clear heads were needed.

The smoke was thicker above stairs, scorching his throat. As he yelled, several doors opened. From one spilled a maid he recognized as Mrs. Hursts', and from another stepped a young woman he guessed was Miss Bingley's. Both took in the smoke with wide eyes. To their credit, neither seemed inclined toward histrionics.

"Is there time to save Miss Bingley's wardrobe?" the younger maid asked.

"No," Darcy said, striding toward them. "Retrieve her jewelry, if you can." He looked to Mrs. Hursts' maid. "Mrs. Hursts' jewelry as well, so long as it takes no more than a few moments. If the fire is severe, you must make haste outside. If it is not, the other items will be awaiting our return."

Both women disappeared back into the rooms from which they'd come.

As Darcy neared the next set of doors, one his own, his valet stepped out, his arms laden. "I have your wallet, sir, watch case and business correspondences. Shall I deposit them outside and return for Miss Darcy's letters and anything else you may need?"

"No. Just get out."

"Yes, sir."

"Are many of the staff above stairs?" Darcy asked before his valet could hurry away.

"I imagine so, sir."

"Thank you," Darcy said, moving past the man to knock on the next door, realizing the risk his voice wouldn't be heard. He'd thought most of the servants would be occupied with the ball, but now realized his error. His were not, after all, so why had he assumed others would be? The door before him opened to reveal a maid. He sent her out, returning to calling out fire as he strode down the hall to the next room.

Once again cursing the size of the place, Darcy took in the rapidly increasing smoke and began unceremoniously flinging open doors. Most of the rooms proved empty, but the smoke was thick enough now that he didn't dare leave any unchecked. Anyone who didn't leave soon may not be able to.

Two more doors down he found a maid sleeping on a bed, atop the linens. She woke with a cry when he entered the room.

"Quickly, get out," he said, gesturing toward the hall. "There's a fire."

"I'm so sorry, sir." She scurried to her feet. "I only shut my eyes a moment. It won't happen again, sir. Please don't tell Miss Bingley."

"I'm not concerned with your nap. Did you not hear me? There's a fire. Go outside."

"Yes, sir. Thank you, sir."

Darcy's cries rousted three more servants as he made his way down the hall, and he found another behind closed door, disregarding the commotion he was endeavoring to make. He reached the end of the hall and peered up the narrow servants' stairs. The smoke was thicker than ever, making breathing difficult. Still, he knew he had to risk the climb. Anyone abandoned in the house would be on his conscience.

He was about to head up when a commotion above warned him back. To his astonishment, Wickham came clattering down the steps. He carried a coughing girl, who looked to be about fifteen. His eyes were red and watering from the smoke, his breath coming in ragged gasps.

"Darcy, what the devil are you doing here? The place is coming down."

"Clearing the house," Darcy said. Wickham shot him a quick grin, and Darcy knew his surprise at seeing the other man must be evident on his face.

"Above here is clear, but we'll have to take the other staircase down. This set's likely impassable below. Is this floor clear?" Wickham dissolved into a fit of coughing almost as severe as what racked the girl he carried.

"Yes, this floor is clear, unless someone is hiding." Darcy held out his arms. "I can take her. How long have you been carrying her?"

"From the attic," Wickham gasped out between coughs, handing the girl over. "I only need to catch my breath."

"Catch it as we move."

Wickham slouched against the wall, smoke induced tears streaming down his face. He waved Darcy away. "I'm half a pace behind you. Take her out while she can still breathe."

Darcy hesitated. Wickham should be fit enough to make his own way out. Darcy had little help to offer, regardless, if he planned to save the smoke-choked form he carried. "Wickham—"

"Go. Egad, you don't have to save me, Darcy." Wickham coughed again, but less violently. He pushed himself off the wall. "I'm on my feet."

Nodding, Darcy turned away. He headed toward the far staircase, hearing Wickham a few paces behind. It took Darcy until they reached the stairs, fighting smoke as they went, to conquer his surprise. Who would have thought, of all people, George Wickham would act heroically? Then again, he'd always been brave, when he wasn't being selfish.

Wickham caught up with Darcy at the top of the stairs. Heat and smoke billowed up, and swirled darkly below. The way appeared barely passable.

Darcy looked at the swooning girl in his arms. "She can't take much more smoke," Darcy said. "Go first and make sure there's a way out that way. Otherwise, we'll have to attempt the servants' stairs."

"I've been on them. I told you, it's bad there too." Wickham peered down. "I think this way will be more passable. Follow a bit behind me. I'll turn round if it seems we won't be able to make it. We can always climb out a bedroom window."

Darcy nodded, though he wasn't sure they could. Not with the girl. Maybe they could use bedsheets to lower her. Hopefully, they wouldn't need to find out. After waiting a few moments, he plunged down the steps.

"What are you doing?" Darcy heard Wickham say and halted. Had he misunderstood their plan?

"I must retrieve my jewelry," a woman's voice said. Darcy recognized it as Caroline Bingley's.

"This place is a deathtrap." Wickham ended his sentence with a cough.

"Unhand me. I must reach my chambers."

Darcy started down. He could assure Miss Bingley it was likely her maid had already secured her property.

"Jewelry won't do you any good if you're dead," Wickham said, his tone exasperated.

Darcy rounded the landing to the sight of Wickham hoisting Miss Bingley from her feet. She struggled, but Wickham flung her over his shoulder, hastening down the remaining steps. Darcy made up the distance between them quickly, for his burden was lighter and not struggling, in fact barely conscious. Miss Bingley turned her head at his approach, spying him from where she unceremoniously hung, Wickham's hands clamped somewhere in the general area of her posterior. Her face blanched with mortification as she met Darcy's eyes. She quickly looked away.

It took a great portion of Darcy's will not to allow his amusement at her predicament to show. He decided she'd be reunited with her maid soon enough to hear news of her jewelry. It would only further humiliate her if he spoke to her now. Together, Darcy and Wickham hurried from the burning manor, both keeping a firm hold on their burdens.

Mary

Mary Bennet saw her father as soon as she emerged. She hurried toward him, pleased she was the first to find him. He would see how well she conducted herself, and that she was the smartest, being the first to leave a burning building, as any reasonable person would.

"Papa," she greeted, hoping he would praise her.

"Mary."

He didn't even look at her. His eyes were on the door. He did mutter, "That's one," but she hardly counted that as praise. Mary sighed, rubbing her arms against the cold. No matter how hard she tried to behave with every aspect of correctness, Papa never seemed to care.

The night was dark, and chilly, and the heavy mist of earlier had condensed into a light drizzle. She could feel the curls she'd labored hours for incrementally flattening. Not that anyone would notice. No one ever complemented her hair. Not the way they did her sisters. Mary sighed again, hugging herself not only for warmth.

She looked up at her father, wondering if he even noticed she was cold. If Elizabeth or Jane were there, Mary was sure he would have thought to offer his coat. If Mama or Lydia were there, they would demand Papa's coat. Mary pressed her lips into a thin line. She wouldn't descend to unbecoming brashness, not even to be warm.

Following her father's gaze, Mary took in the steady stream of people exiting the manor. Where could her mother and sisters be? It wasn't like Lizzy and Jane not to do as Mr. Darcy said. They, and Lydia, had been dancing when Mr. Darcy ordered everyone to leave. Kitty, she recalled, was near the punch, talking with two officers. Mary had secured herself a seat along the wall, not too near her mother, so she could observe the evening without enduring her mother's endless comments.

Long moments went by, smoke and people spilling out. She began to shiver, well soaked now, and reconsidered her resolve not to ask her father for his coat. Her father shook his head, almost as if he could hear her thoughts.

"We must look for your mother and sisters," he said, turning to her. "Mary, I'm asking you to go around the house north. I shall go south."

"Yes, Papa," she said immediately, to show what a mannerly daughter she was.

"Good. I will meet you behind the house. We'll cross ways and return here."

"Yes, Papa."

She made her way around the building, though walking through the garden soaked her hem even more thoroughly. At least moving warmed her. She increased her pace, feeling oddly alone even though she could hear people both in front of and behind the manor. Ahead, around the next corner, she could see flickering light.

Mary rounded the manor to find the back side flickering with flames. Eyes wide, she skirted the fire-filled window embrasures and the glass scattered on the ground. She was so entranced by the horrible sight of Netherfield in flames, she nearly ran into the two coughing figures stumbling through the garden, arms about each other.

"I beg—" Mary stopped, shocked. "Jane? Mr. Bingley?"

"Mary," Jane cried, pulling away from Mr. Bingley to hug her. "I'm so glad you're safe." She let Mary go and fell to coughing again.

Jane's skirts were a rumpled mess and she was soot-streaked, as if she'd walked right through the fire. Mr. Bingley looked hardly better. He coughed as well, his eyes red and teary.

"Miss Mary," Mr. Bingley said, bowing.

He looked slightly abashed. At least he had the sense to realize, fire or no, he and Jane shouldn't be alone and . . . touching. Mary frowned at them.

"Where are the others?" Jane asked, her voice ragged. "Is everyone well?"

"Papa and I met near the carriage steps. We've split up to go around the building, looking for everyone. You're the first I've found." She leaned closer, lowering her voice. "Jane, you shouldn't be out here alone with Mr. Bingley. What if someone sees you?"

Jane blinked several times, looking confused. She cast a glance at Mr. Bingley, his face revealing guilt now. "But, we weren't . . . that is, we were escaping the fire."

"I know that." Mary tried to make her tone soothing, though she was exasperated with Jane's lack of thought. "I'm simply pointing out how it must appear."

"Yes, well, we're headed to join the others," Mr. Bingley said. "Immediately. I must take charge."

Mary looked toward the stable and other outbuildings. She hadn't gone a full halfway around. Should she keep on to find their father, or escort Jane and Mr. Bingley back? She scrutinized them, taking in Jane's rumpled state and weighing it against her unfailing goodness.

"I must keep going, to meet Papa," she said. After all, it was Jane, who never did a thing wrong, and Mr. Bingley, a kind gentleman. Moreover, she didn't want Papa waiting for her and worrying. "You will go out front?"

"We were making our way there," Mr. Bingley said.

"Will you be well alone?" Jane asked.

Better than you'll be in the company of a gentleman you don't even have an understanding with, Mary thought. "I will. I'll meet Papa soon. I don't wish for him to grow worried."

Jane nodded, smiling at her.

Mr. Bingley bowed again. "Miss Mary."

"I'll see you shortly," Mary said, hurrying away.

She didn't find any more of her siblings, or her mama, but her father soon came into view.

"Any news to report, my dear?" Papa asked.

Mary smiled, pleased he'd used an endearment. "I found Jane and Mr. Bingley," she said, trying to keep her teeth from chattering. Stopping to talk with Jane and Mr. Bingley had chilled her. "They were together."

Her father raised his eyebrows at that, but didn't comment. He looked at her, his eyes kind, and took off his coat, finally seeming to see her and realize she was cold in her wet dress. "And I have located Elizabeth. She is in the stable organizing people and carriages. I didn't interrupt, for there were other places to search and she had things well in hand."

Of course she did, Mary thought. Elizabeth always did well and was complemented for it. If Mary tried to tell people what they should be doing, she would be ignored or laughed at. "What about Mama, Kitty and Lydia?" she asked, putting on his coat.

Papa shook his head. "We'll both go back around. People were still coming out the front. I'm sure they're there by now."

He said it calmly. She hoped it was true. "Yes, Papa," she said, and hurried off again.

Lydia

Lydia didn't find Kitty where she expected, and quickly concluded her sister had already fled. It wouldn't be like Kitty to stay in a smoky house, after all. It would surely set her to coughing excessively. Then, none of the officers would want to dance with her anymore. Most of the officers who danced with Lydia would dance with Kitty, if Lydia was unavailable. Some even preferred Kitty, although everyone knew Lydia was far prettier and more fun.

Realizing people were headed to retrieve their cloaks, Lydia quickened her step, weaving between them. She wouldn't be one of those who had to leave their cloak behind to be burned up. Let someone too slow or too stupid to fetch theirs suffer that fate.

She beat nearly everyone else, which made sense as she had wonderfully long legs and was young, but there were no servants there to fetch out her cloak for her. Lydia pouted for a moment, but there was no use pouting when no one was there to be swayed by it. Besides, people were pressing in behind her. She started tossing cloaks aside, seeking hers. Being red, it was easy enough to locate. Snatching it up, she pushed her way back toward the exit.

When she reached the bottom of the marble staircase, someone bumped into her, all but throwing her against the newel. She crashed into it with enough force she was sure she'd be bruised.

"I beg your pardon," she said, her tone nowhere near as pleasant as her words.

She rubbed her hip, turning to glare at the retreating form of her assailant. She quickly recognized him as her cousin, that odious Mr. Collins. He didn't even stop or turn around. Lydia was tempted to go after him. He hadn't gone far, after all but running her down. The mob outside the cloak room was dense now. He wasn't slender like she was, able to weave through a crowd.

She rubbed at her eyes, realizing the thickening smoke was making them water. She would deal with Mr. Collins later, in scorching terms. Right now, it seemed to her maybe it was time to leave Netherfield.

Looking about as she went, Lydia saw many people moving toward the grand entrance hall with her, but none of them were in her family. "Trust them all to hurry off and leave me behind," she said to herself. "You'd think they'd care if I burned up or not."

Hugging her cloak to her as she walked, not wanting to lose it in the press, she allowed herself to be carried along by the flow of bodies. With everyone heading outside and the house full of smoke, she supposed there was no chance of continuing the ball. It was a horrible shame. She'd been enjoying herself ever so much. Dancing with officers, flirting with officers, and dreaming about dining with one on each side. One would have been Kitty's dinner companion, of course, but both would have paid Lydia the most attention. Kitty wouldn't have minded. It was her own fault she was the more boring sister, after all.

Stepping out into the fresh air, Lydia immediately spotted Kitty, who stood shivering violently. Lydia hurried over, holding out her cloak. "Here, take this," she said, handing it to Kitty. Her sister looked quite cold. Besides, Lydia was sure an officer would offer her his coat. That would be much more fun than wearing her own garment.

"Thank you," Kitty said, her teeth chattering. "Where is Mama?"

"How should I know?" Lydia asked, looking about for a likely officer.

"I ran out right away," Kitty said, her concentration on tying the cloak. "Lots of people have come out, but I haven't seen any of our family until you."

Lydia frowned, an unfamiliar feeling of disquiet washing over her. Jane was likely with her Mr. Bingley, and Elizabeth had probably done what Mr. Darcy told everyone to do and left, but what about their mother? "Maybe she went to get her cloak." Lydia hadn't seen her, but there had been many people pressed together. Mama would have been some ways behind her. She recalled their mother had been on the far side of the ballroom, and she wasn't anywhere near as spry as Lydia.

The cloak fastened, Kitty was looking at the dwindling stream of people. "Maybe we should go look for her?"

"I'm sure she'll be out soon," Lydia said. She nibbled at her lower lip, her words having no effect on the strange feeling of dread taking hold of her. "Let's go look through a window."

Lydia led the way back to the house, rubbing her arms against a sudden chill. It was hard to see inside, as the drapes were partially closed and smoke abounded. She made to press her face to the glass, but pulled back from how hot it was. She was about to try a different window when she spotted their mother.

Mrs. Bennet was hurrying down the staircase, while hastily tying on her cloak. A small figure Lydia thought was Mrs. Goulding was at her side, and Mr. Collins was running up behind them.

Lydia pointed. "I see her. She's nearly out." Lydia breathed a sigh of relief. What a silly thing she was, worrying Mama wasn't smart enough to leave. Smart enough to save her favorite cloak, as well. The one Lydia would have someday, because it looked best on her.

"Where?" Kitty asked, shifting from foot to foot at Lydia's elbow.

"She's right there, with Mrs. Goulding."

"Oh, now I see her," Kitty exclaimed.

"And here comes that horrible—" Lydia broke off with a little shriek as Mr. Collins pushed past the two women.

Mrs. Goulding caught herself on the banister, not appearing to hit it nearly as hard as Lydia had when he'd passed her on his way to get his cloak, but their mother was knocked down, falling the few steps that remained. Mr. Collins didn't slow, or even look back.

"What's happening?" Kitty asked. "I thought I saw Mr. Collins push Mama over, but he couldn't have. I can't see well with all the smoke. Is that her on the floor? Why doesn't she get up?"

Mrs. Goulding was pulling on their mother's arm. She was an ancient, frail old woman, though, and making no headway. Lydia reached out to try to push the window open, yanking her hand back in pain. Shoving her burnt fingers in her mouth, she looked about for something to apply to the window. She had to get in to help her mother.

She and Kitty both screamed as the curtains on the other side of the glass burst into flames, jumping back. Able to think of nothing but saving her mother, Lydia abandoned the window route. She ran toward the front door. Mrs. Goulding was coming out.

"Where's my mother?" Lydia cried.

"Mr. Collins ran into her and she fell. I tried to help her up, but she was unconscious. I couldn't move her."

"Mama," Lydia gasped.

She ran around Mrs. Goulding, darting through the door. Scorching air slammed into her. She put her arms up, trying to block the heat enough to see, but there was too much smoke and fire. Hands grabbed her, pulling her back outside. She raged against them, but the arms which encircled her were unrelenting. Inside the house there was a terrible crashing sound, heat whooshing out. Somewhere nearby, she could hear Kitty crying.

Chapter Two

~ Survivors ~

Mr. Bennet

Mr. Bennet continued his circumnavigation of the manor, taking in the smoke seeping from the windows and the dancing flames filling some. He didn't meet with any more of his family, but wasn't surprised. They should be in front by now. His wife and some of his daughters were foolish, but there was a limit to how foolish any being could be. Even Mrs. Bennet, Kitty and Lydia wouldn't stay inside a burning house.

He rounded the last corner of the house to find none of his family waiting, not even Jane. Mr. Bennet wished he'd thought to go alone on his hunt, leaving Mary out front, for they were likely all walking in circles seeking each other. Frowning, he looked about for Mary, who should appear soon, and spied Lydia and Kitty by the house.

He started toward them, to call them away from the heat of the burning building. Apparently he'd been wrong in his estimation of their intelligence. Lydia and Kitty weren't smart enough to avoid a fire. As he drew nearer, they jumped back, crying out. The window they stood at filled with fire, the curtains inside burning. Kitty stumbled toward him, her face white as fresh linens, but instead of running away from the house, Lydia ran toward the door.

Mr. Bennet broke into a trot, then a run. Lydia was perhaps the silliest of his offspring, but that didn't excuse running into a burning house. Someone ran up beside him, a glance revealing Mr. Bingley. Lydia dove into the burning house just before they reached her.

Heat broiled forth from the doorway. Mr. Bennet could hear beams creaking inside. He glanced at Mr. Bingley, took a deep breath, and plunged in after his daughter.

Fortunately, Lydia hadn't gone far. She stood a few paces inside, arms raised to shield her face. Mr. Bennet grabbed her, attempting to haul her out. She struggled, but Mr. Bingley came to his aid. They dragged her back through the doorway. A loud crash sounded behind them, a wall of smoke and heat sending everyone near the door staggering back.

Mr. Bennet wrapped his arms about Lydia, who was now gaping at the house.

"Mama was in there," Lydia cried in anguished tones as he pulled her farther from the burning building.

"Are you certain?" he asked sharply.

"She was. Mrs. Bennet was inside still," an elderly voice said.

Mr. Bennet had to blink several times before his vision cleared enough to make out the diminutive form of Mrs. Goulding.

"Mama was inside?" Mary gasped, somewhere to his right.

Glancing toward the sound, Mr. Bennet could see Kitty beside her. Kitty sobbed madly, her head bobbing up and down in a frantic nod. "I saw, too." Kitty's sobbing words were hardly intelligible.

"Mr. Collins pushed her down," Lydia said. "He pushed her onto the floor so he could get past and she hit her head and didn't get up and now she's—" Lydia's voice crumbled into tears.

Mr. Bennet held her near, stunned. He looked over her head at Mrs. Goulding, who nodded as well.

"It's true," the elderly woman said. "I was with her. He pushed me as well. Ran right between us. I tried to pull her out, but I couldn't. I'm sorry, Mr. Bennet."

"Yes, of course," Mr. Bennet heard himself say. "You should go to the stable, Mrs. Goulding, before you become too chilled. We should all move farther from the house. It isn't safe."

Mrs. Goulding teetered over and patted his hand where it rested on Lydia's shaking back. He was aware of the sound of women crying as he watched Mrs. Goulding hobble away. She was barely five feet tall, elderly and somewhat frail. She couldn't possibly lift his wife. It spoke highly of her that she'd even tried. Mr. Bennet looked back into the fire, quite hot now, unable to pull his eyes away.

"Mr. Bennet, Mr. Bingley, Miss Bennets," a commanding male voice said. "You should move away from the house."

Mr. Bennet pulled his gaze from his wife's pyre to find Colonel Forster, leader of the regiment stationed in the nearby village of Meryton.

"Of course, at once," Mr. Bingley said nearby.

Mr. Bingley put an arm about Jane, who had her arm wrapped about Mary, and led them away. Kitty trailed after, looking small and alone in Lydia's red cloak. Taking Lydia with him, Mr. Bennet followed. He felt oddly numb. He didn't love his wife, or hadn't thought he did, but trying to comprehend she was gone was baffling.

"You should know Miss Elizabeth is safe," Colonel Forster said. He fell in beside Mr. Bennet, but his voice was pitched to ensure all of them could hear.

"Lizzy?" Jane said, glancing back at Colonel Forster with a tear-streaked face. She sounded very relieved.

Mr. Bennet realized he should have thought to say he'd seen Elizabeth. He'd told Mary, of course, behind the house. It seemed like so long ago. He looked back at the manor, his mind feeling slow and unresponsive.

"You should be proud of Miss Elizabeth. When everyone was wringing their hands in dismay, she sent stable hands to get carriages. Mr. Darcy has two carriages here, and they are both ready to take people home. Mr. Bingley, your horses are being harnessed. We have to get people out of the rain. There is room to stand in the stable. With Miss Elizabeth organizing things there, I've been able to do what I can out here. I'm afraid it doesn't seem likely we can save the house, but we'll try, and make sure the fire doesn't spread. It's a good thing, this rain and the lack of wind."

Mr. Bennet pulled his eyes from the evilly glowing fire to squint up into the light drizzle filling the cold November air. He lengthened his stride, steering Lydia up alongside Mr. Bingley, and disentangled himself from his youngest daughter. "Join Lizzy in the stable. I want to talk to Colonel Forster."

"Yes, Papa," his girls answered in chorus.

"I shall see them safely there," Mr. Bingley said.

Mr. Bennet stopped walking, Colonel Forster pausing beside him. He chose to say nothing about the arm Mr. Bingley had around Jane's shoulders, watching her and her sisters walk away. After his daughters were out of hearing, he repeated what Lydia and Mrs. Goulding had told him about Mr. Collins, forcing his mind to pull back from the shock of his wife's death and function with the properness he knew it capable of.

Colonel Forster frowned. "I don't think Mr. Collins did anything he can be prosecuted for."

"I realize that," Mr. Bennet said. "I know we can't take formal action against him, but I do not want him to remain in my home. I don't think any of us would be able to stand it. Can you see he walks to Longbourn? I want to get there prior to his arrival and pack up his things. It would give me some satisfaction to kick him out."

"Now that I think about it, it might be considered manslaughter," Colonel Forster said, looking thoughtful.

"And it might not. I don't want my daughters on the witness stand. It won't bring back their mother and would sully their reputations. Mrs. Bennet wouldn't have wanted that. Part of me wants to see him hang, but not at the cost of my daughters' prospects. Their wedding was my wife's greatest care in life."

Colonel Forster nodded. "I'll see to it." He gestured toward the stable. "Shall we? I should take over organizing from Miss Elizabeth now. She's likely no longer in a state of mind to conduct it."

"Thank you," Mr. Bennet said. He should go to Lizzy and his other daughters to offer what comfort a father could. They started toward the stable. "Oh, and we will have his bedroom available if anyone needs it. Also, we can house three servants easily and more if needed, until it is decided what to do with them."

Caroline

Caroline was sorely tempted to scream. Not in fear, but frustration. How dare Mr. Wickham place his hands on her person? Why, of all luck, had Mr. Darcy come down right behind him, carrying some servant no less. Why was he wasting his time on servants? She was devastated Mr. Darcy had observed her humiliation.

Mr. Wickham carried her outside into a cold drizzle. A few yards from the house, he placed her on her feet in the wet grass. Looking past him, Caroline could see flames leaping into the night sky. Her mouth fell open. Why, half the manor was already engulfed in fire, the other half sprouting smoke from every opening. She'd no idea things were quite so out of hand.

"Where is everyone?" Mr. Wickham said.

A glance told Caroline he wasn't speaking to her, but to a soot-coated footman trotting past.

"Taking shelter in the stable, sir," the footman called, not stopping.

"Thank you," Mr. Wickham said. He turned back to Caroline. Taking off his coat, he held it out to her.

Adopting an expression she hoped let him know she was only accepting due to the desperation of the times, she turned and allowed him to assist her into it, not deigning to speak to him.

"Come, you'll freeze out here," Mr. Wickham said.

She ignored him, looking to Mr. Darcy. He stood nearby, still carrying some silly, fainting girl of no importance. Mr. Darcy's eyes swept the area and Caroline couldn't help but be impressed with how commanding he looked, even with soot on his face and that bit of nothing in his arms. He glanced toward her and she smiled, but his gaze kept moving.

With an exasperated oath, Mr. Wickham grabbed her arm and pulled her in the direction of the stable.

"I believe I asked you not to place your hands on me," Caroline said in vehement, but quiet, tones. It wouldn't do for Mr. Darcy to see her as shrill.

"You don't have the sense God gave a goose."

She opened her mouth to retort, but closed it again, very firmly, as her teeth began to chatter. Ladies did not have chattering teeth, after all. Allowing herself to be propelled along, Caroline looked back once at Mr. Darcy, his broad-shouldered form silhouetted against the flames. For all the light rain seemed to have no effect on the fire raging through Netherfield Park, her hair had already lost the curls that took so many applications of hot irons for her to acquire.

When she and Mr. Wickham reached it, inside the stable was a deal warmer, but Caroline admitted that only to herself, pulling away from Mr. Wickham as soon as they entered. In the dim light, she could make out people huddled together, many wrapped in horse blankets. She was grudgingly glad of Wickham's coat. It smelled of smoke, but then she did as well. At least it was meant for humans, if only for an officer, not livestock.

"Caroline," her sister Louisa called.

Caroline turned to see Louisa pressing toward her through the crowd, her husband Mr. Hurst on her heels. "Louisa," she greeted.

"We were worried about you," Louisa said.

"We were?" Mr. Hurst muttered.

As usual, Caroline elected not to hear such words. "I went back for my jewelry, but I was prevented from reaching it." She cast a glare over her shoulder at Mr. Wickham.

"Oh, how dreadful," Louisa said. Her features turned sly. "I was hoping you would appear beside a certain gentleman."

"Mr. Darcy," Mr. Hurst said rather loudly.

Caroline's eyes went wide. How dare he declare such a thing. She was about to deliver him a set down, her nerves already frayed beyond enduring, when she realized Mr. Hurst and Louisa were turning to greet someone behind her.

Composing herself, Caroline turned as well. Mr. Darcy, no longer burdened and looking heroically disarrayed, strode toward them.

"Hurst," Darcy greeted. "Miss Bingley, Mrs. Hurst." He nodded politely enough, but his eyes didn't settle on them, still scanning as they had been without.

"Mr. Darcy, are you well?" Caroline asked, trying to arrest his attention.

"Yes." He didn't turn to her, but rather to Mr. Hurst. "Have you seen Miss Elizabeth Bennet?"

"She's near the other entrance," Mr. Hurst said, indicating the direction. "Take charge sort of miss, isn't she? She's been organizing people."

"Thank you." Mr. Darcy awarded them a cursory bow and hurried away.

Caroline gaped after him. How easily he'd dismissed her. Why, he'd never been so ill mannered before.

"Caroline," Louisa hissed.

She turned to see her sister giving her a meaningful look. Now what could it be?

"Go after him," Louisa said, sotto voce.

Caroline nodded, scurrying after Mr. Darcy to take advantage of the way people easily gave way to him. She caught up to him as he stopped before Miss Elizabeth. The Bennet girl seemed untouched by smoke or soot. Her unstylish dress wasn't even creased, though the hem was a bit dingy. Although logic said she must have been rained on like the rest of them, her hair was already dry, the moisture making it curl riotously about her face in a way Caroline deemed vulgar. Miss Elizabeth didn't have a blanket about her scrawny shoulders, and stood straight and as tall as her too-short stature could make her, not shivering.

Caroline looked down at her bedraggled, ruined ball gown, putting a hand up to touch hair disarrayed by being carried and matted to her head by rain. She brought her hand back to her side, clenching it. More than anything, Caroline longed to retrieve a bucket of water from the nearby horse trough and toss it on Miss Elizabeth. Low and plain as she was, she still looked far too composed and elegant for Caroline's liking.

"Miss Elizabeth," Mr. Darcy said, bowing to her.

Bowing to a country chit when all Caroline and Louisa had warranted by way of a greeting was the barest of nods? Caroline awarded Miss Elizabeth a nod even less observable than the one Darcy had issued her and her sister.

"Miss Bingley, Mr. Darcy. I'm pleased to see you both unscathed. I was growing concerned. No one had seen you."

"Mr. Wickham and I were clearing the upper floors."

"Mr. Wickham?" Miss Elizabeth stood on her toes, looking past Darcy.

Caroline smirked, taking in the way Mr. Darcy's shoulders tensed beneath his coat.

"He's here as well," Mr. Darcy said, his tone noticeably cool. "He came out with me. He saved a maid's life."

"How gallant of him," Miss Elizabeth said.

"What is the situation here?" Mr. Darcy asked.

Caroline's elation at Miss Elizabeth's blunder in speaking of Mr. Wickham in such a warm manner turned to anger. Her day simply couldn't become any more miserable. She should be the one who knew what was transpiring. She was meant to be calm and in command of the rabble inside the stable. If only Mr. Wickham had brought her out of the house and to the stable with greater haste, she might have been in a position to answer Mr. Darcy's question. It would be her competence he observed.

Miss Elizabeth began naming parties who had left in their carriages. "The Gouldings took two maids with them when they left," she added. "They will keep them there until it is decided what will be done with the servants." She then rattled off four more names of families who had left and who went with them, always taking care to note when extra room was given to servants.

Caroline was further disgusted. No one cared what happened to servants. Why bother Mr. Darcy with such details? Why permit carriages to leave burdened with servants at all? They should wait until everyone above them was seen to before troubling their betters with requests.

"I've been attempting a tally, but it's rather difficult as not everyone took shelter in the stable. I've sent a footman to the carriage house, and have others taking turns making rounds outside the manor. There are some smaller outbuildings as well I hope to hear from. A few may even have walked home, but I doubt that, as this is rather a spectacle. It's especially difficult to account for the servants, as many new ones were brought in for the occasion." She turned to Caroline. "Miss Bingley, I was hoping you would have a better idea how many staff we should be seeking, and of the guest list for the ball?"

"Me? I do not keep track of servants, Miss Elizabeth." Caroline cast Mr. Darcy a conspiratorial look, hoping he would share her amusement at Miss Elizabeth's unseemly obsession with the lower class. He wasn't looking at her, though. "As for the guest list, I simply can't recall all of the countrified names that were on it. They're gibberish to me."

"Put it from your mind, then. I have a fair notion of who should be accounted for, growing up among them as I have."

Was that amusement hidden in Miss Elizabeth's tone? Caroline frowned.

"You must be cold," Mr. Darcy said.

"In truth, a bit," Miss Elizabeth answered. "I wanted to leave the blankets for those who needed them most."

Caroline watched, powerless to intervene, as Mr. Darcy removed his coat and helped Miss Elizabeth into it. To her eye, he took overlong with the process. She'd been wrong, her day could, and had, become more miserable still. She should be the one wearing Mr. Darcy's coat. The dreadfully expensive wool had no place on Miss Elizabeth's stick-like frame. Inwardly, Caroline cursed Mr. Wickham for forcing her into his rough, practically tawdry, red coat. If she hadn't been wearing it when Mr. Darcy found them a moment ago, Caroline would have his coat now.

For what seemed like an eternity, people came in and out of the stable. Elizabeth and Mr. Darcy, side by side, organizing them. Eventually, someone came for the Hursts. Caroline expected to go with them, but was told there wasn't enough room. She couldn't imagine why she hadn't been taken somewhere almost immediately. Any one of these country louts should be honored to have her as a guest in their home. Yet, still, time dragged by and she stood beside Mr. Darcy and Elizabeth, ill-used and annoyed.

Eventually, Miss Elizabeth and Mr. Darcy agreed he should ride into town, in the rain, and see about additional space for some of the servants. Caroline couldn't believe her ears. Not only was Miss Elizabeth asking Mr. Darcy to care about servants, she was sending him away. If Caroline had his attention the way the silly country chit did, she wouldn't be so foolish as to squander it.

As soon as he left, she moved away, lest Miss Elizabeth form some ill begotten notion of asking Caroline to help. Miss Elizabeth obviously wanted to be in charge, so Caroline would allow her to be. It wasn't as if she cared what became of any of these country nobodies or the local help.

The stable grew colder as more people left and the night wore on. Mr. Wickham's coat was inadequate to keep out the chill. Most of the remaining people huddled together for warmth, but there was no one there Caroline was willing to be that close to.

There was a commotion near the door and the other Miss Bennets hurried in. To Caroline's horror, her brother was with them, dancing attendance on Jane Bennet. Caroline pretended not to see, turning slightly away in the hopes Charles wouldn't notice her and make her evening even more abysmal by forcing her to join them.

Miss Elizabeth seemed happy to see her sisters, exclaiming with more joy than Caroline would have. Not for those uncouth girls, leastwise. They clustered about her, babbling in low voices. She burst into tears. Miss Bennet hugged her. The other three started wailing. Really, they were most inconsiderate, making such a fuss in the midst of the stable. Worse, Miss Elizabeth wasn't organizing any longer, likely extending the time before Caroline would be somewhere warm.

She would have come forward and taken charge, it being her right in every way, but she no longer wished to. Let everyone suffer the consequence of allowing themselves to be ordered about by a silly country miss. Maybe next time they would seek out a more reasonable leader, like Caroline. If she stepped forward now, the fools would never learn their lesson, or their place.

Colonel Forster and Mr. Bennet came in. The colonel moved to take charge of those in the stable. Caroline hoped Mr. Bennet would quell his daughters, but he permitted them to keep crying. Miss Elizabeth let go of Miss Bennet, flinging herself into her father's arms like a child. It was really all too ridiculous. Miss Elizabeth was obviously bent on making a spectacle of herself. It was likely the only way she could ever garner any attention, plain as she was.

What could the girl even have to cry about? She'd obviously overset herself by taking on so much responsibility. Well, Caroline had no sympathy. Being overwrought was what Miss Elizabeth deserved for robbing Caroline of her chance to show Mr. Darcy how competent she was.

Caroline tried to compose her face from its glower, not wishing to create unseemly lines. Miss Elizabeth had no right to cry while wearing Mr. Darcy's coat, no matter how taxing she was finding the evening.

All she and her sisters had lost in the fire were their cloaks, although one of the vulgar red ones was still in evidence. Those ought definitely have been burned. The Bennet girls couldn't possibly know Caroline's pain. She'd lost her jewelry and most of her wardrobe. She had a few clothes left at the Hursts' townhouse in London, but they were sadly out of date.

Caroline turned more fully away, sick of the sight of Bennets. She created a mental list of what she'd need new, and how much it would cost Charles. Surely, he wouldn't expect her to pay for it out of her allowance, since it was his home that was burning down. While she was trying to remember how many pairs of shoes he would have to replace, she realized Colonel Forster was walking toward her. She straightened, pushing futilely at her hair. Fortunately, she didn't care much what this lowly colonel thought of her, or anyone else in the stable, now that Mr. Darcy was gone.

"Miss Bingley," Colonel Forster said. "You are to go with Mr. Bennet."

Finally. It had taken long enough. The stable was nearly empty now. She supposed the locals must have been arguing over who had the honor. She could have wished them done more quickly, and that the Bennets hadn't won, but at this point anywhere reasonable would do. Not, of course, that she could think of a reasonable location in miles.

The first thing she realized as she reached the carriage was most of the Bennet girls had already departed. She frowned, affronted those silly twits had been given priority over her. She should have paid closer attention instead of daydreaming about new gowns. If she'd noticed, she wouldn't have stood for it.

The next thing she realized was she was expected to squeeze into a seat meant for two with Mr. Bennet and Miss Elizabeth, who still looked weepy. Opposite them were three servants. Another affront, and even more severe than the rest. Why weren't the servants left for another trip? How dare they put her in so tightly.

Nothing was said for the duration of the journey. Caroline certainly wasn't going to break the silence. At least Miss Elizabeth kept her tears to herself and only sniffled a little. The horses went so slowly, Miss Bingley wanted to scream. It was too dark for her to see where they were taking her, and she wasn't going to ask.

It wasn't until she got out of the carriage that she realized they were at Longbourn and going on to no more stops. She pressed her mouth into a firm line as she marched up the walk. It would have to do. She was not going back out in the cold and rain with those ridiculously slow horses. Could they not have found spryer beasts?

As they entered the cramped entrance hall, she saw a trunk sitting beside the door. She hoped she wasn't going to be asked to share a room. That would be beyond bearing.

"This way, Miss Bingley," Mr. Bennet said, directing her to a doorway. "If you'll wait here a moment," he told the three servants, whom he'd allowed to enter through the front door with them. Country manners disgusted Caroline.

Turning into the indicated parlor, she was dismayed to find the rest of the Bennet girls there. Miss Elizabeth didn't follow her, but hurried above stairs. Caroline was forced to take a seat on a sofa with the odious, sniffling Miss Kitty, deeming that slightly better than being put upon by conversation from Miss Mary. Miss Lydia and Miss Bennet sat in the only two comfortable looking chairs in the room.

Mr. Bennet stayed standing by the door. He turned to a waiting maid. "Please ask Mrs. Hill to attend us."

Mrs. Hill, Caroline assumed, was the housekeeper. She was relieved. She could use some tea.

The maid hurried off and the housekeeper soon appeared. Miss Bennet left her chair to speak with Mrs. Hill in quiet tones. After a few words were said, the housekeeper whisked off the three servants who lingered in the hallway. No one offered Caroline tea, or anything else. She scowled about the room at them, but they ignored her.

"Has Mr. Collins arrived yet?" Mr. Bennet asked, turning to Miss Bennet.

"No. I packed his trunk. His room is ready for Miss Bingley."

"Good," Mr. Bennet responded, looking shockingly grim.

Caroline looked about at the red eyes. For the first time, it occurred to her to wonder if something was more seriously wrong than the loss of a few cloaks.

"I've ordered a light meal for everyone," Miss Bennet continued. "Mrs. Hill will be giving the servants something now. Our meal should be ready in a few minutes. We'll all be the better for it, I hope," she added softly, then cleared her throat. "While we wait, I think we might all go change. We're bringing the smell of smoke to the parlor." She looked at Caroline. "Miss Bingley, if you would follow me, I can show you to your room."

Caroline stood, struck by how subdued the Bennet girls seemed. Why, she wondered, was Miss Bennet requesting meals and giving orders, if they could be called such? Not that Caroline missed her abhorrent presence in any way, but where was Mrs. Bennet?

Chapter Three

~ Reverberations ~

Elizabeth

Her movements seeming slow and almost dreamlike to her, Elizabeth took off Mr. Darcy's coat and carefully hung it up. She changed out of her wet gown, replacing it with a black dress she'd worn four years ago when her grandmother died. She had to dig it from the back of the wardrobe where she'd stuffed it in her hope not to need it again for many years. Logic and the late hour told her she should attempt sleep, but she knew it wouldn't come. Instead, she sat on the side of the bed, fully clothed, her eyes on nothing. She had no notion how long she sat there before she heard footsteps in the hall.

The door opened and Jane came in, closing it softly behind her. She leaned against it, looking worn and sad. "It was meant to be such a pleasant evening."

"Yes, I suppose it was," Elizabeth said. She smoothed her palms over the black dress, pressing out creases she knew would return the moment her hands passed. "Especially for you, dear Jane. I'm sorry."

"It doesn't matter," Jane said.

Elizabeth knew it did, for they'd all thought this evening would result in Mr. Bingley proposing to Jane. She could agree with Jane that it didn't seem to matter at that moment. Nothing seemed to. Her logical mind supposed it would, though, eventually. The future wouldn't hold their Mama, but it could still hold happiness for Jane. Someday.

There was a soft knock at the door. Jane turned to open it.

Lydia rushed in, tears streaming down her face. "I don't have a black dress." She wrung her hands. "I should be wearing black."

Jane put her arms about their tall sister, their mother's favorite, whom everyone said looked like their mother had in her youth. "We'll get something soon," Jane said, stroking Lydia's bright curls, frizzy from the rain.

Below, Elizabeth heard the front door open. "Mr. Collins," her father said in a harsh voice, revealing he'd remained in the hall, waiting.

The door closed. Lydia quieted, pulling away from Jane. She wiped at the tears on her cheeks, her face taking on a hard expression. She edged from the room.

"They said I should walk here." Mr. Collins' nasally voice carried up the steps. "Why should I walk? I am a clergyman and should be treated with respect. Perfectly healthy young people were given places in carriages and I was told to walk. It is dark and raining. I could barely find my way."

"Mr. Collins, we have a carriage ready for you, immediately," Elizabeth's father said. "It will take you to the nearest town where the stage stops. I don't know if the inn has room, but the stage will come in a few hours. You can go to London on it."

Casting a look at Jane, Elizabeth followed Lydia, tiptoeing toward the top of the steps. She could hear Jane behind her, and see Mary and Kitty coming down the hall.

"What is my trunk doing here?" Mr. Collins blurted. "You, put down my trunk." Below, the door opened again, closing almost immediately. "Where are they taking my trunk?"

"They are taking it to the carriage, as I requested they do as soon as you arrived. I've kept it inside only so you could see it. I wouldn't want to be accused of retaining any of your possessions."

"Accused of what? Why are you going on about coaches to London? I'm cold and tired. I require tea and my room. Tell them to bring my things back immediately."

Elizabeth and all four of her sisters were at the top of the steps now. They could see Mr. Collins in the entrance hall. He was facing them, but didn't look up. Although her father had his back to them, Elizabeth could tell by his rigid posture he was furious.

"I do not think you are understanding me." Elizabeth had never heard her father use so harsh a tone. "You are leaving Longbourn this instant. You are not welcome here."

"Why should I leave? This is to be my home someday. I plan to marry Miss Elizabeth."

"Marry one of my daughters?" Mr. Bennet roared. "You killed my wife. Be glad I'm letting you take your things and leave. I wouldn't let you marry any daughter of mine under any circumstances, ever."

Although Mr. Collins was twenty years younger than Mr. Bennet and several inches taller, he shrank back. "Wh . . . I beg your pardon?"

"You are to leave here this instant."

Mr. Collins' eyes darted about. They alighted on Elizabeth and her sister and he stood up straighter. "You are crazed. If Mrs. Bennet is dead, it is because of the fire." He looked up the steps at them. "The loss of his wife has deranged your father."

Elizabeth stared at him, appalled by his attempt to look commanding. Could it be he truly didn't know what he'd done?

Her father took a step forward, bringing himself all but nose to nose with Collins. "Three witnesses saw you knock down Mrs. Bennet on your way from the cloakroom. We can only assume my wife hit her head, because she made no attempt to move or rise. Mrs. Goulding tried to help her up, but she couldn't. Mrs. Bennet was unconscious and didn't move. Finally, the fire was too hot and Mrs. Goulding was forced to leave. You are a large man and surely could have helped Mrs. Bennet. Since you knocked her down, it was your duty to help her."

Elizabeth took in the dawning look of horror on Mr. Collins' face. She didn't know if it made it better or worse that he hadn't realized what he'd done.

"I didn't do it," he said.

"I saw you," Lydia cried. She leapt forward.

Elizabeth reached out and caught her, keeping her from rushing down the steps. She was aware of Jane on Lydia's other side, holding onto her as well. Elizabeth didn't know what Lydia meant to do, but she wasn't about to let her go and find out. She wasn't sure they could trust Mr. Collins not to fight back, should Lydia attack him.

"Mrs. Goulding saw you as well, as did Kitty," Mr. Bennet said, his tone implacable. "That's three reliable witnesses to an act tantamount to murder. I suggest you leave immediately, sir, before I regret my kindness in calling a carriage for you, rather than the magistrate." Reaching past Mr. Collins, her father pulled open the door. Two farm workers stood outside, arms folded over their chests, looking grim.

"I . . . I have to check my trunk. Who packed it? What if they missed something?"

"Check it in the rain," Elizabeth's father said. He gave Mr. Collins a firm push, sending him stumbling backward out of the house, and closed the door in his face.

Mr. Bennet

Mr. Bennet sat alone in his library, a room which usually brought him peace. Tonight, there was none to be had. With Mrs. Bennet gone, he was aware of a hole in his life. What he felt wasn't the deep sorrow waxed over by poets, but more remorse for things done, and not done. Mostly, he was faced with the reality that he was now the only parent of five daughters and when his time came, Mr. Collins would inherit their home.

His eyes picked out a miniature, one which had hung on the wall in his library for over twenty years. Some might think Mr. Bennet kept an image of his wife in her youth out of sentiment, but they would be wrong. He kept it to remind him of past mistakes, almost as a mockery of himself. That beautiful, smiling face was always with him in his library, his one sanctuary.

Mr. Bennet had been madly in love with Jane Gardiner when he married her. It hadn't taken long for him to realized he loved a dream. She was as beautiful as the daughter they'd named after her, but there was nothing else about Mrs. Bennet that was lovable. While they'd courted, he'd taken her agreeing with him to be intelligence and her silences to be contentment. He'd soon learned that her agreeing with him had been policy and her silences a calculated method of keeping him from knowing her, until it was too late.

Jane Gardiner had used what little guile and intellect she had to achieve a married state. While disgusted he'd been fooled and dismayed by her artifice, he hadn't blamed her. Mr. Bennet knew that was the world in which they lived, and knew as well Jane Gardiner's behavior was expected, even applauded. She accomplished what she'd been raised to achieve and could not be criticized for it. It was a gentleman's responsibility to steer himself clear of just the sort of blunder he'd walked into.

While women must endure the world, a man had the right to attempt changing it. To that end, Mr. Bennet vowed he would bring up his daughters better. He worked hard to educate Jane and Elizabeth, but when Mary came along, he was stymied. All he achieved was to give her a desire to please him. She attended diligently to her learning and accomplishments, not realizing he couldn't love a woman, even his own daughter, if all her intellect was capable of was regurgitation without comprehension.

Worse, she wasn't even pretty. The one asset her mother could have offered her somehow went awry. Mr. Bennet was sure he could love Mary had she at least the advantage of charm.

No, he was being unfair to himself. It wasn't that she wasn't pretty, but that she had no common sense. She had the diligence to read sensible sayings from morn till night, but could never be sensible. He had higher regard for Charlotte Lucas, their twenty-seven-year-old neighbor. Miss Lucas was harder on the eyes even than Mary, but had a keen intellect, which was likely why she and his Lizzy were friends. If Mary had half of Miss Lucas' sense, Mr. Bennet would be able to respect his third daughter.

His youngest two offspring, he hadn't even attempted to better. He recognized early on they were very much their mother's children. Discouraged by his lack of success with Mary, he hadn't had the forbearance to attempt instilling brains in their pretty heads. And pretty they were, even beautiful, but they had less sense even than Mary. They didn't know the meaning of applying themselves to anything except flirting and enjoyment.

Mr. Bennet sighed. The worthlessness of his younger children was his fault, and he knew it. Having made a bad choice, he'd succumbed to the path of least resistance. He took what pleasure he could in exposing his wife's stupidity and hid in the library to enjoy his books. The result was he only respected two of his daughters.

But he was responsible for all of them, and he had allowed his dislike of confrontation and his contempt for his wife to keep him from fulfilling that responsibility. If he had saved more, his daughters would have some security. If he died now, they would be dependent on the charity of his wife's relatives, because the interest on the five thousand pounds settled on his wife would not be enough to support them.

Mr. Collins was the closest relative on his side, and after the recent events, he doubted Mr. Collins would do anything for his cousins. Mr. Bennet didn't regret kicking Mr. Collins out. In a way, he'd done the odious gentleman a favor, though he doubted Collins would see it as such. Too many people already knew what had happened, and everyone else in Hertfordshire would learn it soon enough. There was the real risk of the community attacking Mr. Collins. Mrs. Bennet had been neither liked nor respected, but she was a part of the community and Mr. Collins was a stranger. Likely, though, people would be satisfied with him kicking Collins out. With the man gone, at least Mr. Bennet need not worry over a mob coming to Longbourn demanding justice.

He looked around his library, his gaze once more coming to rest on the miniature. The room where he spent most of his happiest hours seemed sterile now that his wife was dead. Maybe he would replace the little picture from her youth with a more recent one. Jane had done several lovely sketches of her mother. Mr. Bennet shook his head. The woman who'd done nothing but torment his days for half a lifetime was dead. Why was it the nature of man that, now, he missed her?

Well, perverse or not, he did miss her, and casting Mr. Collins out seemed a paltry retribution for what the clergyman had done. Mr. Bennet wanted to do something, anything. No, he didn't love Mrs. Bennet, hadn't loved her for more than twenty years, but she deserved better than to have the estate she was so proud to live in go to the man who'd caused her death. He had to do something.

An absurd idea occurred to him. The more he thought about it, the more he liked it. Alone in his library, with his wife's miniature looking on, Mr. Bennet smiled.

Chapter Four

~ Departures ~

Caroline

The afternoon following the fire found Caroline seated in the Bennet's small parlor, thoroughly bored. There was absolutely nothing of interest to do, and no one worth talking to. Especially not with them all weepy-eyed and sniffling. That Caroline couldn't credit their tears with being real made them all the more annoying. Mrs. Bennet had been a horrible woman, after all. It was impossible they weren't grateful she was dead. It improved their prospects tremendously. She considered pointing that out, but knew they would only pretend not to see it.

As she was all but a prisoner in Longbourn, since neither Charles nor the Hursts had made proper arrangements for her yet, Caroline had attempted to make the best of it. That morning, she'd engaged both Miss Mary, who ought to be grateful anyone spoke to her, and Miss Kitty, who was as intellectually limited as a jar of pebbles. Caroline had spoken from the heart about her tragedy, the loss of her home, clothing, jewelry and other property, but had been almost completely ignored. No one seemed to care at all that she was suffering. Caroline could see they were too self-involved to pay the appropriate amount of attention to her.

She'd thought perhaps the condolence calls would offer some relief, but was sorely disappointed. One dreadful country nobody after another filed through the parlor, offering no amusements whatsoever. They all pretended they cared Mrs. Bennet was gone, and none of them treated Caroline with the respect they ought. It was obvious even the family grew tired of it, for by the time they neared the hour for tea, only she and Miss Elizabeth remained in the parlor.

Caroline was considering leaving as well, for Miss Elizabeth was the very last person she wished to converse with, when Mr. Darcy was announced. He stepped into the parlor, every inch the ideal gentleman. He set a valise he carried on the floor, coming forward to bow to Miss Elizabeth. Mr. Darcy was dressed impeccable and Caroline experienced a twinge of jealousy, realizing he must have sent for clothing from London, though the fire had taken place less than a day ago.

"Miss Elizabeth, may I offer my sincerest condolences on your family's loss," Mr. Darcy said.

"Thank you, Mr. Darcy. It is kind of you to come." Miss Elizabeth stood. "If you'll excuse me a moment?"

He bowed again, turning to follow her progress as she left the room.

Caroline couldn't imagine how the girl could be such a fool. She had Mr. Darcy, as prime a catch as walked through all of England, almost completely to herself, and she'd dashed off. Perhaps Miss Elizabeth had some silly notion of not wanting Darcy to see her in black. She did look excessively dreadful in it.

Caroline knew the feeling. She was being forced to wear one of Miss Mary's dresses. It was an insipid pale yellow with a too-high neckline and a complete lack of embellishment. She hated for Mr. Darcy to see her in it. Realizing he wasn't, as he was still looking in the direction Miss Elizabeth had gone, Caroline cleared her throat.

"Miss Bingley," he said turning back around. "I am pleased to see you looking well. I have this for you." He retrieved the valise, and placed it next to her on the sofa.

"Thank you, Mr. Darcy." She gave him her best smile, wondering what the case contained. It didn't matter, of course. What mattered was using this moment alone with Mr. Darcy to her best advantage. "It's very kind of you to think of me."

"Not I, but your sister. I am merely the errand boy."

"You are never merely anything."

He frowned slightly, his gaze going back to the door Miss Elizabeth had departed through.

Caroline realized she was losing his attention. "Won't you sit, Mr. Darcy?" She gestured to the seat on the sofa, which he took. There was the valise between them, but at least they were on the same piece of furniture.

"I believe the case contains things your sister had brought from London for you."

"Let us find out, shall we?" She gave him a coy smile.

He shrugged, his eyes returning to the door.

Schooling her face from a scowl, Caroline opened it. It contained a dress and various other small necessities. The dress was two seasons out of date, but better than wearing Mary Bennet's dreadful clothing.

"Your maid was able to save your jewelry case. Mrs. Hurst has it," Mr. Darcy said.

"That's a relief," Caroline said, but in truth it vexed her.

If her maid had her jewelry, there'd been no reason for Caroline to attempt to return to her room. If the silly girl had only found Caroline and told her, as she ought to have done, Caroline wouldn't have run into Mr. Wickham. She would have been saved the embarrassment of Mr. Darcy seeing her thrown over the horrible lieutenant's shoulder, had the glory of organizing everyone, and got to wear Mr. Darcy's coat. Why, it was as if the whole affair had been staged to torment and humiliate her.

Caroline realized Mr. Darcy was looking at her now. She put a grateful smile on her face. "It's so kind of you to reassure me. I was afraid I'd lost everything."

Mr. Darcy raised an eyebrow, looking at the valise.

Did he think the existence of a few undergarments and outdated clothing made up for the clothes she'd lost? If he weren't so wealthy, she'd be angry with him for that look. She tilted her chin up a notch to show her displeasure.

"The Hursts will be taking you to London tomorrow," he said. If he was chastened by her look, it didn't show.

"Will you and my brother be going with us?" Perhaps she was to have a proper carriage ride this time, with Mr. Darcy beside her.

"No. Bingley has to see about the servants. I'm going to stay to help."

"Servants? Can't the local populace be counted on to handle anything?" Where had this unseemly obsession with servants come from? And now, it seemed, Mr. Darcy had infected her brother with it as well. Footsteps sounded in the hall and Mr. Darcy turned away from Caroline again.

Miss Elizabeth entered, carrying his coat. "Thank you for the use of this." She held it out to him. "I appreciated having it."

"I appreciated your seeing to the carriages and leaving the ballroom promptly," Mr. Darcy responded, standing.

Caroline wondered if that was another barb, like his glance at the valise. Was Mr. Darcy subtly chiding her for not leaving promptly? Taking in the way he was looking at Miss Elizabeth, Caroline pressed her lips into a thin line. No, it was worse than that. Chiding would imply he cared. He wasn't criticizing her. He'd completely forgotten her presence the moment Miss Elizabeth walked in.

"Thank you, but it was an obvious thing to do," Miss Elizabeth said with a demureness Caroline was sure she faked.

"But you were the one who did it."

Mr. Darcy gazed at Miss Elizabeth in a way that made Caroline wish to slap him. She considered standing, anything to break into their exchange and remind Mr. Darcy she was there.

"I do not mean to belabor the point," Mr. Darcy said. "Yet I must reiterate how sorry I am about the loss of your mother. This must be a difficult time for you."

What about me? Miss Bingley thought. It is a difficult time for me as well, and you aren't making it any better, ogling that country chit.

"Thank you," Miss Elizabeth said. "We all appreciate you and Mr. Wickham behaving so heroically, even though not everyone was saved."

Caroline smiled, relieved. She might have realized all she need do was wait for Miss Elizabeth to attempt stringing more than five words together. The girl couldn't help but show her ignorance, lack of breeding and lack of understanding. Anyone with half a brain could see Mr. Darcy did not care for Mr. Wickham.

"Mr. Wickham was never a physical coward," Mr. Darcy said.

There was a faint emphasis on the word physical. Caroline was sure Miss Elizabeth missed it.

"That is a good thing for someone in the militia," Miss Elizabeth said. If her expression was any indication, she had more to say on the subject.

Mr. Darcy looked toward the door, clearly about to take his leave.

Continue, Caroline urged Miss Elizabeth silently. Push him further away with your ignorance. Caroline wished Mr. Darcy would return to London where he ought to be, away from Miss Elizabeth Bennet. London was a much better place for Caroline to attract him. He would see her belonging in London society, which Miss Elizabeth clearly didn't.

A servant appeared in the doorway. "Mr. Wickham," he

announced.

Mr. Wickham entered the parlor, his eyes alighting first on Miss Elizabeth and Mr. Darcy, who both stood. He bowed, the gesture including them both. His eyes slid past them to land on her and he nodded politely.

"Miss Elizabeth, Miss Bingley, Mr. Darcy," he said, his tone one of cool courtesy.

"Mr. Wickham," Mr. Darcy answered in a like tone.

"Mr. Wickham, do come in and sit, please," Miss Elizabeth said, moving to a chair.

Mr. Wickham shot Darcy a look, then took another chair. Caroline thought Mr. Darcy would leave, since he appeared to be ready to do so and she knew he abhorred Mr. Wickham. Instead, to her surprise, he sat down on the sofa again.

"May I express my condolences on the death of your mother?" Mr. Wickham said, leaning toward Miss Elizabeth as he spoke. "It is a terrible loss you and your family have suffered."

"Thank you," Miss Elizabeth murmured. "I shall pass your kind words on."

Caroline wondered if Miss Elizabeth was truly fooled by Mr. Wickham's soft tones. She wasn't. How could anyone mourn the loss of Mrs. Bennet? She turned to Mr. Darcy, expecting to exchange a look of condescending amusement for Miss Elizabeth's gullibility. Instead, Caroline found Mr. Darcy's gaze locked on Miss Elizabeth with disturbing intensity.

"I'm sure you and your sisters are devastated," Mr. Wickham said. "Mrs. Bennet was the cornerstone of your household."

"She was," Miss Elizabeth said.

"If there is anything I can do?" Mr. Darcy offered, capturing Miss Elizabeth's attention.

"Perhaps, being his friend, you could ask Mr. Bingley . . ." Miss Elizabeth trailed off. She took a deep breath, seeming to gather herself. "That is, I believe we would all feel better if we could see her properly interred."

Caroline shuddered. "What a gruesome topic. Surely, this is not for us to discuss?"

"Efforts are already being spoken of," Mr. Darcy said, once again ignoring her. "We must wait for the remains of the house to cool. It's still too dangerous. There are also three servants unaccounted for. I will make sure your family is kept abreast of the search."

"Thank you," Miss Elizabeth said.

Caroline rolled her eyes. Servants again. As if anyone cared about them.

Mr. Wickham turned to her. He offered a smile she would have found charming if he'd any income to speak of. "I believe you have my coat."

Caroline blinked at him. He wanted his coat back, after how he'd humiliated her? She turned to Elizabeth. "Miss Elizabeth, could you send someone to retrieve Mr. Wickham's coat from my room?"

"Of course," she said, standing. She crossed to the hall door. Caroline could hear her speaking to the maid who waited without.

"They've checked with all of the families, then, and in Meryton?" Mr. Wickham said, looking to Darcy. "I know quite a few of the staff made their way there."

Miss Elizabeth returned to her seat, not looking at Caroline.

"Yes, I rented them rooms," Mr. Darcy said.

"Ah." Wickham nodded. "Well, then, the count of three is firm?"

"They were all kitchen staff, and we believe that's where the fire started. A young girl working with them was brought forward to say she was ordered to leave, and they were all still within."

"That's a shame. I take it Bingley will undertake something for the families?"

"Really, I don't see why Charles should be held responsible for this," Caroline said. She would put that idea to rest. Charles would do better to spend his money refurbishing her wardrobe, as he ought, this being entirely his fault. Caroline's potential marital connections were of much greater importance than the families of some servants they'd had on for hardly any time. "From what you've said, it was the servants who started the fire, after all."

All three turned to look at her. A maid hurried into the room, carrying Mr. Wickham's coat, still bundled up the way Caroline had left it when she'd tossed it on the floor of the inadequate room they'd provided her. The girl stopped before Caroline.

"Give it to him," Caroline said, gesturing to Mr. Wickham. "I don't wish to touch it. It's filthy."

The girl bobbed a curtsy and held the coat out to Mr. Wickham. As he took it, it unfolded and cinders fell out, scattering on the floor. Mr. Wickham grimaced. "I'm sorry. I didn't realize how bad it was," he said, looking to Miss Elizabeth.

She made a dismissive gesture. "I should have thought to warn you. Mr. Darcy's coat was similarly bad. I had my father's man brush it."

Everyone looked at Caroline again. Mr. Wickham appeared annoyed and Mr. Darcy frowned. Caroline shot a glare at Miss Elizabeth, who was still faking a sorrowful demeanor. How dare she imply Caroline was thoughtless?

"Yes, well, I daresay I can brush it out myself," Mr. Wickham said.

His tone was amiable enough, but Caroline knew a set down when she heard one. She retargeted her pique on Mr. Wickham. "First you keep me from retrieving my jewelry and then you complain about my not acting as your valet?" It didn't matter that her jewelry wasn't there to be retrieved. He hadn't known that. "I lost everything in that fire. Really, sir, your thoughtlessness knows no bounds."

"Thoughtlessness? I saved your life," Mr. Wickham said. "At some risk to my own, I might add, as every second we lingered was dangerous. If you had any decency, you would offer me a reward, or at least your gratitude."

"How dare you speak to me in that tone?" She turned to Mr. Darcy. "Aren't you going to stand up for me?"

Mr. Darcy's face took on the same look it had earlier, when he'd silently reprimanded her over her valise.

"I don't have to sit here and be treated like this." Caroline snatched up the valise, standing. "I won't be down for dinner, or breakfast, but expect them to be served in my room. Send someone to inform me when the Hursts arrive. I can't wait to be back in London among civilized people." She stormed from the room.

Darcy

Darcy turned from the door after watching Miss Bingley storm out, to find Elizabeth looking at Wickham.

"I don't think she gives you much credit," Elizabeth said.

"Alas, no. Perhaps I will make a nuisance of myself over it." Wickham gave her a wry grin, which Darcy thought was a good deal more charming than called for. "It does rankle somewhat to save a life and receive only derision in return."

"Yes." Elizabeth turned her gaze on Darcy. "It does seem as if someone ought to reward you for your valor."

Darcy frowned. Why did Elizabeth look to him with such insistence as she uttered those words? He was not responsible for providing for Wickham or rewarding him for saving Miss Bingley, so why should Elizabeth look at him as if he were? Darcy wondered what lies Wickham had been telling behind his back.

He didn't press the issue, concentrating instead on recalling Wickham's valor. Darcy could admit to himself that he preferred being able to be in the same room with Wickham without the other man's presence ruining all attempts at civility. Wickham's deeds of the night before made that possible, at least for the moment. Still, at some point he should like the opportunity to put Elizabeth straight on whatever it was she thought she knew.

"I believe we are in danger of overstaying our welcome," Darcy said, standing. He gave Wickham a stern look. It was nearly time for tea. The Bennet's didn't need the additional expense of feeding Wickham, and they were in mourning.

"Right." Wickham stood. He bowed to Elizabeth. "Again, I am sorry for your loss. If I may be of any service to your family, please don't hesitate to ask."

Darcy bowed to her as well, a bit taken aback by Wickham's manners. Of course, he'd always possessed an easy charm, and pleasant manners were a part of that. He didn't normally apply them to women so lacking in fortune, however. "Miss Elizabeth," Darcy said as he rose from his bow. "Please pass on my regards to your family."

"Thank you both," she said. "I will share your kind words. I am sure they'll bring solace."

She smiled, but the expression was obviously a courtesy. No happiness reached her eyes. She looked wan in her black gown, somehow more delicate than was usual. It was her vivacity, Darcy realized. The loss of her mother had dampened it.

Wickham turned away. With a last nod to Elizabeth, Darcy forced his feet to follow. He wished he were in a position to comfort her further, but he couldn't. Even if, through some miracle she should wish it, he would never press his attention on her while she grieved.

He and Wickham stepped outside. Looking around, Darcy could see Wickham must have walked to Longbourn. All that way for a likely ruined coat and Miss Bingley's disdain. Elizabeth was correct, that didn't seem like much of a reward. Gallantry, especially in Wickham, should be encouraged. Darcy turned to his one-time companion, one-time enemy and said, "Would you care for a ride back to town?"

"Thank you. That would be agreeable," Wickham said, though he eyed Darcy with mild suspicion.

"Where are you quartered, Mr. Wickham?"

After repeating Wickham's answer to his driver, Darcy climbed into the carriage. Wickham clambered in after. He looked around as he took his seat opposite Darcy, as if seeking to reassure himself nothing was amiss.

"I didn't offer you a ride in order to accost you," Darcy said.

"You can't blame me for being wary. Since when are we being so polite to each other?"

Darcy considered his answer. Would it push Wickham away from honorable behavior if Darcy commended it?

"Offering me a ride, calling me Mister Wickham." Wickham made a vague gesture around the inside of the coach as he spoke, emphasizing the word mister.

"Your behavior last night earned you some respect," Darcy finally settled on saying.

"Respect? Not friendship?"

"Friendship is long gone. Your attempt to elope with my sister makes its return impossible." Darcy would have thought even Wickham would understand that.

"Would you believe I genuinely loved Georgiana and knew you would never consent to a marriage?"

"No." Not, at least, the love his sister deserved. The love of a man who would have taken her penniless and would have respected her enough to allow her to mature.

No, Wickham was a man who would press a fifteen-year-old girl into running off with him. Darcy clamped his mouth closed over the words. They had an entire carriage ride to get through. Had he really thought he could be civilized to Wickham? Not leaving people to die in a fire was the first noble thing the man had done since they were children.

"Well, I did love her." Wickham let out a sigh, leaning back against the thickly cushioned seat. "I loved her as a child, and loved her in a different way once she blossomed."

Darcy's resolve to be polite faltered. He couldn't sit and listen to Wickham wax poetic about loving Georgiana. "Would you have loved her if she didn't have a dowry of thirty thousand pounds?"

"Probably not," Wickham said ruefully.

"You've become more honest," Darcy said. One should give the devil his due.

"And that pleases you, I can tell. You always were aggravatingly sanctimonious, Darcy." Wickham grimaced at his own words, looking away. After a moment, he turned back, his expression thoughtful. "I will humor you with a bit more honesty. I had another incentive for marrying Georgiana. I wanted your respect. I knew I'd lost it and as Georgiana's husband, you would have had to treat me with respect."

Darcy was shocked. He'd not realized his opinion mattered so much to Wickham. "Treating someone with respect is not the same as respecting them."

"It would have been enough."

"Is there ever enough for you?" Darcy asked.

"Probably not. I keep hoping."

"Which is why you gamble, even though you always lose in the long run."

"You should know. You've paid my debts." Wickham frowned.

"Why? I've never understood why you kept paying them for so long."

Darcy was the one who was wary now. Was this so-called honesty of Wickham's some sort of trap? Were there more debts he was trying to lure Darcy into paying? He shook his head. This once, he would give Wickham the benefit of the doubt. What would he lose by taking the bait, if that's what this was? He could afford the money, and relegating Wickham back to the roll of vermin would be almost a relief, not a punishment. "Because your debts were partly my fault."

"What?" Wickham's expression was as stunned at his tone.

Darcy shrugged. "If I'd told my father the truth about you, he would have disowned you. I covered up your gambling and womanizing because it would have broken his heart. He was still recovering from my mother's death, and ill as well. He didn't need more to burden him." He held up a hand when Wickham would have interrupted. "I didn't give you the opportunity to learn. Things were too easy for you."

"I can't believe I'm about to say this," Wickham said slowly. "You're wrong, Darcy. That's the biggest load of manure I've ever heard from your mouth. You and I were raised the same. We had the same tutors, the same schooling, even the same choices in clothes. We rode the same horses. If I was corrupted by a life that was too easy, why weren't you?"

"Because I was punished for even the slightest error. I was raised to manage Pemberley, and therefore much scrutinized. You were raised in a privileged way, but without the weight of responsibility. The truth remains that I covered for you, making it so you never faced the consequences of your behavior."

Wickham waved that aside with a gesture. "You take too much on your high and mighty shoulders. Can't you see how arrogant you sound, saying you caused me to become the man I am? I made my own choices. I knew what I did was wrong, just as I knew you would clean up after me, though I truly thought you'd give up the task sooner. You were always too conscientious. If anything, I used you abominably."

"We agree there," Darcy said, irked. He'd tried to do right, and done right, and Wickham disdained him for the aid?

"Don't be sore, Darcy. You have something I'll never have. Although I know plenty of people who find you arrogant, I'm willing to admit everyone respects you. They always have. You need only walk into a room with that lord of the manor bearing you were born with."

Wickham accompanied his words with a bitter smile. "Brought up the same or no, I was never able to master that. I've always had to use my charm for anyone to attend to me."

"As a result, you learned charm. You won't deny my ability to command respect? I cannot deny that people find you unfailingly charming." Darcy drummed his fingers on the carriage seat. He wasn't at all comfortable with their conversation. It was far too personal. Yet, it was better than the outright animosity that usually existed between them. "Perhaps if I'd been born a younger son, or to no station, I would have been forced to learn more tact, and charm. It could be I would move through life with greater ease and cease offending people." Thinking of that, Darcy recalled Elizabeth's coldness when they'd danced. Had he already managed to offend her? She'd seemed pleasant enough today, though it was hard to read any emotion in her other than grief.

Wickham laughed. "You, charming? I'm sorry, Darcy, but the idea is ridiculous. Quite impossible. You could no more learn to be charming than I can learn to command instant respect."

"Why not?" This time, Darcy found himself more curious than angered. Wickham employed charm. How difficult could it truly be?

"I told you, you came forth from the womb as lord of the manor. The midwife likely bowed to you before cutting the cord."

"I'm sure that's amusing." Darcy allowed sarcasm to color his tone. "I could learn to be charming. I've simply not required the skill."

"Never," Wickham said with certainty. "I can't say there may not have been a slim window at some point in your formative years, but it's long since closed."

"How can you be so certain?" Darcy knew he was being baited, but he didn't care for being told he was incapable of achieving something.

"Because you consider yourself superior to almost everyone. It shows." Wickham shrugged.

"And if I am superior?"

"You should hide it, or at least have the grace to recognize most of it is not of your doing. You are good looking, but that is an accident of birth. You are well read, but you have a library to choose from. Books are too expensive for most of us."

"You didn't read much when you had access to the same library," Darcy felt obliged to point out.

"You are sanctimonious, as I believe I already mentioned once today. That is a choice, I think, not an accident, and I read when I had the time." Wickham held up a hand, ticking off points on his fingers. "You are probably a better horseman than I am, because I get little practice and you ride daily. Your clothes cost many times what mine cost and you have a valet to keep them in shape. Would I command more respect in clothes like yours? Definitely." Wickham shrugged. "I could go on about you being a better shot or better at fencing, but we both know that as I no longer have the advantages we both grew up with, I don't have the luxury of practicing gentlemanly arts. You consider yourself better than most people. You probably are, but it's because of an accident of birth, not from any unusual effort on your part."

"You are hardly one to talk about effort. At Cambridge you learned almost nothing." Darcy was stung by Wickham's criticisms, his reason balking at the truth in them.

"I'm not one for weighty studies, Darcy. I charm, lie and deceive," Wickham said, shrugging again. "If anyone ruined me, it was your father. He was my greatest friend ever, and he ruined me. He brought me up with all of the advantages of wealth and privilege, but on his death, I had no better future than that idiotic clergyman, Mr. Collins. What could he have been thinking?" Wickham's eyes took on a faraway look. "Me, a clergyman? The very idea is laughable." His gaze refocused on Darcy, his expression bitter. "I've never had any incentive to do well, because nothing I could do would get me the one thing I wanted. Nothing could make me you."

Darcy stared at him, stunned. He didn't know how to respond to this brutally honest speech. Wickham opened the door of the carriage. It took Darcy a bewildered moment to realize they'd stopped. They must have reached their destination.

"The smoke must have addled my brain," Mr. Wickham said. "I should never have said anything."

"It hardly matters," Darcy made himself say, though he knew it did. "Bingley and I should be leaving in a few days. Our paths may never cross again."

"But we can be on good terms for the time you are here. There's a group of us having dinner at The Lion Inn tonight. I'm headed there now. Join us."

Darcy agreed, with misgivings, but Mr. Wickham behaved well

throughout dinner. He was his usual charming self, but used his charm to make the evening run smoother, not make himself look better. When dinner was over and tables were set up for gambling, he didn't join. He responded to their invitation by laughingly saying, "You only want me for the money I lose."

Darcy declined as well. He was in no mood to gamble, especially not in the company Wickham kept, which was mostly other officers. Eventually, as their dinner companions moved on to more entertaining pursuits, Darcy found himself seated at a table vacated by everyone save Wickham. Under the cover of three tables of cards, they could talk without being overheard.

"I can recall when you more often made the effort to be this." Darcy made a gesture at Wickham, at ease, sober and not engaging in any disreputable occupations. "With a little determination, this could be you. I don't understand why it isn't."

Before giving up and cutting Wickham from his life, Darcy had endured watching this version of Wickham slip ever further away, replaced by one who spent far too many evenings losing at cards or flirting with whatever woman was available. He'd also had to endure listening to Wickham tell stories very different from what he'd said earlier. Ones meant to garner sympathy, implying he hadn't been brought up as Darcy had, but instead as a lower member of the household. In reality, the only real difference between them was their expectations. Hardly minor, but not apt to gain Wickham favor.

"I don't know," Wickham said. He toyed with his glass. "This isn't half so entertaining, for one. No offense intended."

"Yet here you sit."

Wickham shrugged. "The card game doesn't serve my purpose. If I win, they may resent it. If I lose, I lose."

"You usually lose." Having paid them, Darcy knew the extent of Wickham's gambling debts.

"Sadly, yes."

"Then why play?"

"For the dream of winning."

"Is the dream worth the cost?" Darcy couldn't imagine it was.

"It must be," Wickham said, his sweeping gesture taking in the tables of gamblers.

"Yet you aren't joining them."

"As I said, it doesn't suit my purpose. I'm riding high on public opinion now. I'm a local hero. I don't want unpaid gambling debts to ruin that."

"If you could stop gambling, your life would be better," Darcy said. "You know I'm right."

"If you could stop offending people with your pride, your life would be better." Wickham cast Darcy an amused look. "The difference is; you don't realize I'm right."

"My inferiors are too easily offended." It was Darcy's turn to shrug. If people weren't able to appreciate being around someone of his standing, what did it matter to him? They likely weren't worth his time, or effort, anyhow.

"Your inferiors, as you call us, include most of the world. At least, according to you." Wickham leaned forward in his chair. "I'll make you a wager, Darcy, my last one for a while," he said in a low voice. "I'll take your advice and reform, for a time, to see how being the man you think I should be works out for me. I bet you I can behave as you think I should for a longer time than you go without offending people you don't want to offend with your pride."

Darcy frowned. It was tempting. Not because he needed to reform, but because Wickham did. It seemed like folly to think making a wager with someone addicted to gambling could help them, but was it an opportunity Darcy should seize?

"It will do you good, Darcy." Wickham's eyes glinted with challenge. "Even your father thought your manners were lacking."

Darcy straightened in his chair. He didn't care what most of the world thought of him, but he had cared about his father. He also knew, in this case, Wickham was once again telling the truth. Darcy's father had said it often enough, that his single criticism of his son was Darcy's inability to be affable unless surrounded only by people he considered his friends and equals. Once again, Wickham's words found their mark. "You expect me to kick off your reformation from gambling with a bet?" Darcy was aware his tone was harsh.

"There are bets and there are bets," Wickham responded. He leaned back, looking enviably at ease. "And we aren't speaking only of my gambling, but my overall behavior," he added, obviously aware of the allure reforming him held for Darcy. "I will bet you a shiny ha'penny that your pride will get you into trouble before my bad behavior does me."

Darcy took in the slight smile on Wickham's face. There was a glint in his eyes Darcy recalled from their youth. Usually, it accompanied phrases like, 'I bet I can climb to the top of that tree quicker than you,' or 'I bet you aren't brave enough to jump off the stable roof.' Wickham had rarely won those bets, and he wouldn't win this one either. Darcy stood, holding out his hand.

Wickham came to his feet as well, and they shook.

"George," Darcy said, amused by Wickham's obvious surprise at the name. "Try to behave."

"Behave?" Wickham grinned. "I will if you will."

Turning, Darcy walked away.

Chapter Five

~ Schemes ~

Mr. Bennet

Mr. Bennet, a widower and respected, had little trouble contriving to walk with Miss Lucas alone. It had taken merely a request sent by a servant. It was odd, he thought, that he should so easily be allowed to walk out with her. A younger man, never married, would have seen the request passed to her father or mother, who would then insist on a chaperone. Instead, Mr. Bennet was certain his message had been relayed without any parental intervention, and that their meeting was completely discreet.

"Thank you for seeing me, Miss Lucas," he said once they'd wandered a distance from her home. Whatever her answer, he didn't want to be overheard. Fortunately, it wasn't too cold for a walk of some length.

"Curiosity was incentive enough," she said. "I can't imagine what you wish to speak to me about." She didn't look at him as she spoke. She was dressed demurely, and kept her face forward. There was nothing clandestine about her attitude.

"I ask that you allow me to be blunt in explaining myself. I'm going to say things you may not approve of. If you are offended, I am sorry. I do not mean to upset you." He was aware of his heartbeat quickening slightly, which surprised him. He wasn't a green boy, or infatuated in any way. What he was proposing was little more than business, really. Hopefully she would understand that. Mr. Bennet had no use for emotional entanglements. He'd learned the first time.

"I am even more intrigued," Miss Lucas said.

"Then I shall not keep you in suspense. You understand Longbourn is entailed to Mr. Collins?"

"It is common enough knowledge."

"Until now, I didn't care who inherited Longbourn. I have regretted I never managed to save enough to support my wife and daughters after I die, but I never regretted it enough to overcome my distaste for quarreling with my late wife over her spending. Yet the truth is, if I had saved even a tenth of my income, my daughters would have more security."

He stopped walking, turning to her. Obligingly, she followed his lead, halting her steps and turning to him. Her face was composed, so very different from Mrs. Bennet's overly expressive features. He wondered if Miss Lucas realized what he was going to ask her. He knew she wouldn't say anything if she did. Miss Lucas knew how to hold her tongue. "I don't want Longbourn to go to Mr. Collins."

"No one does, now," she said. "No one would want such a man for a neighbor."

"There is only one way I can keep Mr. Collins from inheriting; marry and father a son. I realize there is a risk my wife might not get pregnant, and if she were able to conceive, she might give me more daughters. It's a risk I'm willing to take." He watched her face as he spoke, pleased he saw not enlightenment, but confirmation. She had already guessed where he was going before he'd mentioned marriage. Good. He'd known she was intelligent.

She kept silent, watching him.

He was a bit leery of that but, really, what could she say if she wanted him to continue? "I am forty-five. I could die tomorrow. I wish to marry quickly, since time is not on my side. I also want a wife who will run Longbourn well. My daughters will be in mourning for months. Expenses could be curtailed. You would make an excellent mistress of Longbourn. I would like to post the banns this Sunday. Will you marry me?"

She made no fuss or exclamation, indeed, hardly gave an outward sign of what he'd asked. Still, somehow, he felt it was a yes. Mr. Bennet allowed himself to relax, feeling foolish for succumbing to tension to begin with.

"You have proposed in a practical way, so I'm going to answer you in kind," Miss Lucas said. "My father will only give me five hundred pounds."

"It will all be yours," he said.

"I suppose you don't want to settle any more on me."

"That's correct. Mrs. Bennet had five thousand pounds. I propose to leave that to accumulate interest for my daughters. I will give you the same allowance I gave her. She used the interest on the five thousand pounds as well, but she was very extravagant."

"You believe I can save more money, even given less?"

"I know you can."

"Then let me make a suggestion. Any money I save will be divided into three equal amounts. One third will be added to your daughters' shares. One third will be given to me. I will put it with my five hundred pounds, for my future security. One third will be used to make improvements in your estate."

"Improvements?" Even though he felt he knew her moderately well, he'd no idea Miss Lucas was quite so practical. She also sounded exceedingly reasonable. Mr. Bennet was beginning to think, this time, he'd made a commendable choice.

"You know you haven't paid much attention to your farm," Miss Lucas said, seeming unaware of his pleasure in her tone, bearing and words. "You are using the same techniques that were used when you were a boy. I think you can improve your income if you risk a little money to try some new things."

"You sound as if you've investigated them." He was surprised to find his heart beating faster again. For the first time, he really looked her up and down. What a mind the woman was turning out to possess.

"I've investigated some of them. My father has permitted me to implement a few. They've worked."

"I can see you have some passion in this area," he said. "May I take it, then, that your suggestion is, in truth, a term for acquiescing?"

She smiled. "You may."

Really, she was prettier than he'd thought, and her figure quite fine. He'd never properly attended to her attributes before. "In that case, I accept your terms."

"Then yes, I will marry you. However, I believe it more appropriate to defer reading the banns until after Mrs. Bennet's funeral. It would be best not to tell your daughters until the funeral is over as well."

"Both reasonable suggestions." He held out his hand. She took it. Mr. Bennet felt a bit odd, walking hand in hand with a woman as he'd not done in many years. He was not, however, opposed to it.

They held hands until they drew within sight of Lucas Lodge, where he met with her father. Mr. Bennet encountered no difficulty when he asked for permission from Sir William. He was happy to finally have his daughter settled and amenable to the financial arrangements agreed to by Charlotte.

The details settled, nothing more was said on the subject. Mr. Bennet did not see Miss Lucas in the days leading up to the funeral. When he returned from putting his late wife to rest, he made the announcement to his daughters.

Elizabeth

Elizabeth prepared for church in a higher state of anxiety than Sunday services usually induced. She'd been trying, unsuccessfully, to wrap her head around her father's announcement. Her father, only hours after laying her mother to rest, had gathered all five of his daughters and informed them he'd asked Charlotte Lucas to be his wife. Perhaps even more shocking, Charlotte had accepted.

No, Elizabeth thought, fiddling with the ribbon on her bonnet as she followed her father and Jane toward the church with Mary at her side, it was more shocking her father had asked. Charlotte accepting was not expected, but should have been, when she looked back at some of the things Charlotte had said in the past. As Elizabeth's closest friend, at least until now, Charlotte had conversed with her on marriage. Elizabeth knew her friend didn't wish to be a burden on her family forever. Knew, as well, that Charlotte devoted herself to pursuits that would make her a desirable wife.

No, Charlotte leaping at the opportunity wasn't, strictly speaking, surprising. Elizabeth suspected her friend would have accepted nearly anyone at this point. In truth, the only single gentleman Elizabeth knew whom she could say with a certainty Charlotte would not marry was Mr. Collins. No one in Hertfordshire would, after his behavior.

For Elizabeth's father to ask Charlotte was, well, astounding. He'd hardly acknowledge Charlotte Lucas existed, let alone shown any interest in her. Elizabeth recalled him saying once, when she and Charlotte had first become friends, that he was forced to approve as Charlotte was the least silly choice. Elizabeth stifled nervous laughter as she couldn't help but wonder, was her father's decision making in this case the same? Was Charlotte simply the least silly choice for a wife?

Elizabeth understood, but did not condone, her father's haste. He'd been clear enough when he told them of his decision. He wished a son, so Mr. Collins couldn't inherit Longbourn, and he felt he was too long in years to wait any more time than necessary to begin begetting one.

Her face heating, Elizabeth banished that thought. She could not possibly bear to ever, ever, think about her father and her closest friend begetting. It was not to be endured. If she ever did gain a baby brother, or sister, she would be quite sure Charlotte had plucked it from the cabbage patch, or been visited by a stork. Inane as they might seem, such notions were much more calculated to secure her sanity than pondering the truth.

Seeing Charlotte and her family approaching, Elizabeth felt the heat suffusing her cheeks increase. Greetings were exchanged with such normalcy, however, that she began to relax. She was relieved Kitty and Lydia had remained home, still too distressed to be out. Elizabeth couldn't imagine their lack of deportment, given how Mary gawked at Charlotte and muddled her way through the usual courtesies. At least Jane behaved as if nothing were out of the ordinary. In fact, all save Mary proceeded so smoothly, Elizabeth began to doubt her memory in recalling her father's announcement.

"Miss Lucas," Mr. Bennet said as the two families neared the church. "Will you sit with us during the sermon?"

"No, thank you, Mr. Bennet. I believe I shall retain my customary place until my change in station."

Her father nodded. Elizabeth was surprised to see he looked a touch disappointed. He would never have been disappointed had their mother wished to sit away from him.

Charlotte and her family moved away and all were seated, the service commencing as usual. If there were some sidelong looks and whispered words, there was no way to know whether they were related to rumor of the upcoming nuptials or to Elizabeth's mother's death. Elizabeth steeled herself for greater scrutiny when the time came for the banns to be read, but they were read for a couple on the Goulding's estate only. Their rector, Mr. Preston, then began the offertory. Elizabeth glanced at her father in confusion, wondering if he'd somehow changed his mind.

Her father cupped his hands about his mouth. "You will read all the banns," he shouted from his pew.

Mr. Preston looked up from the pages before him, his face reddening. "I will not. It is indecent for you to remarry so quickly. Your wife is not cold in her grave."

"By now she is," Mr. Bennet muttered, the words nearly lost in the low babble of voices that quickly filled the church. Mr. Bennet stood up. Elizabeth made a move to follow, but he gestured for her to stay. As she watched her father march from the church, she saw Mr. Bingley leave his seat and follow.

The remainder of the service was uncomfortable for Elizabeth. She and Jane slid over, covering the empty space beside them, but Elizabeth could feel the eyes of the neighborhood on them. Finally, the service was concluded and she and her two sisters joined the line of parishioners filing out. Elizabeth fortified herself as best she could against the curious stares and hum of gossip. When they reached Mr. Preston and the exit, he didn't look at all pleased.

"I hope Mr. Bingley talked some sense into your father," the clergyman said.

Elizabeth managed a weak smile in response. She didn't think Mr. Bingley was the kind of person who would take it upon himself to talk sense into anyone.

"We shall ask them," Jane said, looking past Mr. Preston.

Elizabeth followed her gaze to observe their father and Mr. Bingley talking earnestly and apparently cordially.

"It was a wonderful sermon," Mary said. "Do you know, some of the greatest minds of our time maintain—"

Elizabeth took that opportunity to dip a hasty curtsy and hurry away, Jane beside her. Neither of them wished to hear Mary repeat whatever she happened to be reading. Likely, Mr. Preston didn't wish to either. Unlike Elizabeth and Jane, he was obliged to.

Their father bowed to Mr. Bingley, who cast a longing smile their way before hurrying off. Elizabeth could feel Jane's disappointment and her sister's steps slowed. Mr. Bennet came toward them, only to pass them by. Turning, Elizabeth watched him march up to Mr. Preston, who was greeting the Lucas family. Elizabeth took Jane by the arm, tugging her back toward Mary, Mr. Preston and Charlotte's family. Given the chance, Jane would likely stand and watch Mr. Bingley depart for an unseemly length of time.

Mr. Bennet stopped before Mr. Preston. "I presume you will marry us when we have the proper documents."

"Certainly. I will even read the banns next Sunday." Mr. Preston glanced nervously at Charlotte, who was standing between her parents. "Assuming you all wish me to."

"We'll be certain to advise you," Mr. Bennet said. He held out his arm and Charlotte took it. The two of them walked away, their heads close together as they spoke rapidly, their paces falling with seeming ease into a common stride.

Elizabeth watched them go, aware of a stirring of emotion within her, which she was dismayed to realize was jealousy. She wasn't sure of which, her father talking so easily with her friend, or her friend speaking so intimately with her father. Either way, she was resolved to subdue the emotion. It simply wouldn't do to be jealous of what happiness they could find with one another.

On the way home, they were silent, except for Mary's voice. Elizabeth's younger sister seemed to feel it her duty to expound at length on the prescribed role of matrimony in English society. As all Mary did was repeat various passages she'd read, it wasn't possible to tell if she argued for or against their father's right to remarry immediately. Elizabeth only half listened.

When they reached the front door, Lydia and Kitty came out of the parlor to greet them, watching them enter, their eyes red from crying. Lydia opened her mouth to speak, but sobbed instead, turning to put her head on Kitty's shoulder.

"Jane, would you please join me in my library at your earliest convenience," their father said as Jane moved to comfort their younger sisters.

"Yes, Papa," Jane said, her arms about the sobbing pair.

Elizabeth waited a moment to see if their father would address her, but he went to the library without saying anything more. Feeling that slight more than she knew she ought, she suggested to Mary that she pin up the hem of the black dress Mary was nearly finished sewing.

Lydia lifted her head, sniffling. "Kitty, I should pin your dress, too."

"Thank you," Kitty said, and started sobbing again, covering her face with her hands.

Mary retrieved the dresses, pressing Kitty's into her hands, and both changed while Elizabeth and Lydia got out the pins. The hems were set in silence, punctuated only by the occasional cough from Kitty. When she was done, Elizabeth stood, gesturing for Mary to turn so she could inspect her work.

"I hate black, but I have to wear it for Mama, even though it makes me look horrible," Mary said.

"You're not looking at yourself properly," Lydia said, straightening from working on Kitty's hem.

"What do you mean?" Mary asked.

"Look in the mirror."

Mary moved to the small mirror near the door of the parlor.

"No. Not that one. The long one in Mama's room," Lydia said.

Elizabeth, Mary and Kitty exchanged glances. It seemed shocking and disrespectful to talk about going into their mother's room.

"Mama's mirror?" Kitty whispered.

"It will soon be Charlotte's mirror, and Charlotte's room," Lydia said, her tone touched with anger. "It won't hurt to use the mirror."

"No, it won't," Elizabeth said. Lydia was right, and Elizabeth realized they should take this chance to see their mother's room as it always was, for soon it would change.

Marching from the parlor, she led her younger sisters upstairs and into their mother's room. Lydia crossed to the window and threw open the curtains, letting in more light. Elizabeth made a slow turn, taking in all the beautiful, and sentimental, things her mother had collected over the years. This room held Mrs. Bennet's most treasured items, especially with four of her daughters in it.

Mary moved to stand in front of the mirror. "I look pathetic."

"No, you look dramatic," Lydia said, coming to stand behind her. "You need to make your hair more severe, but with a ribbon. Curls don't really suit you."

"I can't wear a ribbon. Not when I'm mourning."

"You can wear a black one. Come, let me fix it for you." Lydia led them to the room she and Kitty shared and picked up some discarded black cloth. After a few snips with scissors, she created a strip of cloth. She folded it. "Lizzy, you're quickest. Could you sew it here?"

Elizabeth took the folded cloth. Looking about, she spied a needle already threaded with black. She took it up and began sewing with quick, sure stitches. Kitty sat down on the bed, toying with the other black scraps of cloth, her expression sad.

"Sit here," Lydia ordered Mary, pointing to the chair before the dressing table.

Mary looked at her younger sister with slightly wide eyes, and did as she was told. While Elizabeth sewed, Lydia brushed Mary's hair out straight, the curls needing little encouragement to disappear. Elizabeth finished her work, turning the tube she'd sewn inside out and handing it to Lydia. Mary would be able to sew the end later.

"Thank you," Lydia said. She braided the newly-fashioned ribbon into Mary's hair with competent ease. It made a sharp contrast to Mary's pale hair.

"There. Now go look at yourself," Lydia said, smiling at her work.

They all returned to their mother's room. Mary stood before the long mirror, turning from side to side, her expression slightly surprised. Elizabeth was as well, having believed the dull black fabric wouldn't be attractive on anyone, but Lydia was correct. Mary was much more striking than usual. Her pale skin, which generally looked washed out and wan beside the pastel dresses she favored, looked dramatic against the black. The more severe hair style, instead of emphasizing Mary's overly bland face in an unflattering way, gave her an arresting allure.

"You look beautiful," Kitty said.

"It is very becoming," Elizabeth supplied. "Lydia, how clever of you."

"It will only work for Mary," Lydia said, her tone envious. "I've always thought it's too bad she can't wear black unless she's in mourning. Now she has an excuse to wear it. I've tried to tell her to wear dark colors, but she says they aren't right for a young, unmarried woman."

Elizabeth knew that was true, but hadn't given it much thought. Now, no one could criticize Mary for wearing something that made her more attractive. She would only be condemned for not wearing black.

Mary put a hand to her hair. "Is it truly that becoming?"

"You can see for yourself," Lydia said, shrugging.

"You aren't simply trying to be kind?"

Lydia snorted, shaking her head.

"We are not," Elizabeth said. "You truly look pretty. Mama would be so pleased." She regretted the words as soon as they left her mouth, for all four of them set to looking about the room. Elizabeth knew her face must match the sorrowful expressions on her sisters'. Kitty sniffed, wiping her eyes.

"Here you all are," Jane said, coming into the room. She made a slow turn, her countenance mournful as well, and Elizabeth guessed she was thinking the same thing Elizabeth had: Soon, their mother's room would change. "Mary, you look lovely," Jane said as her gaze came to rest on Mary. Jane smiled, the expression at odds with her sad eyes. "I didn't think anyone could wear black well."

Mary blushed. "Thank you, Jane. Lydia did it."

"Well, Lydia did a wonderful thing for you, then."

Lydia didn't blush. She stood up straighter, looking proud.

Jane turned to Elizabeth, her smile fading but a serene, almost happy, look taking its place. Elizabeth couldn't imagine the cause of that look was simply by Mary's appearance. She wondered what Jane and their father had talked about.

"Lizzy, Papa wishes to speak with you," Jane said.

Elizabeth nodded. "Mary, you should sew more ribbons. It looked as if Kitty and Lydia have more scraps."

"We do," Kitty said.

"You can have them," Lydia said. She wrinkled her nose. "I don't need them. I don't look half so pretty in black as you do."

They all filed out of their mother's room, Mary blushing again. Elizabeth hurried down the steps, aware of Jane entering the bedroom they shared, not following their younger sisters to Kitty's and Lydia's room. As she walked down the hall to their father's library, Elizabeth wondered again what he'd said to put such a peaceful look on Jane's face, and what he would say to her. When she reached the door she knocked. "Papa, it's me, Elizabeth."

"Come in," was the muffled reply.

Elizabeth entered the familiar room. Her eyes went immediately to the wall where a miniature of her mother always hung. She was surprised to find it replaced with a slightly larger, more recent rendition. Elizabeth wondered when her father had done that, for she hadn't noticed the newer portrait of her mother, one of Jane's best works, being absent from its usual place in the dining room. She was foolishly glad to see it there, having worried he would have replaced the miniature with Charlotte as well.

"Please, sit," her father said, gesturing to a chair across from his desk.

Elizabeth did as she was bidden, sinking into the comfortable leather. How many times had she sat there, absorbing her father's humor and wisdom? She waited with mild anxiety to learn what he would impart today.

"Lizzy, this marriage will be particularly hard for you," her father said. "You think of Charlotte as a peer and she will become a parent. If all goes as I hope, Charlotte and I will become closer than you are either to me or to her. To put it bluntly, for many years you have been the person I cherished the most. I hope to replace your position in that role with Charlotte. Perhaps it won't happen. Perhaps I'm an old fool, but I think I could come to love her. That doesn't mean I will love you less."

Elizabeth sat for a moment, digesting that. She recalled her earlier jealousy, and her resolve to lay it to rest. "I hope it does happen. I must admit to some uncharitable thoughts, but I truly hope Charlotte becomes dearer to both of us."

"You wouldn't be human if you didn't have uncharitable thoughts."

"Unless I was Jane," Elizabeth said with a smile. "I don't believe there to be a harsh bone in her." She hesitated, for there was more she wished to say, now that the subject of unhappy thoughts had been broached. "I don't see why you must wed with such haste. I know you told us you don't wish Mr. Collins to inherit and you are old, but you aren't that old, Papa. Are you unwell? Is there some reason you feel you need to wed so quickly? Something I should be aware of?" Elizabeth kept her tone even, but inside she was shaken. She couldn't endure losing her father, especially not so soon after her mother.

Mr. Bennet shook his head. "The most salient reason for quite so much haste is not myself or Charlotte, but rather Kitty and Lydia."

Elizabeth blinked, thoroughly confused. "Kitty and Lydia?"

"Charlotte is going to run things very differently than your mother did. I want us to marry quickly, before your younger sisters get over the shock of losing your mother and return to their old habits."

"Differently?"

"Very," he repeated. "And I expect you to obey her and support her."

"I promise to try to," Elizabeth said, wondering what Charlotte's changes would entail. Knowing her friend as she did, Elizabeth couldn't imagine they would be anything unendurable. For her and Jane, at least.

"That is enough of a promise for now," her father said, smiling. "Send Mary in when you leave."

"Yes, Papa." Elizabeth stood. "Be sure to complement her on her look. Lydia has transformed her."

"I will," her father said, looking slightly bemused.

Elizabeth left her father's library resolved to be happy for both him and her friend. Though she was still shocked at the speed at which her father sought to replace her mother and taken aback by Charlotte's quick acceptance of a man so much her senior, she could understand the logic on both sides. Elizabeth's rational self could even agree with their thinking, though her heart was sore over the loss of her mother and resented their behavior. At least, she reflected as she sought Mary, with the banns not being read this Sunday, she and all of Hertfordshire would have weeks more to grow accustomed to the idea.

The following evening found Elizabeth with the rest of her family, together in the parlor. The day had been one of condolence calls, though those were tapering. Elizabeth was glad of that, for each one raised a fresh bout of weeping in Kitty and Lydia, and sometimes her, Jane and Mary as well. Though she knew it had been but a short while, Elizabeth was weary of black, of sad words and of being cooped up indoors surrounded by both.

A knock at the door made her wince, for she'd thought visitors done for the day. A maid appeared, but no one followed her. Instead, she presented their father with a letter.

"Is anything wrong?" Elizabeth asked, exchanging a worried look with Jane. For the letter to arrive so late, it must have come by special courier.

Her father chuckled, opening the envelope. "No. Everything is right." He held up a piece of paper. "This is a common license. Charlotte and I can be married without banns. I wonder how Mr. Preston will like keeping his promise to me."

Elizabeth exchanged another look with Jane, this time of shock. At least, she was shocked. Jane's face was almost devoid of emotion, which was instantly suspicious. Elizabeth knew that blank look as the one her sister assumed when attempting to conceal her emotions. Elizabeth was sure Jane had known about the special license. Why would her father tell Jane and not her?

Mr. Bennet stood. "Please send a servant to my library to take a letter to Lucas Lodge," he said, leaving the room.

Lydia burst into tears, which set Kitty crying. Jane went over to comfort them.

Mary sniffed. "Do you think Charlotte will be a good mama?"

"She will never be any sort of mama to me," Lydia sobbed. "I hate her, and I hate father."

"I'm sure she'll be a welcome addition to our home," Elizabeth said staunchly. She crossed the room to ring for a servant to send to Lucas Lodge.

The marriage took place the following morning. Mr. Preston put a good face on, seeming to wish the couple well with all sincerity, as did Jane, Elizabeth and Charlotte's family. After the ceremony, there was a hastily arranged wedding breakfast at Lucas Lodge. It was a pleasant enough gathering, though Kitty and Lydia were sullen and Jane seemed hardly to attend to what they were about.

Elizabeth and her sisters walked back. Mr. Bennet and Charlotte were to use her family's carriage, which was being packed with her possessions, things still being added when Elizabeth and her sisters left Lucas Lodge. It felt odd to Elizabeth, leaving Lucas Lodge with Charlotte and all of her belongings following her home.

"I will not call her mama," Lydia said, kicking a pebble down the road.

"I daresay she doesn't wish you to," Elizabeth said.

"I won't, either," Kitty declared, as if Elizabeth hadn't spoken.

"She's your friend, Lizzy. How could you let her do this?" Lydia said.

"It isn't as if she consulted me, any more than Papa did us."

"Still, if you two weren't friends—"

"Papa would still have known her," Jane put in.

"And think, if he didn't, he would have chosen someone else," Elizabeth said, silently thanking Jane for taking her side. "Who knows who? There are plenty of women I'd care for much less than Charlotte."

"Elizabeth is right," Mary said. "Father was determined to marry, to keep Mr. Collins from inheriting. We should be pleased he chose someone we know and like."

"I don't like her," Lydia muttered.

"I do worry we shall end up with more sisters," Mary said.

"They're sure to be hideous little things, like their mama," Lydia said.

"Lydia." Jane's tone was reproving.

Lydia shrugged and quickened her pace, striding ahead. Kitty raced to catch up with her. Lydia slowed down enough to lean over and say something to Kitty, who giggled. Elizabeth smiled slightly, pleased to see them somewhat themselves.

They arrived at Longbourn the same time as the carriage. Elizabeth watched, silent, as their father offered his hand to help Charlotte disembark. With the same courtesy, he escorted her over the threshold. Through the open door, they could see him bend his head and bestow a kiss on her lips. Beside Elizabeth, Lydia made a gagging sound. Though the sight of their father kissing Charlotte was similarly disquieting to Elizabeth, she kept her face neutral.

Mr. Bennet looked out at them and gestured. "Girls, come here."

Obediently, Elizabeth started forward. She couldn't quite force herself to meet Charlotte's eyes as she entered. It still seemed too awkward, Charlotte being their new mother.

"I haven't emptied the former Mrs. Bennet's rooms," their father said once they were all gathered inside. "I'm sorry to hand that job to you, Charlotte, but it should be done. I will be in my library." With that, he left them.

Elizabeth turned to Charlotte, who appeared commendably calm. Charlotte met her look and gave the barest hint of a grimace before moving her gaze over Elizabeth's sisters. "Come with me."

Charlotte headed up the stairs, Elizabeth and her sisters trailing behind. She led the way to their mother's room. Stopping in the center, she turned in a slow circle, much as Jane had done a scant two days ago. Elizabeth allowed her gaze to likewise traverse the space, trying to see it how Charlotte must. The room was not as artistically decorated as the public spaces, holding several items kept more for sentiment than attractiveness, but the room showed the first Mrs. Bennet had an eye for beauty.

"Where did she keep her jewelry?" Charlotte asked. "We should tend to it first."

"In this box," Elizabeth said. She moved to the dressing table, picking up an ornately carved, but not overly large, box.

"If you would, please?" Charlotte said, holding out her hand.

Elizabeth nodded and handed her the box.

"She kept the key hidden," Jane said, and retrieved the key from a small compartment concealed in the dressing table. She offered the key to Charlotte, who took it.

"Come with me. I think a larger table is wanted, and your father's blessing," Charlotte said.

They all followed her back downstairs and to their father's library and Charlotte knocked.

"Enter," their father said.

Charlotte pushed the door open. "Mr. Bennet, I wish to supervise the dividing of your first wife's jewelry and other possessions as you told me she did not leave a will. I believe this must be done before the room can be cleared up."

"Certainly, my dear."

"Thank you." Charlotte closed the door, leading the way into the dining room.

To Elizabeth's surprise, her father came out of his library, following them. He took his place at the table as they took theirs. Charlotte unlocked the box and carefully spread out the jewelry. The pieces varied from those few that were valuable to the merest trinkets.

When Charlotte was finished arranging them, she looked up. "Jane, you pick first."

Jane looked over everything very briefly. "I'll take the box."

"The box? Not her pearls?" Elizabeth asked in surprise. She and Jane had admired the pearls often enough, and Elizabeth thought they would look splendid on her older sister. Never once had she heard Jane speak of the jewelry box itself. It was a pretty box with delicately carved designs, but hardly worth much compared to the jewelry.

Jane picked up the box and the key. "The box," she said firmly.

"Elizabeth, you may select second," Charlotte said.

"I'll take the pearls, then." Elizabeth felt if she left them for Jane one of her other sisters would take them.

"Mary," Charlotte said.

"I'll take the cross." Again, it wasn't the most valuable piece left.

Kitty reached for a heavy chain, but Lydia elbowed her. Kitty looked to Lydia. "Which would look best on me?"

Lydia pointed to a delicate chain, which Kitty took. One by one, the pieces were allocated. When the last piece was given to Kitty, Mr. Bennet rose and returned to his library, still smiling.

After they all put away the jewelry, they returned to their mother's rooms. Charlotte took a brief tour, then told them what things she wanted left. She wished to dispose of all of the clothing and ornaments, as well as some of the furniture. Elizabeth was surprised that this time, when allocating their mother's possessions, Charlotte started with Lydia, who took the mirror. That pleased Kitty, because the mirror would be kept in the room they shared. Their mother's rooms looked very bare when they were through. Charlotte told Mrs. Hill to have them cleaned.

"Thank you all for your assistance," Charlotte said as they left Mrs. Hill and her staff to their work.

"Are you going to do the same thing to the rest of the house?" Lydia asked sullenly.

"No," Charlotte said with a smile. "I needed to clear those rooms for my things. That is more than enough space for them. Your mother had wondrous taste. I see no reason to change things."

Over the next two weeks, Elizabeth found Charlotte's statement not to be strictly true, for things did change in Longbourn. The table was set with little more food than they ate, meaning if company came, it must be planned in advance. Charlotte told Elizabeth and her sisters the maids would now only clean their rooms once a month and all of them should make their own beds and see that their rooms were tidied daily. They were told to sweep and dust at least once a week. They were informed each of them was expected to contribute at least an hour a day to the running of the household, and to seek out charity work, in addition to ladylike pursuits. Mary tried to claim her pursuit of so many accomplishments took precedence, but Charlotte said Mary's choice of activities did not exempt her from doing what the others did.

Jane took over mending the linen. She could sew better than any of them, and the mends were hardly noticeable. Elizabeth kept books for the household and helped in the kitchen, which she found quite educational. Charlotte's requirement of an hour a day was hardly onerous, but Kitty and Lydia complained to each other. They quickly formed a dislike of their father's new wife, and took to whispering about her as Char-little, for she permitted little decoration, little food, and little fun.

If Elizabeth found her time in the kitchen educational, she found her time managing the household accounts even more so. The kitchen was interesting because it had never occurred to Elizabeth to wonder how things actually got done. She hadn't known how to light the very modern closed stove her mother had insisted on buying, and why the cook shaved wood to gradually add small amounts to keep the temperature constant, or what dishes were best to serve when you hoped, or feared, leftovers.

The books, on the other hand, were a more empirical pursuit and pleasantly challenged Elizabeth's mind. The calculations involved were not arduous, but seeing where her mother allocated coin and where Charlotte chose to was eye-opening. Elizabeth had always known her mother was a bit frivolous, but never realized quite how much so. Why, what she would spend on one special ingredient for one dish, something she felt they simply must serve, was boggling when compared to how much food could have been purchased, or money saved. She would buy ducks when she wanted them, disdaining the chickens they raised. She would order peaches, though they had apples going to waste. In no short time, Elizabeth began to realize her mother had been squandering their futures, and her father had been permitting it.

She took to working more than her one hour, and she and Charlotte could often be found in the little office at the back of the kitchen. It was on one such occasion Mrs. Hill came in with hardly a knock. Looking up, Elizabeth could see the housekeeper was agitated.

"Mrs. Bennet, Miss Elizabeth," Mrs. Hill greeted.

"Mrs. Hill, what is troubling you?" Charlotte asked, turning from her work.

"One of the maids quit and another is talking about doing so. They say we don't give them enough food, and they don't like the additional work you've given them."

"They don't have additional work, they have different work," Charlotte said. She'd set them to making candles and soap now that they didn't spend as much time cleaning and tidying, saying they had too much idle time. Elizabeth agreed with the economy of the idea. "You know we feed them well. I have no objection to feeding them, but they'd colluded with the cook to deliberately make too much so they could bring food to their families."

Mrs. Hill nodded, obviously knowing that was true. "They say, too, it isn't prestigious to work here anymore, missus."

Charlotte regarded Mrs. Hill with her usual calm. Elizabeth had always known her to be like that, but respected it more now that she'd seen Charlotte maintain the poise in more varied situations. "I admit to having expected as much. I've arranged to hire Sally Smith instead."

"Sally Smith?" Mrs. Hill was clearly incredulous.

"Yes. She was working in Netherfield when it burned. She needs a place. If we don't take her, her father is going to send her to work in a mill. We can't permit that in our community."

"But she's only a girl, missus. She can't take over the work of two experienced maids."

"She won't have to. There's much less work to be done. The Miss Bennets are being far more active in that regard. In fact, I don't think we'll need Sally to work full hours. I believe she can come for two fewer a day than the former maids did, before the reduction."

"Two fewer, missus? And what is a girl like that to do with extra hours, I ask you?"

Elizabeth reflected that Mrs. Hill was clearly of a mind with the maid who left and the other who might leave. The housekeeper obviously didn't approve of Charlotte tampering with the prestige of Longbourn. Elizabeth had never realized how much the staff cared about such things.

"I imagine she'll find something to occupy her," Charlotte said.

"Aye, but nothing good. It's our duty to keep her here all hours, missus. Idle hands do the devil's work."

Charlotte's eyes narrowed. "I doubt Sally Smith will so be suborned by the devil in two hours a day. Actually, as I think on it, in addition to shorter days, give her a full day off every other week so she can visit her family. Also, I believe we shall remove much of the ornamentation in the common rooms. That should greatly simplify the dusting." Charlotte regarded Mrs. Hill steadily. "I daresay if I put my mind to it, I could find a way to do away with the need for more of the remaining staff. Don't you agree, Mrs. Hill?"

Mrs. Hill stared at her for a long moment. Finally, she nodded. "Yes, Mrs. Bennet."

"Sally will be here the day after tomorrow," Charlotte said. "I expect you to treat her kindly and explain her duties to her."

"Yes, Mrs. Bennet." Mrs. Hill left the room.

Elizabeth turned to Charlotte. "I'd no idea you were so ruthless."

Charlotte smiled. "If the staff cannot gossip about the ostentation of Longbourn, let them gossip about my harsh treatment of them. Either way, they will be satisfied. They want only something to create tales of to impress their fellows. No one wants to be employed in a boring household."

Elizabeth nodded, returning to the books. Charlotte had given her much to think about. Two days later, Sally Smith came and the two maids left. Sally was so young, Elizabeth was glad she was able to go home every other week, although she knew it was an unusual indulgence. Soap and candles were bought at Meryton again, making

Elizabeth suspect the exit of the maids had been planned, though she suspected if they really needed to cut back more, she and her sisters would end up making soap and candles.

Over the next several days, Elizabeth realized they'd hit a social lull. The condolence calls had stopped, which was a relief. Not only had they grown arduous for Elizabeth and her sisters, but they'd been made awkward by Charlotte's presence. The lack of society chaffed Elizabeth only slightly, that slightness being Mr. Wickham, for everyone else she most enjoyed conversing with now residing in Longbourn. It seemed to perturb Jane and Mary not at all. Lydia and Kitty, however, were quite distressed. They'd begun to bemoan their lack of interaction with officers with a frequency that required the mustering of forbearance.

"A note has come from your Aunt Phillips," Charlotte informed them as they all gathered in the parlor one afternoon before tea. She held up a piece of stationary. "She has invited us all to an evening of cards. She has extended this invitation to various other suitable company as well."

"Officers? Shall there be officers?" Lydia cried.

"I love an outing with officers," Kitty said, her tone dreamy.

Elizabeth all but held her breath, unsure if Charlotte meant to permit them to go. They were still in mourning, after all. It would be the height of cruelty to mention the invitation if she'd no intention of allowing them to attend, but Elizabeth had witnessed Charlotte's set down of Mrs. Hill. "May we go?" Elizabeth asked.

"Of course we may, mayn't we?" Lydia asked, looking stricken. "Please say we may. I shall die of boredom if I remain here another moment."

"Then you shall die, for the invitation is for tomorrow night, not for a moment from now," Charlotte said. "I do believe the rest of you should attend, however, but you are to wear black. It is only seemly."

"You don't truly mean I can't go?" Lydia wailed.

"Of course you may go," Charlotte said. "That I ask you to dust your room doesn't make me a monster, I hope. Besides, your father and I shall enjoy an evening with only each other's company."

"You aren't attending?" Elizabeth asked, surprised. Charlotte used to quite enjoy an outing.

Charlotte shook her head. "I don't think you need a chaperone with your aunt and uncle."

It wasn't only that they were related. Elizabeth knew if there was dancing it would be hard to keep Lydia and Kitty from joining in, but since the Phillips didn't own a pianoforte and had relatively little space, there would not be dancing. She suspected Charlotte knew there was little trouble Kitty and Lydia could get into at the Phillips.

"Who cares if Charlotte and Papa are going?" Lydia said. "We are. I shall need to think of some way to make myself look splendid. Black doesn't look good on me. I may have to wear more of my hair down, don't you think?"

Lydia and Kitty prattled on in that fashion for the rest of the evening, causing dinner to end quickly. Their father and Charlotte retreated to his library. Elizabeth tried to stay behind the pianoforte, but Mary wanted her turn to practice. Jane, as usual, seemed unaffected by their youngest two sisters' inane babbling. She stitched away, a soft smile on her face, almost as if the rest of them weren't even there.

When they arrived at their aunt's the following day, Elizabeth was pleased to see several officers had been invited. Card tables were set up and Elizabeth maneuvered to play at a table with Mr. Wickham, even though it included Lydia and Mr. Denny. There was no possibility of private conversation at their table, but that didn't prevent Lydia from flirting with both officers so outrageously Elizabeth thought perhaps Charlotte should have kept her home. Mary, Elizabeth could glimpse from where she sat, didn't flirt, but attracted more attention than usual. Thanks to Lydia's help, she had a look of tragic allure some of the officers clearly appreciated.

When it was time to return to Longbourn, Mr. Wickham and Mr. Denny kindly insisted on escorting them home, along with Captain Carter and Colonel Forster, who had played with Mary and Kitty. Jane hadn't played cards, sitting instead in a somewhat dreamy near-silence that rebuked even the most gallant attempts made to attract her attention. Elizabeth, who'd observed Jane all evening, thought it beastly unfair of her sister. Jane knew she was the prettiest girl in Hertfordshire. She owed it to the young men of the town to at least acknowledge she could see them.

The evening was cold, but Elizabeth didn't mind. She'd been too long cooped up indoors to care if there was a chill in the December air. As they walked, the nine of them soon broke into smaller groups. Lydia and Kitty strode rather far ahead, with Captain Carter and Mr. Denny. Colonel Forster walked at a more sedate pace between Jane and Mary.

Elizabeth felt for him, as she suspected he'd taken the spot to be near Jane, but must pay the price of listening to Mary in order to take in Jane's fair visage. She wouldn't rescue him, however, for the arrangement left her lingering behind with Mr. Wickham, which was very agreeable to her.

From far ahead, Lydia's and Kitty's laughter drifted back to Elizabeth. Looking down at her somber skirts, she supposed she should find their frivolity objectionable, but couldn't bring herself to. They'd been mourning their mother for weeks. While sorrow still clung to them all, it was impossible to maintain it continuously. Before learning of this outing, Lydia and Kitty had been somber enough, for long enough, Elizabeth had begun to worry about them.

Trying to banish her own pall of sadness, she glanced at Mr. Wickham, mustering a smile. "You are quite the hero, saving some of the servants and Miss Bingley."

He awarded her a smile of his own. "True enough, but I never did convince Miss Bingley to offer me a reward."

"I didn't think you would, though I say it would have been good of her. Still, it must be satisfying to be acclaimed by so many."

"It would be more so if I could make money out of it."

"Make money?" She repeated, surprised by the turn of conversation.

"If I had enough money, I could marry where I would." He cast her a sidelong look. "As it is, I can't afford to."

"I see." She did see. She wasn't surprised. At least, not that he should want to wed for wealth. Most did, men and women. She was, however, surprised he felt the need to tell her he wouldn't offer for her. Yes, they'd enjoyed a certain amount of comradery, and she'd some vague thoughts on the matter, but nothing at all substantial. "Money is the crux of many things, I suppose. I'm sorry you didn't profit more from your bravery, in a pecuniary way, at least."

"Oh, I did somewhat. I owed a bit to some local merchants and two of them forgave my debts for my bravery. Sadly, the others still wanted cash."

"You had intended to pay them at some point, of course," she said. She and Mr. Wickham had never discussed money before. She was appalled he was so cavalier about it. Of course, she'd been more so herself, before taking up the family accounts. She supposed it was the mark of a gentleman not to care over much about money.

"To be honest, I hadn't intended to, no, but I did."

"I'm pleased to hear it. They can't afford to stay in business if they aren't paid. I imagine you had a change of heart. The fire must have awoken a valent streak in you."

"I doubt that's possible," he said with a slight smile. "I paid them because I was worried it would tarnish my image not to."

Elizabeth didn't know what to say to that. The Mr. Wickham she knew was entertaining and lighthearted. Was he also a man who racked up debts and left town without paying them?

"I had my gambling debts forgiven as well," he continued. "I am now debt free, astonishing for me. I plan to keep it that way for now, which will be difficult."

Trying to make sense of the man beside her she asked, "You truly weren't used to paying your debts?"

"Darcy paid…" He stopped. "Perhaps I'm taking this attempt at honesty too far, and money isn't really an appropriate topic, is it?"

"No, please, tell me. I must confess to some confusion over how the two of you interact. I should like to understand better."

Mr. Wickham sighed. "Then I have a confession to make. Darcy had some justification for keeping the living from me. He paid many of my debts."

"Enough to be worth the value of the living?"

Mr. Wickham shrugged.

"One thing that has baffled me is your trust in him when he told you to whistle. It was such an odd request. From what I thought I knew of your relationship with him then, I assumed at the time he was trying to make you look like a fool." She shook her head. "I saw your face. You didn't realize there was a fire until after you whistled."

"No, I didn't."

"Yet you trusted him."

"Yes. Darcy is arrogant, but he isn't petty."

Elizabeth digested that. "I disliked him when I stayed at Netherfield Park. He is haughty in the extreme. His pride goes before all other traits, yet he acted heroically during the fire. I don't understand him."

"Darcy is a strange one. He's very proud, yes, but that runs in the family. Only his father didn't have the Darcy arrogance. His sister is as snobbish as he is," he added, a bitter edge creeping into his voice.

Taking in his glower, Elizabeth turned the conversation to lighter things, determined to enjoy herself, but as they conversed her mind kept returning to what Mr. Wickham had revealed about the living Mr. Darcy had denied him. It shed new light on both men. She wondered if she'd managed to misjudge them.

Both had been similarly brave during the fire, but she doubted Mr. Darcy was seeking advantage from his bravery. Of course, Mr. Darcy needn't. He already had every advantage of station, finance and appearance.

She glanced at Mr. Wickham's handsome face, wondering how a man could look so attractive, so honest, so sincere, and be so brave, but have some of the characteristics of a spoiled child. Did she see more than was there in Mr. Wickham? Did that means she saw less than she ought in Mr. Darcy?

Elizabeth shook her head. It didn't matter. Mr. Wickham wouldn't remain in Meryton forever, and she was unlikely to ever see Mr. Darcy again. They walked on, the gentlemen escorting Elizabeth and her sisters all the way home.

Late that night, in the wee hours before dawn, Elizabeth found her mind restless. Though a part of her knew she was asleep and dreaming, knew she'd walked home and readied for bed, she couldn't summon wakefulness to stave off the terrible images plaguing her. She watched, unable to intervene, as Mr. Collins pushed her mother down. She saw the curtain's burning as Kitty and Lydia had described, and heard the hungry crackling of the fire. Unlike in Lydia's recounting, Elizabeth watched her mother struggle to rise, but fall back to the floor. Twisting her head at an odd angle, Mrs. Bennet glared at Elizabeth. "Elizabeth, why didn't you save me?"

She sat up with a gasp, fighting down a sob, the message in the dream painfully clear. If she'd sought out her mother before leaving, or gone back to find her instead of helping the people in the stable, Elizabeth might have saved her. Their father and the mild burns Lydia had suffered confirmed Lydia had run back into the fire to get their mother. What had Elizabeth done?

"What's the matter?" Jane asked, her voice muddled with sleep and confusion.

"I was dreaming," Elizabeth said.

"About what?"

Jane, due to her gentle nature, would assume the guilt Elizabeth felt tenfold if the thought of it ever came to her. Knowing she couldn't burden her sister with her dream, Elizabeth said, "It was about Mama. She said she wished she'd lived long enough to see us married."

"You seemed afraid."

Elizabeth shook her head, though it was too dark for Jane to see. "No. Merely startled to find her speaking to me."

"Well, hopefully she'll let you be now," Jane murmured in a drowsy voice.

"Yes. Hopefully," Elizabeth said, but it took her a great while to return to sleep, guilt over not being there to save her mother weighing on her.

Darcy

It was a chilly December day in London, the sort that cleansed the city and left quiet in its wake. It was also the sort that lent itself to a warm fire and prolonged reading, which was why Darcy sat in his favorite chair in Darcy House, engaged in just that activity. As the book he was occupying himself with drew to a close, he fingered the scrap of paper he'd been employing as a bookmark, reading the words one more time.

Darcy,

I'm going to Hertfordshire and will return tomorrow evening. Don't tell anyone.

Bingley

It was now 'tomorrow' and Bingley hadn't returned, at least not to Darcy House. Shutting the book, Darcy decided the note offered no further clue to Bingley's behavior. He tossed it into the cheery blaze, still perplexed as to what Bingley could be doing in Hertfordshire. The staff had long since been seen to. Bingley had no obligation to a burnt out shell of a house and was dealing with the financial implications of the fire through the owner's attorney in London.

Darcy stood and crossed to look out a window. The sun would be setting soon. He and Bingley had an engagement that evening. Darcy didn't want to be put in the position of explaining Bingley's absence to his sisters, who would be in attendance. Turning from the window, which offered as little in the way of answers as Bingley's note had, Darcy called for tea. He shelved his book, and began browsing for another one. He hadn't yet made his selection by the time the tea arrived, brought by Moreton, his butler.

"Thank you. Put it on the table," Darcy said, glancing over his shoulder in that general direction. "Any news of Bingley?"

"No, sir."

"Let me know if you hear from or set eyes on him."

"Yes, sir."

Darcy pulled another book from the shelves, flipping through the first several pages. He wasn't usually so unable to settle on a choice. It was dissatisfaction, he knew, for dealing with Bingley's sisters would add an additional layer of annoyance to what was already sure to be an abysmal outing. Then, most outings were. Darcy hardly knew why he bothered.

He closed the book, sliding it back into place on the shelf. A rustle of fabric behind him, bespeaking of someone shifting their weight from one foot to the other, caught Darcy's attention. He turned to find Moreton standing beside the table on which he'd set the tea.

"There was something more?" Darcy asked, intrigued to find his butler still in the room and looking nervous.

"I try not to pry into your guests' affairs, sir, but in view of Mr. Bingley's unexpected absence I thought I should mention something."

Darcy was aware his staff was observant of the conduct of both himself and his guests. What else did they have to entertain them, after all? For Moreton to bring something to his attention was unusual, though. "Yes?"

"Mr. Bingley has been receiving letters from a Mr. Bennet in Hertfordshire about twice a week. I believe he writes Mr. Bennet equally often. He's asked those letters be put in his room in a drawer if he is not home when the mail arrives. He looks for them immediately when he comes home and they are never left out."

"Thank you," Darcy said, frowning at Bingley's odd behavior. "Mr. Bennet of Hertfordshire is also an acquaintance of mine." Knowing his butler's level of discretion, Darcy didn't feel the need to reprove Moreton for observing and passing on Bingley's conduct.

"I felt it my duty to mention it, sir."

Darcy nodded. "If there's nothing more, that will be all."

"Yes, sir."

After Moreton left, Darcy sat at the table. He applied himself to his tea while pondering Bingley's letters. Darcy remembered Mrs. Bennet, the first Mrs. Bennet, commenting that her husband was dilatory in writing letters. Bingley was also. What could they possibly be corresponding about, and with such ferocious secrecy and consistency?

Thoughts of Mr. and Mrs. Bennet quickly gave way to ones of Elizabeth, who never seemed far from his mind. In fact, Darcy knew he thought about her much too often. Resolve as he might, he was unable to help but wonder yet again how she was coping with her mother's death and her father's hasty remarriage.

He remembered his condolence call and saw her red-eyed and somber, wearing an ill-fitting black dress. The image was an extreme contrast to her at the ball at Netherfield Park, but both images came to his mind, and in both she was beautiful. He was glad he was no longer in Hertfordshire to be tempted by her, even though he was confident her low connections would keep him from becoming too seriously involved.

Darcy finished his tea while musing about Elizabeth Bennet, finding it a pleasant enough way to while away an hour. By the time he heard Bingley's footfalls in the hall, the tray had been cleared and Darcy was once again seated before the fire. He'd not yet begun to read, his mind still on Elizabeth, but he flipped the book open as his friend approached. Darcy knew it to be deceitful, but when Bingley entered the library, he was the picture of a man quietly reading, however false that picture was. It wouldn't do for Bingley to find him mooning over a woman, especially one he had no intentions toward.

"I'm glad to see you've returned," Darcy said, closing the book. "I've been contemplating how I might explain your absence tonight."

"Oh, I'd forgotten about tonight," Bingley replied as he sat down. "My sisters would have wondered." He smiled cheerfully. "But I'm here now, so you won't be obliged to explain."

"I couldn't explain," Darcy said pointedly. "I've no notion what you've been about."

"I left a note saying I'd gone to Hertfordshire. Don't tell me you somehow missed it?"

"I did not miss it. However, it requested secrecy and gave no indication as to purpose, nor can I guess at one. Hertfordshire is a large place."

"Surely you can guess where I went."

"Netherfield Park is hardly fit for visitors," Darcy said dryly.

"No, I didn't get that far north." Bingley stood up and walked to the bookshelves.

Darcy was certain Bingley wasn't looking for a book. He kept his silence, waiting.

"I promised Mr. Bennet I would keep it a secret, but you won't tell anyone, will you?" Bingley asked, turning to face Darcy.

"If you are asking me to keep a confidence, of course I will, unless you are confessing to a felony."

Bingley smiled slightly. "I'm not. You must have realized I'd been thinking of asking Jane Bennet to marry me?"

Darcy nodded. He had guessed as much, and been prepared to argue against it should his opinion be sought.

"The only trouble was, I wasn't quite sure if she loved me," Bingley continued.

Darcy could think of other obstacles, but held his tongue. He was relatively sure his opinion was not, in fact, being sought and would likely be tardy and unwelcome to boot.

"When Jane saved me in the fire, I realized she loved me." Bingley's gaze was unfocused now, directed somewhere over Darcy's shoulder. "I was nearly overcome by the smoke. She saved my life, and at risk to her own."

"That isn't a reason to marry her. By that reckoning, your sister should marry Mr. Wickham."

Bingley chuckled and shook his head. "Caroline and Mr. Wickham? I won't tell her you suggested such a thing." Sobering, he dropped his gaze. "I asked Jane to marry me then, as soon as we made it out of the house. She accepted, so I went to see Mr. Bennet the day following the fire to ask permission. He pointed out I don't have a home to take Jane to. I hadn't thought of that. I agreed not to publicize our union until I was in a more stable situation." Bingley held out his hands, palms up, looking pained. "I didn't know what kind of problems I would have. I thought things would be settled by now. I didn't realize how long it will be until I once again have a home. It's devilishly slow working something out with a person who keeps himself in India." He sighed, leaving the bookshelves emptyhanded and returning to his seat.

Darcy had followed the problems Bingley was having with the aftermath of the fire. The owner of Netherfield Park was a missionary in India. He'd used the income from the estate to support his mission. His attorney said Bingley should be responsible for the house, but no one knew what the owner thought. "So Mr. Bennet asked you to keep your engagement secret until such a time as you're able to provide a home for his daughter?"

"Yes and, well, he said he was going to do something outrageous and we should keep our engagement secret because of that as well." Bingley looked bemused. "I didn't know what he was talking about until the church service."

"At least he admits it was outrageous," Darcy said.

"But understandable," Bingley replied.

"Yes. I've heard the gossip. Most people feel it will be fitting if Mr. Collins is kept from inheriting Longbourn. There is no sympathy for Collins, and some amused respect for Mr. Bennet."

"Well, I'm one of those who respect him, so much so that I helped him."

"You helped him?"

"I talked to him after the church service, the one where Mr. Preston refused to read the banns. I believe I mentioned the incident?"

Darcy nodded.

"After the service, I told Mr. Bennet I would get a common license for him in London."

Darcy allowed himself a slight smile. "I hope Mr. Preston understands that if he had read the banns as requested, the wedding would have been delayed a seemlier amount."

"I think it safe to assume he does, but I'd prefer to bring the conversation back to Jane." Bingley smiled. "Mr. Bennet said because I assisted him, and as things with Netherfield Park are taking longer than expected, he would make arrangements for Jane and me to meet in person. He already permits us to write through him. Jane says he doesn't read either of our letters."

Darcy couldn't imagine Mr. Bennet would wish to. Letters between Bingley and Miss Bennet were likely saccharine in the extreme. "So you went to Hertfordshire to see Miss Bennet," Darcy asked, steering away from speaking of the letters. That was slightly shaky ground, for he didn't wish to reveal his servants were spying and passing along gossip. "How did you arrange for that to appear innocent? Did you simply happen to be in the neighborhood and dropped in?"

"No. No one knows I was there, and very ingeniously too, I might add, all thanks to Mrs. Bennet. The new Mrs. Bennet, that is," Bingley immediately clarified, though the previous Mrs. Bennet could hardly have been involved. "Mrs. Bennet has been making many changes, you know. Among other things, she is worried the younger girls are too enamored with officers. She made each of them spend a day helping an officer's wife. You know the type, the ones who have no more than their husband's pay and are up to their ears in children."

"That should cure anyone of wanting to end up in that situation," Darcy said, impressed with Charlotte Bennet's ingenuity. The militia didn't pay its lower ranking officers very much. Many officers received allowances from their families to support their lifestyle, but the ones with families of their own and no outside income were poor.

"Mrs. Bennet sent Miss Mary to help a curate's wife and Miss Elizabeth to help one of their tenants who'd broken an arm. I think those were simple acts of charity. Jane was sent to watch the children of a woman whose brother is one of Mr. Bennet's tenants. The brother was getting married. Jane went in a carriage to the cottage so the carriage could bring the sister back for the ceremony. As soon as she left, I went and helped Jane. We had four hours together." Bingley's face took on a sublimely happy look.

"Won't the children talk?" Darcy asked, though he suspected not. Mrs. Bennet sounded too intelligent not to consider that detail.

"They are twins, a boy and a girl. They're a little more than two years old."

"So you had plenty of time together."

"Yes and no. The children were into everything. Jane said we should take them outside to tire them, but the girl wanted to climb everything. She managed to climb up an apple tree. I could barely reach her. She ran all over the place. The boy wanted to play in the mud." Bingley grinned. "Jane and I did talk, but we had to keep our eyes on both children and they were never together. It was as marvelous a way to spend an afternoon as I've ever encountered."

Darcy raised an eyebrow. He could see Bingley was well and truly besotted. "Did you succeed in tiring them?" He asked out of courtesy, sensing his friend was happy to relive the events of the day, not out of any actual desire for greater detail.

"Eventually. We brought them inside and fed them. The girl fell asleep right away, but the boy started crying. He stopped when Jane picked him up, but when she tried to put him to bed, he cried again. We ended up sitting on a bench with her holding him."

"That doesn't sound very amiable," Darcy said.

"It was," Bingley said, a dreamy expression on his face.

"It looks like Mr. Bennet found the perfect chaperons. They kept you honest and won't tell any tales."

"True, but the opportunity probably won't arise again. He did promise me another meeting in a month, if this Netherfield Park situation still hasn't righted itself."

"How is the Bennet family faring?" Darcy asked with every attempt at nonchalance. He didn't wish Bingley, or anyone for that matter, to gather that he had any special interest in the Bennet family. Rather, in one member in particular.

"Very well. The new Mrs. Bennet has made a number of changes."

"So you said. What other changes aside from the charity?" And how was Elizabeth bearing up? Darcy wished he could get Bingley to come round to that detail.

"The girls spend some time every day helping around the house. Mrs. Bennet told them she wants three hours a day from each, in addition to them looking after their own rooms and clothing. One hour is to help the household, one hour is to improve themselves and one hour is for them to be together in the evening. Jane says they often take turns reading. That's in addition to the charitable work I mentioned."

"I imagine Miss Mary spends more than an hour a day on accomplishments," Darcy said, thinking of her technically good playing with no heart and her inadequate voice. Surely hinting at Miss Mary's playing would bring Bingley around to Elizabeth, for who could help but recall her at the pianoforte?

"Miss Mary is required to read books her father selects. None of them are religious."

"What about the others?" Darcy said, impatient. Bingley was frustratingly obtuse.

"Miss Elizabeth is practicing the pianoforte more than she used to. All of them are spending more time in practical sewing."

"Practical sewing?" He asked, while trying to think of a way to keep the conversation directed toward Elizabeth.

"Making clothing instead of embroidering. You know, shirts for Mr. Bennet, caps for the maids, that sort of thing. The former Mrs. Bennet had servants doing that."

"What are they doing in the way of helping around the house?" Darcy realized he didn't like to think of Elizabeth being forced into such drudgery. He was surprised to find himself in agreement with the former Mrs. Bennet on anything, but Elizabeth's rare beauty and keen wit should be nurtured and encouraged to flourish. She shouldn't be bent for long hours stitching caps or prevented from spending her days playing the pianoforte and reading to expand her mind.

"They help in the kitchen, clean the parlor and hallways. Their meals are much simpler than they were. If they want fancy food, they have to budget for it."

"Have they let go some of their servants?" He didn't approve of letting servants who had done no wrong go. It was sometimes difficult for them to find another decent place to work.

"They didn't need to. Two maids quit."

Darcy nodded. He wondered why they'd quit, and hoped the current Mrs. Bennet was not being unreasonably harsh. Bingley kept up his chatter, mostly a direct repetition of all he and Miss Bennet had spoken of for four hours, until it was time to ready for dinner. Darcy humored him, aware his friend was violently in love and with the hope of hearing more about Elizabeth. That hope was little rewarded, as Darcy supposed was to be expected. It was obvious Bingley had no eye, thought or inclination for any woman but Miss Bennet. By the time they went out for the evening, Darcy was forced to admit it seemed Bingley's attachment was quite genuine, and already proving to be of a much sterner sort than previous infatuations. In short, Darcy thought this time Bingley might genuinely be in love.

This quieted his concerns, as did Bingley's tales of Mrs. Bennet's changes. While Darcy felt Elizabeth somewhat in need of rescuing from the situation, he deemed the measures Mrs. Bennet was taking the best thing for the younger three girls. In fact, the more he thought on it, the more he realized most of the objections he would have given Bingley over Miss Bennet, and often reiterated to himself in the middle of the night pertaining to Elizabeth, were no long in effect. The two no longer suffered from a ridiculous mother. Nor did they, apparently, have younger sisters hell bent on ruin. Or if they were, the strong will of the new Mrs. Bennet seemed determined to hold them back.

There was still the matter of the original Mrs. Bennet's low origins, though, and the relations in trade. That couldn't be denied or changed. It was well enough for Bingley, who had trade connections in his own lineage, but would never do for the Darcy line. As Darcy had realized Elizabeth Bennet was beneath him from the start and deemed he therefore could not form an attachment where she was concerned, he didn't know why that rankled so.

Chapter Six

~ Reunions ~

Elizabeth

Elizabeth hadn't slept well yet again. It had been months since the fire, but she was still having nightmares about the event and her lack of an attempt to save her mother. Logically, she knew she hadn't killed her mother, but her mind seemed entangled in guilt. If only any one of them had realized Mrs. Bennet would require help to exit the building, any one of them would have returned to get her. Unfortunately, it hadn't become apparent until it was too late.

Her mother and guilt weren't foremost on her mind as she climbed into the carriage with Jane, though. She was still unsure why they were going to London. She would have thought it a normal, and greatly appreciated, trip to visit their Aunt and Uncle Gardiner, if not for the odd look on her father's face when he'd wished them well and Jane's care in packing. Jane, it seemed to Elizabeth, had packaged up most everything she owned. She also clutched a small satchel as they rode. Having watched her sister ready, Elizabeth knew the satchel contained all of Jane's jewelry and their mother's carved jewelry box. Or, as Elizabeth had come to think of it, Jane's locked box.

The journey was slow, the two horses needing to stop often to rest. Elizabeth had plenty of time to wait for Jane to enlighten her on the purpose of their trip. When it eventually became apparent Jane's mind was elsewhere and no explanation was forthcoming, Elizabeth's forbearance deserted her.

"Why are we going to London?" Elizabeth asked. "And why are you bringing so much?"

Jane didn't answer, gazing fixedly out the window.

"Jane? Are you listening? Do you know why we're going to London?"

"Yes, I do." Jane turned to look at Elizabeth, a radiant smile on her face. "I'm sorry, I can't tell. I promised Papa." Jane's voice trailed off with the last word. She remained silent for a few minutes, her smile replaced by a contemplative look. "I hate not telling you, but I did promise. Don't worry, Lizzy, you'll know everything soon enough."

"Can you assure me it is for a good reason, at least?" Elizabeth put fourth, for Jane seemed happy.

"The best of reasons."

Elizabeth was flummoxed. Jane looked almost irritatingly happy, not like a sister in agonies over being forced to keep a secret. Elizabeth clamped her mouth closed around her questions. If Jane was even half as joyful as she seemed to be, it truly couldn't be anything terrible. Elizabeth would have to consider what was coming a pleasant surprise and use that as solace during the wait.

They finally arrived at the Gardiners and were let in by a maid, who sent a manservant to collect their luggage. The maid escorted them into the formal parlor, where Elizabeth was surprised to find her Aunt Gardiner entertaining Miss Bingley and Mr. and Mrs. Hurst.

"Jane, Elizabeth," Aunt Gardiner said, coming forward to meet them. "It's so good to see you both."

Elizabeth hugged her aunt, greetings proceeding around the room. She could tell by Miss Bingley's and Mrs. Hurst's expressions they were as baffled to see her and Jane as she was to see them. Mr. Hurst's thoughts were his own, his face evidencing its usual lack of concern.

Greetings exchanged, they were all seated. Still clutching her satchel, Jane sat on the sofa next to Miss Bingley. Elizabeth sat opposite them, next to her aunt, leaving the Hursts to occupy the sofa across the far end of the room. For a long moment, they all looked at one another in strained silence, though Jane still smiled.

Elizabeth turned to Miss Bingley. "I trust you've been well since last we saw you, Miss Bingley?"

"Very well, thank you," Miss Bingley replied.

Elizabeth waited for a courteous extension to the conversation, but none was forthcoming. Shrugging, she made another foray. "And how is Mr. Bingley?"

"Overdue," Miss Bingley said. "He asked us to meet him here, though I can't imagine why." She looked about as if the parlor contained something repugnant, though it was a modestly elegant room. "We arrived only moments before you and were about to inquire as to how Mrs. Gardiner knows my brother."

Elizabeth frowned. "Do you know Mr. Bingley, then, Aunt?"

"I've not yet had the pleasure," her aunt said. She smiled at Jane, who gave an answering smile back.

"Charles has been terribly strange of late," Mrs. Hurst said in her nasally voice. "No interest in society at all, and he's informed us he intends to visit Pemberley next week, but will not permit Caroline and us to join him."

"I can explain that," Miss Bingley said.

"You can?" Both Jane's face and voice revealed her surprise.

"He's obviously going to Pemberley to further his courtship of Miss Darcy."

Jane's face turned red. "That's not possible."

"Of course it is." Miss Bingley looked down her nose at Jane. "Why else would he travel to Pemberley without us? It's Georgiana Darcy who has him ignoring society."

"No." Jane shook her head, her blush deepening. "All else aside, Charles wrote that Miss Darcy is fixed in town for the whole winter."

A scattering of gasps met Jane's words, Elizabeth's among them. To call Mr. Bingley by his first name and pronounce that he'd written to her was tantamount to declaring he and Jane were engaged. Now Elizabeth knew why her sister was so happy. She opened her mouth to issue a congratulatory exclamation.

"How dare you," Miss Bingley screeched, surging to her feet. "How dare you imply Charles has written you?"

"I did not imply it." Jane stood too, but her voice was calm. "I stated it. As a fact."

"This is slander. You're liable."

"It most certainly is not slander." Jane hugged her satchel tight. "Miss Bingley, I was hoping this would be pleasing news to you. When we met, you were nothing but kind."

"Pleasing?" Mrs. Hurst cried, surging to her feet as well. "How can it be? Mr. Hurst, do something."

"Such as?" he mumbled, remaining seated.

Elizabeth rose, wondering if she should go to Jane. Her aunt, likewise leaving her seat, was probably having the same thought.

"I refuse to believe a word of this," Miss Bingley said.

"I do have proof," Jane said in a quiet tone. "If I show you proof, will you try to make peace with this before Charles arrives? This is meant to be a happy occasion."

"What proof could you possibly have for something that's so outrageously false?" Miss Bingley demanded.

Jane sighed. She reached into her bodice, pulling out a small key. Elizabeth recognized it as the one that unlocked their mother's jewelry box. Setting her satchel where she'd been sitting, Jane retrieved the box as well, unlocking it under Miss Bingley's and Mrs. Hurst's angry glares. As did they, Elizabeth leaned forward to see the contents.

She needn't have bothered moving nearer, for as soon as Jane lifted the lid, the mass of letters all but sprung free. The box was crammed with them, undoubtedly over twenty. Jane smiled down at them as if they were the most precious items their mother's jewelry box had ever contained. Maybe, Elizabeth mused, they were.

Miss Bingley snatched up one of the letters. "It's addressed to Mr. Bennet," she said triumphantly.

Jane reached to retrieve the letter, but Miss Bingley handed it to her sister.

"Please return that," Jane said, her tone still calm.

"It says, 'my dearest Jane, I miss you more every day.' " Mrs. Hurst grimaced as she read. She scanned a bit more before handing the letter back to Jane. "It's rather private, and it is Charles' writing."

"I suppose you persuaded him he had to marry you, since you saved his life," Miss Bingley snapped. "That was a cheap thing to do. You should have been looking after your mother."

Jane blanched. Elizabeth realized it still hadn't occurred to Jane, as it had to her, that their mother might be alive if they'd acted differently. The look Jane gave her was so tortured, Elizabeth felt tears form in her own eyes. She crossed to her sister, carefully taking the letter, key and box she clutched from her ice-like fingers. Casting Miss Bingley a glare, Elizabeth slipped the letter back in with the others, pressed them down firmly, and locked them inside the box.

She was looking about for where to set them, so she could hug her sister, when she spotted Mr. Bingley and her Uncle Gardiner in the doorway, Mr. Darcy behind them. She nodded her head toward Jane. Obviously taking her meaning, Mr. Bingley hurried into the room. Elizabeth set the box on Jane's satchel, tucking the key into her own bodice for safe keeping. Hoping no one was looking, she quickly dabbed the corners of her eyes.

"Charles, what is the meaning of this?" Mrs. Hurst demanded.

Mr. Bingley didn't even look at her. He crossed to Jane and took her into his arms. Elizabeth could hear her crying as she clung to him. She stepped back by her aunt, feeling bereft. Her uncle came to stand on her other side, making her feel a bit better, but Mr. Darcy remained in the hallway, his gaze oddly intent as he watched her. Elizabeth supposed he'd seen her both put the key in her bodice and wipe her tears. He likely thought it all quite low of her, but she was resolved not to care.

"Tears," Miss Bingley said with contempt. "That's what weak women do when they are in the wrong."

"Caroline, that's enough." There was no real force behind Bingley's statement, but Elizabeth felt he meant it.

"No, it's not enough. I don't know why you've let this woman think you will marry her and why you are going to Pemberley without me but you should do your duty to your family. She is nothing." Miss Bingley's voice took on a desperate note. "What are you thinking? Why would you do this? You should be going to Pemberley to court Georgiana, and I should be going with you. If you would simply follow my and Louisa's plan for you, it could someday be me journeying to Pemberley and inviting you."

Frowning, Mr. Darcy stepped into the room, his firm footfalls drawing eyes. Miss Bingley gave a start of surprise. She'd obviously been so focused on her brother and Jane, she hadn't realized Mr. Darcy was there. "Mr. Darcy," Miss Bingley gasped, coloring.

"Miss Bingley, you are my friend's sister, and if he chooses to bring you to Pemberley, I will accept you, but you will never, under any circumstances, be coming to Pemberley without him." The eyes Mr. Darcy leveled on her held more condescension than Elizabeth had imagined even he could bring to bear.

"My friendship with Georgiana—"

"I will actively discourage my sister from any relationship with someone so cruel. That is, assuming she wants to pursue a friendship with you, which I doubt."

"It's not cruel to remind Miss Bennet she was derelict in her duty," Miss Bingley said with nearly as much arrogance as Mr. Darcy possessed.

"It was your duty as well," Mr. Darcy said. "As hostess, you were responsible for seeing the guests got out. Instead of looking after them, you required rescuing."

"Mr. Wickham did not need to rescue me," she said.

"Mr. Wickham saved your life." With a final look of disdain, Mr. Darcy turned to Jane. "Miss Bennet, no one could have foreseen what happened to your mother," he said in a much kinder tone. "She was an adult and perfectly capable of leaving a building on her own, if she hadn't been interfered with. You are in no way to blame for not being omniscient."

Jane pulled away from Mr. Bingley. Her cheeks were wet with tears. "It never occurred to me. I . . . I am shocked it never did." Suddenly, Jane turned to Elizabeth. "Is that what your nightmares are about?"

"Some of them," Elizabeth admitted. "I didn't see what happened, but I dream I did, from Lydia's description. In my dreams, I don't save Mama, as I didn't in reality. Instead, I did what Mr. Darcy said I should do, and I've felt guilty about it ever since." She glanced at him apologetically. She didn't mean to imply he was at fault for her mother's death. She'd made the decision to obey him.

Mr. Darcy looked more concerned than she would have credited. "You shouldn't feel guilty, either," he said. "According to Colonel Forster, you almost certainly saved lives through your actions. He praised your quick thinking. According to him, if you hadn't sent for the carriages, some of the guests, particularly the elderly ones, may have sickened and died."

"Thank you," Elizabeth said, surprised by his kind words. "Truly, I don't believe I killed my mother. As you said, she was perfectly capable of walking out of a burning house on her own. No one made her try to retrieve her cloak, and certainly no one is responsible for pushing her down except Mr. Collins. I'm beginning to learn to live with what happened, but I believe it's the sort of shock that takes some while to recover from."

The smile Mr. Darcy gave her was at once warm and kind. Elizabeth blinked in surprise. She'd never seen his features shaped into such an amiable expression before. It lent him considerable appeal.

"This isn't about Miss Elizabeth," Miss Bingley said. "Miss Bennet has behaved like a hoyden by writing to a man she isn't engaged to."

"I received her father's permission to marry her three months ago," Mr. Bingley said.

Miss Bingley gaped at him in shock.

"You what?" Mrs. Hurst blurted.

Elizabeth saw her aunt and uncle exchange amused looks. She wanted to go to Jane and congratulate her, but Mr. Bingley still had his arms around her, and Mrs. Hurst and Miss Bingley still glared.

"I believe I spoke clearly," Mr. Bingley said, looking between his sisters. "Mr. Bennet stipulated Jane and I must keep our engagement a secret until he deemed me able to properly care for her and the hubbub around his own marriage sufficiently dulled. We'll be married a week from tomorrow at St. Andrews, at ten in the morning." He smiled down at Jane. "I wanted to make it sooner, but your father thought it looked better this way."

"Why did you ask us to come here?" Mrs. Hurst asked.

"To meet your future sister's family," Bingley said. "Also, for Darcy and I to clear up the last obstacle. Mr. Bennet assigned Mr. Gardiner to evaluate my plan for where Jane and I will be living, since I don't have a home. Darcy said we could stay at Pemberley, for a year if necessary, and came here to confirm that fact with Mr. Gardner."

"I don't understand," Elizabeth said, confused to learn her sister wouldn't have a home of her own if she wed Mr. Bingley. "How is it you haven't found a new residence yet?"

"I'm not sure if I shall be required to rebuild Netherfield Park. If I am, I might continue to rent it, or offer to purchase it outright."

Looking around, Elizabeth could see the others knew what he was referencing, but she still wasn't sure she did. "You don't know yet?"

"The owner is in India, so corresponding takes quite some time," Mr. Bingley said. "His attorney thinks I should be held responsible for the loss, but it isn't settled yet. I hired the housekeeper, the butler, and Mrs. Nicholls on the owner's recommendation and they hired the other servants. We'll likely never know if it was a servant or sheer mischance which caused the fire, but neither would be my province."

"I offered him residence at Pemberley while he gets his affairs settled," Darcy said. "And seeing how upset Miss Bennet is, I suggest Miss Elizabeth come to Pemberley as well, to help her sister overcome her irrational guilt."

For a second time, Elizabeth turned to him in surprise. She was unsure how she felt about the idea. The last time she'd dwelled in the same household as Mr. Darcy, he'd been excessively disagreeable to her. She knew more good of him now, but that wouldn't change his manners. Aside from which, he'd made it clear on their very first meeting that he took no joy in having her about.

Jane's face lit up, however. "Would you allow her to come? That would be so very kind. Elizabeth is very dear to me and I now feel more guilt because I didn't realize the extent of her distress."

Elizabeth went to her sister, gently freeing her from Mr. Bingley to hug her. "I knew you hadn't thought of it, but why should you? Neither of us could have guessed what Mama would do."

"If I'm going to be Jane's sister, I should be coming to Pemberley as well," Miss Bingley said.

"No." Mr. Darcy didn't even turn to look at her.

"Caroline, give it up," Mr. Hurst said, his tone bored. "The story of your rescue by Mr. Wickham has already made you the laughing stock of London. Don't make things worse by begging in the midst of a crowd."

"Laughing stock? But people praised me when I told them what happened."

"That was before they heard about it from Hertfordshire. Lady Lucas and Mrs. Goulding have friends in London," Mrs. Hurst said, her tone gentler than her husband's. "I didn't think it right to tell you. You've been under enough strain."

Miss Bingley looked around the room with wide eyes. "A laughing stock," she whispered. She burst into tears, rushing into Mrs. Hurst's arms.

Mr. Hurst turned to Mr. Bingley, offering his hand. "Congratulations Bingley. You've picked a lovely and amiable woman to marry. You're a lucky man. Louisa and I will be at your wedding. Caroline too, if she has any sense. Right now, I think we serve you best by leaving."

Later that evening, when everything had settled down and all of the guests save Elizabeth and Jane had departed, they retreated to ready for sleep in the little room they shared at their aunt's and uncle's. As soon as they were alone and the door firmly closed, Jane turned to face Elizabeth, entreaty on her face.

"Lizzy, I am so sorry I didn't tell you. If I hadn't given my solemn promise to Papa, I should have. He said one hasty marriage in the family was enough of a scandal, but he gave us permission and he let us write."

Elizabeth didn't believe Jane and Mr. Bingley's wedding would have been much of a scandal, expected as it had been. More likely, their father had wanted to test whether Mr. Bingley was steadfast, which he'd certainly proven to be. She saw no reason to enlighten Jane on her thoughts, though.

"Charles even came to Hertfordshire twice for secret meetings, but I only could see him for a few hours and parting was difficult," Jane continued, her expression still beseeching. "I so wanted to tell you, but I promised."

"Oh, Jane, don't be sorry. I'm only sorry I didn't share it with you. Talking about it might have made it easier on you."

"Keeping it from you was very difficult for me. Charlotte understood that, but said there really wasn't much point in defying Papa on this, since he'd agreed to the main point. They both feel the story will get out that I met Bingley again in London on this visit and we precipitously married."

"I don't think Miss Bingley or the Hursts will contradict that," Elizabeth said, thinking with amusement on how Miss Bingley would react to good wishes expressed about her brother's marriage. Jane responded with a smile and they readied for bed. Maybe falling asleep amused helped, for Elizabeth had no troubling dreams that night.

The following week, Elizabeth was pleased to attend Jane and Mr. Bingley's wedding. She was a bit sad for Jane because no one else from their immediate family was there, but their aunt and uncle were, as well as the Hursts. Miss Bingley did not show herself. Mr. Darcy attended, of course, and his sister Georgiana. Elizabeth found her, as Wickham had suggested, aloof and withdrawn.

Jane didn't seem to mind who was or was not attending, having eyes only for Mr. Bingley. After a meal hosted by the Gardiners, the newly wedded Bingleys, Elizabeth, and Mr. Darcy all embarked toward Mr. Darcy's home. In an obvious change of plans, Mr. Darcy's sister Georgiana and her companion, Mrs. Annesley, traveled to Pemberley with them.

Not long into the trip, Elizabeth was forced to reevaluate her opinion of Miss Darcy. She was not overly proud. In truth, she seemed timid, modest, and exceedingly shy. When her shyness showed quick evidence of dwindling in the presence of Jane, though they spoke only at stops, Elizabeth wasn't surprised. Jane's good and gentle character was evident to even a poor observer of human nature.

While Elizabeth was relieved to find Miss Darcy to be a sweet young woman, not another Miss Bingley, the entourage they traveled in seemed especially ostentatious. Its heart was a wagon and three carriages, including one for the servants, all trundling north. When Elizabeth saw how many outriders accompanied them, she was certain they would never be able to change horses, but each stop proceeded smoothly.

After much travel, they finally rolled into the inn yard where they were to make their last stop in the journey. Elizabeth, wanting to stretch her legs, followed Mr. Darcy from the carriage and inside. The inn was rather fine, she soon saw, with carpets where most would have simple wood floors, and leaded glass windows with heavy curtains. Knowing that no matter how fine the inn she still shouldn't wander unescorted, she trailed Mr. Darcy up to the desk.

"May I help you, sir, madam?" The liveried man behind the desk asked.

Mr. Darcy glanced at her, smiled slightly, and turned back. "I commissioned a change of horses, for Darcy," he said, not correcting the man's misconception that Elizabeth was his spouse.

"Mr. Darcy, we've been expecting you." The man looked up, clearing his throat uneasily. "Sir, I'm exceedingly sorry, but your horses aren't ready."

"Not ready?" Mr. Darcy said with an admirable lack of inflection.

The man behind the desk glanced at Elizabeth. She gave him a sympathetic look, sure he was about to become acquainted with the less amiable side of Mr. Darcy's nature.

"That is, they were ready, sir." He cleared his throat again. He then gave a name coupled with the title of the lord who had arrived unexpectedly and insisted on using the horses. Elizabeth didn't recognize the name, but Darcy appeared to. He glanced at Elizabeth again, his lips pressed into a thin line. She watched annoyance flicker across his face. She tensed for an outpouring of arrogance. He turned back to the man behind the desk,

"I see," Mr. Darcy said.

"We did suggest to his lordship that the horses had been arranged by someone other than himself."

"I'm sure you did your utmost," Mr. Darcy said.

"Indeed sir, we truly did."

"Thank you."

"Sir, we have secured some replacement stock. We set about it immediately."

"That was considerate of you."

In the end, a greatly relieved innkeeper put together enough horses that all Mr. Darcy needed to do was order two of the outriders to remain behind with the wagon carrying extra luggage. It was less the speedy and amicable resolution to the issue that left an impression on Elizabeth, and more Mr. Darcy's forbearance. She'd been sure he would revert to the level of snobbery she'd first observed, and so disliked in him, but he did not. He and the innkeeper even parted cordially.

Soon enough, Elizabeth found herself once again ensconced in a carriage, heading north. As Jane and Bingley had a carriage to themselves, she traveled with Mr. Darcy, Miss Darcy and Mrs. Annesley. She found nothing offensive in the company, but do to Mr. Darcy's reserved nature and Miss Darcy's excessive shyness, she and Mrs. Annesley had been carrying the bulk of the conversation thus far, when they made the effort to.

As they set out again, Elizabeth felt no need to fill the silence. The country they traveled through was new to her, and she was pleased to look out the window. Miss Darcy sat opposite her, beside her brother, taking in the terrain as well. She kept glancing at Elizabeth, however, and soon Elizabeth observed that Miss Darcy looked as if she wished for courage enough to join in conversation. Elizabeth recalled that sometimes in the past she had ventured a short sentence when there was least danger of its being heard. Finally, wishing to encourage the girl, Elizabeth said, "That is a singularly lovely tree, don't you feel, Miss Darcy?"

"I see what you mean," Miss Darcy said quietly, after a long pause. "The outline of such sweeping branches against the gray sky is beautiful." She stared out the window until it was out of view. "I would love to try to paint it."

"After the recent difficulty with the horses, I think it would be a trial to your brother's good temper if we stopped to do so," Elizabeth said.

Miss Darcy shot her a shocked look. Elizabeth smiled, to let her know she was teasing. Miss Darcy relaxed somewhat, providing a tentative smile of her own in return.

"Aren't there beautiful trees at Pemberley?" Mrs. Annesley asked. "I remember a big oak near the bridge."

"What makes this tree beautiful is how it stands out from its surroundings," Elizabeth said. "It's on top of a small hill with nothing near it. Also, I believe the lighting of the afternoon, while not encouraging in the usual manner, lends great drama to the scene."

Miss Darcy nodded. "We have many roses at Pemberley," she said slowly, looking thoughtful. "I enjoy looking at them and smelling them. Sometimes I cut off a bud, bring it to my room and put it in a vase. Early last spring I noticed a single yellow crocus in the woods. It was a cold, misty winter day, and that single bright flower standing out against the winter-browned vegetation gave me more pleasure than a garden full of roses usually brings." She dropped her gaze as she finished speaking, a blush coloring her cheeks.

Elizabeth was surprised by the eloquence of Miss Darcy's speech. A glance at Mr. Darcy revealed he was as well. As Miss Darcy seemed once more too shy to converse, Elizabeth returned her scrutiny to the world without. She knew they were near their destination, and felt an unaccountable excitement at the idea of seeing Mr. Darcy's home.

When Mr. Darcy's home finally did come into view, Elizabeth was unabashedly impressed. In truth, she could, in that moment, better understand some of Darcy's pride. She had never seen such a magnificent home as Pemberley. As for the grounds, she had never seen a place for which nature had done more, or where natural beauty had been so little counteracted by an awkward taste.

Darcy

Darcy stood in the doorway to the parlor, watching Elizabeth and Georgiana play. They were too absorbed in their duet to notice him, and Mrs. Annesley's head was bent toward her sewing, affording Darcy an excellent chance to study them. He had never heard his sister play so well. Elizabeth somehow put more feeling into her music, giving it life and vitality of its own. He doubted anything had been said, but by practicing with her Georgiana appeared to be learning that music was about more than dutifully playing the notes as written.

Why, he wondered, had he invited Elizabeth to Pemberley? His reasoning at the time had seemed sound, he had that as solace. When they met at the Gardiner's, he'd been too much affected by seeing her again. Even though he'd known Elizabeth would be there, he'd been forced to linger in the hall for a time to gather himself. That was how much the sight of her moved him.

Which was why he'd leapt at the opportunity to invite her to his home. Not out of regard, but in the hopes of affecting a cure. Elizabeth Bennet, as he'd told himself numerous times, was much too low for him. She was also far too low for Pemberley. Darcy had thought, once he saw her here among the elegance and finery of his world, her unsuitability would manifest in uncountable small ways and grate on him, scouring away any feelings he might harbor toward her. He'd even brought Georgiana back, both to help contrast with Elizabeth and to keep her away from Miss Bingley.

Unfortunately, his reasoning was not bearing fruit. Unworthy as he knew her to be, she seemed at ease in his home. She complemented the tasteful surroundings. Darcy had only succeeded in making his situation worse.

He wondered if Elizabeth was like Georgiana's crocus or the lone tree they'd passed on the road; beautiful because the surroundings were so plain. After all, she was the only young woman in Pemberley not already wed or directly related to him. As well, in Hertfordshire, there had been a dearth of beautiful women.

No, that wasn't completely true. Elizabeth's two younger sisters would be considered beautiful if they had enough rank, poise or money. Mrs. Bingley would be considered beautiful without standing or income. Now, she had both, and she was Elizabeth's sister. Elizabeth's connections had grown.

Still, in the carriage, Darcy had taken his sister's words as a sign he was doing the right thing by bringing Elizabeth to Pemberley. At the time, he'd imagined Georgiana's soliloquy about the lone flower an affirmation of the idea Elizabeth had gained a hold on him simply because she was the most fascinating of the women he'd been forced to endure in Hertfordshire. Now he found himself considering that perhaps he was a man ill equipped to interpret portents.

Standing there, watching Elizabeth's agile fingers move effortlessly across the keys, Darcy realized acts of providence or no, he'd had enough of English roses. The eligible women of his class were uninteresting, one much the same as the next. He wanted that singular, perfect yellow blossom that bespoke of the promise of spring.

"I hope you don't mind if we take a break," Elizabeth said when the piece they played came to an end. "I would like to walk around after sitting for so long."

"I would as well," Georgiana said. "If we were in town, I might have to go to another master and get a lesson in Italian or drawing. Mrs. Annesley is much more forgiving of my idleness here than in London."

Mrs. Annesley glanced up and smiled, her eyes noticing Darcy in the doorway.

Darcy stepped into the room. "That's because she knows you are learning other things here."

Elizabeth and Georgiana turned.

"What am I learning?" Georgiana asked.

"You're learning to entertain company. Also, to work with someone else."

"But it is no task to entertain Miss Bennet," Georgiana said.

"Task or not, I am being entertained very well," Elizabeth said.

"I'm also learning to play better. You've a lovely cleverness with the keys. I'm afraid I've always neglected the nuances of timing, but I strive for better for the sake of our duets."

"Miss Darcy's skill has improved since she began playing with you as well," Mrs. Annesley said.

Georgiana looked surprised. "Has it?"

Darcy nodded. "I am in agreement with Mrs. Annesley. With Miss Bennet as well. Your playing is improving, and it is reasonable for both of you to take a break from it."

"May I show Miss Bennet our mother's room?" Georgiana asked. "I've told her about Uncle Fitzwilliam's paintings and she said she would like to see them."

"Certainly," Darcy replied, bemused his sister would do so. They were not great works of art.

"Perhaps you would accompany us? You remember him and I don't."

"It would be my pleasure," Darcy said, surprised how much he meant it.

He led the way toward his mother's room, offering an explanation as they walked. "The current Earl of Matlock is actually the second son. The older son never lived to be earl. Before he died, he spent several years in Italy, where he took up painting. He loved it there, but left when Napoleon entered. He came back to England to meet his responsibilities as heir, but died a few years later. He enjoyed painting works showing paintings and other art. It was something of a secret passion, I suppose."

"Do you mean he copied paintings?" Elizabeth asked.

Darcy glanced back to see her frowning. "Not quite."

They reached the room and Darcy opened the door, allowing Elizabeth and his sister to precede him. He watched Elizabeth's reaction to the paintings, curious how they would be received. Two were paintings of paintings, including the frames, walls on which they hung, and any other accents which may have been in the room, such as a potted plant or draperies. The other two were of statuary, given a like treatment. Although all were painstakingly reproduced, each was copied at a slight angle, distorting the perspective.

"He always maintained they permitted only those with true talent to sit directly before the greater works. He was routinely allotted a space six feet to the side," Darcy said.

Darcy watched Elizabeth approach the nearest painting. It depicted the statue of David, but was done from a position oddly near the base and at an inauspicious angle. After a moment, she moved on to the two paintings of paintings, and then to the fourth, a statue Darcy had never identified. None of the four were very good. Darcy had always wondered if his uncle, aware of his lack of skill, had elected to paint at the strange angles he used to poke fun at the whole concept of copying art.

After examining the final painting with as much interest as she'd shown the first three, Elizabeth turned back toward Darcy and Georgiana. "Your mother must have loved her brother very much."

"Why do you say that?" Darcy asked. That was not the reaction he'd expected.

"Your mother had excellent taste. Pemberley is a work of art. Every room, every object in every room, is beautiful. It's largely a simple beauty. The picture frames are plain, showing the pictures. These are in elaborate gilt frames." She gestured toward the paintings. "I don't think your mother selected the frames. Her brother did." She cast a glance toward their uncle's work. "They aren't terrible paintings, but there are far better ones all over Pemberley. Your mother could have any of those beautiful works here and allocated her brother's to a different room, or not be hung at all, yet she elected to have his paintings here. It's unlikely it's because she thought they were beautiful. More likely is that she loved her brother."

Darcy couldn't help but admire both her honesty and her deduction. Most women, especially young misses in wont of a husband, would have showered the works with false praise. He could easily imagine, for example, what Miss Bingley would have said. Something that would have bored him into a numb stupor halfway through, certainly.

"You praised the simplicity of our decorations, but you spent a lot of time looking at the ceramic shepherdess in the Rose Room," Georgiana said, her tone tentative.

Elizabeth smiled at her and Darcy could see his sister instantly grow less tense. He should have realized Georgiana would take to Elizabeth. Who couldn't? All the more reason Elizabeth belonged in Pemberley, not some English rose of Miss Bingley's ilk.

"That's because it is so like one my mother had," Elizabeth said. "I was trying to figure out if they were done with a mold or individually sculpted."

"What did you decide?" Darcy asked.

"I couldn't. I have no idea how they were produced. They look the same, although I think there are minor differences in the glazing."

"I believe they use molds," he said. "The shepherdess comes from Staffordshire. I believe the Wood family sells them."

"I was simply surprised to see one here. My mother was very proud of hers."

"As she should have been," Darcy said. He hesitated, realizing he didn't wish to part ways yet. Directing himself to Georgiana he said, "However, I don't think this constituted much in the way of a walk. Would you care for a stroll about the grounds? I don't believe it to be that cold a day."

"That would be pleasant, thank you, Fitzwilliam," Georgiana said. She turned to Elizabeth. "You will accompany us, I hope, Miss Bennet?"

"It would be my pleasure," she said, and Darcy wondered if she echoed his earlier words consciously.

That was the beginning of an agreeable habit for Darcy. Each afternoon, unless the weather proved to be unendurably foul, he, Elizabeth and Georgiana would take a stroll about the grounds. Darcy greatly enjoyed showing Pemberley's estate to Elizabeth, and could tell Georgiana did as well. Elizabeth's obvious pleasure in all she saw made the task exceedingly rewarding.

Their walks quickly grew into such a firm habit, Darcy felt it wasn't at all awkward to propose they take one several afternoons later, even in view of Georgiana's absence. His sister had been carted off by Mrs. Annesley for a lesson with a local drawing master. Elizabeth seemed quite pleased by the offer. The weather being particularly fine and he being acquainted with her joy in the outdoors, Darcy had expected her to be. He liked to think, also, she might desire this time in his company.

"I notice you never ask Mr. Bingley and Jane if they wish to walk," Elizabeth said as they strolled a tree-lined path near the house.

"We don't permit Bingley and his wife enough time alone. They are too polite to avoid us, but I think they would prefer to spend more time without us." He hoped she would allow the exaggeration, for in truth Bingley and his bride would often disappear to their rooms or walk the grounds together.

"That's very thoughtful of you," she said with a smile.

Darcy guessed she was joking and she understood it wasn't Bingley's wellbeing he was considering. They walked on in silence after that. He supposed many men would be displeased by her lack of verbosity, but he enjoyed their friendly silences. He also enjoyed the cold-induced rosy cheeks and brightened eyes of his walking companion.

Yes, he decided, he would be happy with her at his side. Giving up his reservations, Darcy permitted himself the pleasure of anticipation. Elizabeth would be overjoyed when he made it clear to her she needn't return to her former low company and surroundings. This was to be her home, with him as her husband.

Chapter Seven

~ Proposal ~

Elizabeth

Elizabeth enjoyed her walks with Georgiana and Mr. Darcy, and the ones she and Mr. Darcy took without his sister, as they did on days when Georgiana attended one of her various lessons. When Elizabeth walked with Mr. Darcy it was the best of worlds, for it was nearly like being alone and unfettered, but with the reassurance of him by her side.

He spoke rarely, not burdening her with conversation. When he elected to break the silence, he mused thoughtfully about his tenants or details of his property. At these times, Elizabeth supposed him speaking more to himself, for the sake of appearance. It wouldn't do, after all, if they were never seen to converse. Jane and Bingley might hear of it and realize they were deliberately being given time together. Elizabeth appreciated Mr. Darcy's thoughtfulness in arranging it so it looked as if they were enjoying themselves.

On one such comfortable afternoon, a particularly warm day in a series of unseasonably warm days, they meandered down what was less a trail than a path. Trees surrounded them on all sides and Elizabeth supposed it might be scandalous, if she walked with anyone other than Mr. Darcy. In the pleasant quiet between them, she took in the still bare branches interlaced against the blue sky above, following a ray of sunlight to the forest floor. There, glorious for its bright yellow petals, stood a single crocus.

"Look," she said with a laugh. "It's Georgiana's flower. We shall have to walk this way tomorrow, in the hopes it will remain for her to see."

Mr. Darcy followed the direction of her gesture. To her confusion, he stopped walking.

Turning back, Elizabeth was perplexed by the odd expression on his face. "Mr. Darcy, are you quite well?"

"No, no I am not," he said, one long stride closing the distance between them. "Nor have I been for some time."

She held out her hands to him, alarmed. Indeed, he did look exceedingly peculiar, though not ill. "Whatever is the matter?"

His hands, large and warm, engulfed hers. "I am suffering," he said. "In vain I have struggled. It will not do. My feelings will not be repressed. You must allow me to tell you how ardently I admire and love you."

Elizabeth stared at him, stunned. What was he speaking about? Admiration and love? In spite of the many hours they'd spent together, they'd exchanged fewer words than she had with Mr. Bingley. True, she'd softened somewhat toward Mr. Darcy since the ball at Netherfield, but she'd never imagined he viewed her in that way. She certainly didn't him. Why, it was only recently she'd set aside an active dislike of the man.

"I thought myself safe from your charms because of your family's low status, but your beauty and your wit overcome my reason and judgment. After how admirably you behaved during the fire, I feel it not to be completely against my character to consider marrying you. When I met your aunt and uncle in London, I realized you have at least some relatives who will not be a constant embarrassment to me. Your father's hasty marriage did create a minor scandal, but it was understandable, possibly even admirable under the circumstances, and the gossip has mostly passed now. Besides, when I learned what steps the new Mrs. Bennet is taking to curtail the offensive behavior of your younger sisters, I realized your father's marriage is an advantage to me as well."

Elizabeth was too astonished to speak and Mr. Darcy wasn't pausing to let her.

"Mrs. Bennet is curbing the wild and inappropriate behavior of your younger sisters. She is bringing respectability to a family that didn't have any. Your older sister's marriage also raises you to a level somewhat closer to mine. I no longer need to be as concerned about the degradation of marrying so far beneath me. Having you here at Pemberley had made me realize how unhappy I will be if you ever leave. Elizabeth, will you marry me?"

She stared at him in shocked silence for a long moment. Never had she imagined to hear such a cutting, cruel proposal. She struggled with her temper, attempting to dredge some level of civility to her thoughts. "No, I will not marry you, sir. I must decline." She took in the surprise on his face. "Furthermore, I am sorry to make you unhappy, as my departure apparently stands to do, but I must ask that you arrange for me to return to Longbourn immediately. With this proposal between us, it would be awkward for me to stay."

He yanked his hands away, letting them fall clenched to his sides. "And this is all the reply which I am to have the honor of expecting! I might, perhaps, wish to be informed why, with so little endeavor at civility, I am thus rejected. But it is of small importance." To this pronouncement he added a repressive frown.

"I might as well inquire," replied she, "why with so evident a desire of offending and insulting me, you chose to tell me that you liked me against your will, against your reason, and even against your character?" How, she wondered, had she even for a short time been fooled into thinking Mr. Darcy had decreased in arrogance?

"I am not ashamed of the feelings I related. They were natural and just. Could you expect me to rejoice in the inferiority of your connections?—to congratulate myself on the hope of relations, whose condition in life is so decidedly beneath my own?"

"No, I cannot. The very natural and just nature of all you have related, coupled pleasantly with my absence, should make it easy for you to overcome any lingering disappointment aroused by my refusal. I'm sure in very short order you will be inclined to be grateful for my rejection and forgive me the lack of civility with which I administered it."

Taking a deep breath to hold back angrier words, Elizabeth bundled her hands into her skirts, lifting them to a slightly indecorous height so she might, with excessively quick strides, hurry back toward Pemberley. She did not hear Mr. Darcy follow immediately, for which she was considerably grateful. Though she knew it not possible, she vehemently wished never once to set eyes on him again.

Darcy

Darcy raged silently as he watched Elizabeth storm away, the sight of her shapely ankles inflicting opposing sentiments in mind and heart. Though part of him heated with an emotion quite different from anger, his reason and logic pointed out how her lack of decorum only confirmed her total unsuitability as a wife. What had he been thinking, asking such a low person to become mistress of Pemberley? Why, she didn't even have the intelligence to seize the opportunity he'd presented her. What sort of a dullard would turn down his offer and ask to be carted back to Longbourn? She was right; he was relieved she'd refused him. Therefore, he concluded, the tangle of strong emotions hurtling through him must be a combination of disillusionment and rage.

That established, he started after her, not permitting her out of his sight. It was, after all, the gentlemanly thing to do. Her being a lowborn hoyden didn't exempt him from properly seeing her returned to Pemberley.

When she reached the drive, she stopped, glancing back at him with a look of consternation on her face. She let go of her skirts, hiding her ankles, and smoothed her hands over the wrinkles she'd made. Darcy was perplexed, thinking for a moment she was going to turn to him and apologize, until he noticed a carriage coming up the drive. He reached Elizabeth's side slightly before the vehicle came to a stop. A glance showed her face composed, bearing only a lingering undertone of displeasure.

"I realized I'd been seen and must remain to greet your guest," she said, her tone cold.

"Do not on my account."

"Because you think me low and rude will not make me behave so, sir."

Plastering a smile on her face, Elizabeth stepped forward as a footman opened the carriage door. Darcy was impressed her smile didn't so much as waver when Miss Bingley was helped down. It was only years of training that permitted him to bow eloquently in greeting, hiding both annoyance and surprise.

"Mr. Darcy, you didn't need to come out to meet me," Miss Bingley said. She glanced at Elizabeth, nodding politely. "Miss Bennet."

"Miss Bingley, what a singular surprise," Elizabeth said.

"We were returning from a walk," Darcy said, not wishing Miss Bingley to think he was paying her any special attention.

"Oh?" She looked between them with probing eyes. "Was it a pleasant sojourn?"

"The weather was particularly fine," he said. In an effort to curtail the conversation, he gestured toward Pemberley. "Shall we?"

She nodded again, smiling up at him. He escorted her inside, wishing Elizabeth would retreat to her room in shame, or sorrow, or any fit of strong emotion. Instead, she followed them into the parlor, where they found Georgiana, Mrs. Annesley and the Bingleys conversing.

"Miss Bingley," Mrs. Bingley said in apparent astonishment.

"Please, call me Caroline."

"Caroline, what are you doing here?" Bingley demanded, standing. He edged over so he stood between his sister and his wife, as if Miss Bingley might accost Elizabeth's sister.

Georgiana looked on with wide eyes. Under the circumstances, Darcy wasn't even irritated with her for not acting as hostess.

"I'm here for advice," Miss Bingley said. She didn't wait for an invitation to sit, claiming a vacant chair.

Mrs. Bingley tugged lightly on Bingley's sleeve. He glanced at her. "Charles, do sit," she said.

Bingley did as ordered. Seeing Elizabeth also seat herself, Darcy took the remaining chair. To his relief, it wasn't near Miss Bennet.

"What are you seeking advice about, Caroline?" Mrs. Bingley asked.

"How did you get here?" Bingley demanded.

"I am staying at an inn in Lambton with the Hursts, who are traveling to visit relatives north of here," Miss Bingley said to the group in general. She turned to Darcy. "I want to speak to you."

"Then speak," he said.

"In private."

"I think not." The last thing Darcy needed to add to his day was a private moment with Caroline Bingley. He'd rather be locked in a room with a poisonous snake.

"Very well then." Miss Bingley adjusted her position in her chair, not, he suspected, to make herself more comfortable, but to delay. "Mr. Wickham has been asking me for money."

Darcy kept his face immobile, but he was surprised. Of all the ways he'd imagined Miss Bingley could be there to stir up trouble, her mentioning Wickham hadn't occurred to him.

"Tell him no," Bingley said.

Miss Bingley pursed her lips. Darcy suspected she was containing a tart reply.

"Money?" Jane Bingley prompted.

"Yes, and he has been most insistent," Miss Bingley said. "At the start, I laughed it off. I didn't think he'd really saved my life. I thought he'd erroneously kept me from retrieving my jewelry. In truth, if my maid hadn't already salvaged it, I should have been on to Mr. Wickham for money, to replace that which he'd forced me to lose."

"He saved your life," Darcy said. Even Wickham deserved credit for a good deed. "I was right behind him. You would never have made it out of Netherfield if you'd gone upstairs."

"That is the conclusion I've reluctantly come to." She looked down at her interlaced fingers. "I am the laughingstock of London."

"It will be forgotten soon enough," Mrs. Bingley said.

Darcy wasn't so sure. Miss Bingley had few, if any, real friends. She tended to alienate people, so most would revel in her fall. She was proud, overbearingly so, and . . . his own line of thought surprised him. Could a person be too proud? Shouldn't Miss Bingley embrace her station?

"Perhaps, but until, or if, it ever does, it limits my choices." Miss Bingley sighed. "I am not getting any younger. I'd intended to wed this season. When I think of all the suitors I've turned away in years past . . ." She shook her head. "My sister is not willing to risk her social position to advance mine. I understand her point of view." Miss Bingley finally looked up, training her gaze on Jane Bingley. "I behaved badly and owe you a deep apology."

"You were distressed," Mrs. Bingley said. "The fact that I didn't rescue my mother would have eventually occurred to me."

"One apology isn't enough, Caroline," Bingley said. "You can't expect Jane to sponsor you."

"Since you don't have a home yet, and the only eligible man here wouldn't marry me under any circumstances, I'm not asking that."

Her words taking him by surprise, Darcy almost laughed. He eyed her with a modicum more respect. "What are you asking?"

"I'm asking for information. I have a chance to marry a man with a title, but he has some rather strict ideas. If I publicly atone for my mistake, I believe he will propose. In one sense, Mr. Wickham is right. I owe him something. The man I am considering marrying might think more of me if I give Mr. Wickham a reward. Yet, I don't trust Mr. Wickham. His coming after me for money suggests he isn't worthy of having any. I don't want to squander what I have, or come over as even more of a fool than I seem already."

Darcy frowned, thinking that over. Miss Bingley's assessment of Wickham wasn't far off the mark, despite some of his recent laudable behavior. No true gentleman would accost a lady for money. On the other hand, it was a shame not to reward Wickham for one of the few truly good deeds of his life. Possibly he could be encouraged toward better behavior through monetary reward.

Darcy realized everyone was looking to him, as the one most acquainted with Wickham, and he must formulate a reply. "I do not consider Mr. Wickham a worthy individual, but in this instance he behaved heroically. Are you judging his life or his actions in this one case?"

"Both," Miss Bingley said, staying Darcy when he would have continued. "You should know there is a rumor going around. Mr. Wickham is said to have told people he was to receive a living from your father's will and you denied it to him."

"The story is true, but incomplete." Darcy shot a glance at Elizabeth, unable not to wonder if she'd been told, and believed, that about him. He recalled having the impression at one point that she was fond of Mr. Wickham, perhaps even looking to champion him in some way. "I denied it to him after he requested three thousand pounds in lieu of the living. I paid it, thinking it best for him and the community. He would have been an abysmal clergyman."

Another glance showed Elizabeth watching him with thoughtful eyes. Darcy's heart twisted painfully. He wrenched his gaze away, summoning his indignation at her hasty and ill-mannered refusal.

"There's something else you should know, if you wish to know George's worth," Georgiana said.

Darcy winced at his sister's use of Wickham's Christian name. All heads turned to her in surprise. Her eyes went to the floor, her cheeks coloring.

"Georgiana, it isn't relevant," Darcy said, wishing to spare her.

"Tell them."

Her whispered words hardly reached his ears. Darcy frowned, but the damage was already done, and his sister was correct; the tale was relevant when assessing Wickham's nature. "Wickham tried to elope with Georgiana last summer. She came to me and I sent him away."

"It's worse than that," Georgiana said, looking up. Darcy started to speak, to stay her, but she held up her hand. She was quite pale now. "I agreed at first. He didn't… We didn't…. He kissed me. I let him."

"But you're only fifteen," Mrs. Bingley exclaimed.

Georgiana hung her head.

Mrs. Bingley and Elizabeth both went to Darcy's sister. Mrs. Bingley put an arm about her and Elizabeth knelt beside her, taking her hands and murmuring something Darcy couldn't make out. He felt a strange ache in his chest, watching Elizabeth soothe his little sister.

"Old enough to marry without the consent of a parent or guardian in Scotland," Miss Bingley said, her words crisp. "So he is a bad man. He still saved my life. If I give him a thousand pounds, I can be considered generous."

"That might not win you respect in London," Darcy said, forcing himself to look away from the tableau of Elizabeth comforting his sister.

"I only need the respect of one person," Miss Bingley said confidently. "Thank you." She stood and walked out of the room without waiting for anyone to acknowledge her departure.

Darcy stood as well, bowing at her retreating back, as did Bingley. Elizabeth stayed with Georgiana, but Mrs. Bingley hurried out of the room, calling for Miss Bingley. Darcy didn't try to sort out their words as they spoke in the hall. He settled back into his chair, frowning at the wall behind Bingley.

What world was this where Wickham was doing good deeds and being rewarded, in spite of the man they all knew him to be, and Darcy couldn't even obtain the hand of a low born country miss? He risked a glance, finding Georgiana and Elizabeth still speaking in quiet tones, his sister looking much restored. Whatever world it was, Darcy hoped it soon righted.

Elizabeth

All the way back to Longbourn, Elizabeth thought about Mr. Darcy's proposal. She'd never been so insulted in the entirety of her life, and his view of her family, it was simply intolerable. She couldn't help but rehearse their interactions, wondering when she'd lost sight of the arrogance she knew him to possess, which had reemerged with such vengeance.

Before the proposal, she was beginning to think he was a pleasant, decent man. She'd known he was proud, but somehow that pride wasn't displayed at Pemberley. Perhaps the obvious wealth and beauty of the place made it so he did not need to show any additional pride.

Or perhaps he was at peace there? She could almost think his pride as much a veil as Miss Darcy's shyness. He'd been heroic during the Netherfield fire. He was clearly kind to his sister and to Mr. Bingley. In Pemberley, Elizabeth was aware he was liked and respected by his servants. Her belief in his greatest offence, denying Mr. Wickham his living, had turned out to be incorrect. If she'd known that sooner, she could have seen herself warming to Mr. Darcy.

No amount of warmth would have induced her to accept his proposal, however. He'd made it painfully obvious he had no respect for her. He may have spoken of her wit and beauty, but all else out of his mouth had made it seem as if she'd crawled out of the mud and would be grateful for anyone who would allow her to be clean.

Arriving home, Elizabeth put Mr. Darcy firmly from her mind. His pride and his horrendous proposal had no place in her life at Longbourn. Though in truth, there were times she felt she didn't have a place there, either.

She found it odd to be home after her more than two-month

absence, and struggled to fit into the rhythm of family life Charlotte had created. Elizabeth found herself lonely, and yet constantly wishing for more privacy and space. The combination made her short tempered and dull.

The loneliness she easily attributed to Jane's absence, but as it lingered she realized it ran deeper than that. Not only was her dearest sister gone, but her mother and father were as well. Her father because he had, in her absence, done as he'd hoped. He and Charlotte seemed quite close. They were often together, when neither was occupied by caring for Longbourn. This made the quiet chats with him in his library rare.

Her mother's absence contributed most to Elizabeth's lonesome state, however. As much as her mother had been a source of torment, she'd filled their home. Filled it with people, talk, pestering and laughter. She'd filled it with beauty, too, which Charlotte had stripped away in the interest of economy. Devoid of her and the elegance she'd loved, Longbourn seemed almost like a place abandoned by comparison.

Elizabeth realized that, while in a deep state of sorrow when she'd left, she had not at the time fully grasped that her mother was gone. Going away had permitted the unacknowledged delusion her home remained little changed. Now that she had returned, her grief muted by the months, she was struck anew by the reality of her mother's death.

It didn't help that they entertained rarely, and much more modestly than before. Elizabeth would not have considered herself one for entertaining, but it was much more pleasant than hours spent in the company of only one's family, listening to each sister take turns reading while Charlotte and her father made eyes at each other. Simply put, little was as it had been before her mother's death, and Elizabeth was only now being forced to truly come to terms with the abiding changes in her life. She knew this, but knowledge did not make the trial of it more pleasant to experience.

Some few weeks after her return found Elizabeth pushing spinach about on her dinner plate. She didn't care for spinach. It wouldn't have signified before, but Charlotte allowed them so few choices, it was spinach or no vegetable at all. Elizabeth was perversely certain Charlotte, having once been her dear friend, knew of her dislike of the cooked leaves and had added them to the menu purposefully.

"I have pleasant news," Lydia said, smiling cheerfully around the table.

"Then please share it," Charlotte said.

"Mrs. Forster has invited me to join her in Brighton as her particular friend," Lydia said with obvious delight. "Colonel Forster said I must ask you for permission. I told him you are trying to save money and would surely be happy for someone else to have the cost of feeding me. My expenses can't be higher than my allowance."

"Mr. Bennet?" Charlotte said, frowning at Elizabeth's father.

He looked up from his plate. "Yes, my dear?"

"It is for you to tell Lydia she may not go."

"Papa," Lydia cried, casting a glare at Charlotte.

"Quite right. Lydia, you cannot go." He returned to eating.

"But Papa, why? It's Brighton! It shall be ever so much fun. We never get to have any fun anymore."

Charlotte shook her head. "You are too young to be in the care of someone who is but a few years your senior. Mrs. Forster is not a suitable chaperone for Brighton."

"I'm not too young," Lydia said. "By the time I leave, I'll be sixteen."

"I wouldn't let Kitty go," Charlotte said.

"I want some fun. You won't let us dance or wear bright colors."

Elizabeth could see Lydia was working herself up into a full fit. Beside her, Kitty began to cough. Mary mimicked their father, concentrating on her plate as if nothing else transpired.

"You are still in mourning," Charlotte said. "Bright colors and dancing are not appropriate."

"I'm sick of mourning," Lydia wailed. "I've mourned. I've followed your stupid rules. Nothing I do will bring Mama back." Lydia turned to their father. "You said we would mourn for six months. That's until a couple of days after the regiment leaves. I shall have no chance to do anything. I want to dance. I want to laugh. I'm tired of mourning. Mama wanted me to have fun. She would have wanted me to go."

Mr. Bennet looked at his wife with some concern. "Charlotte?"

Charlotte's expression was resolute. "Good behavior does not end with the mourning period. Yes, you will be able to dance and wear bright colors, but you will behave with decorum. Your current display confirms my misgivings. You will not go to Brighton."

Lydia let out an anguished howl. Elizabeth winced at the sound, gritting her teeth. Perhaps Mr. Darcy did have a slight point in his criticism of her younger sisters' behavior.

"Lydia, that is enough," their father said. "You won't go. I don't want to hear any more about it."

Though her father spoke with a firmness that convinced Elizabeth of his stance, they did hear more about it. In fact, over the next week it was all anyone heard from Lydia. She cajoled, wheedled, whined, and finally screamed. For that outburst, she was confined to her room for two days. After one, she meekly asked permission to do her usual work and was allowed out. She spent the entire day working in the house. The next day, she was given permission to work outside and she spent several hours weeding the kitchen garden. When that was done, she went inside and did housework for the rest of the day.

Elizabeth observed with misgivings her father's and Charlotte's obvious pleasure in Lydia's reformed behavior. She thought they were right to set an example for how poor behavior would be received, but wrong in thinking Lydia had reformed. One day spent in boredom in her room wouldn't be enough to change Lydia.

Several days after Lydia's release, at another dinner where spinach was prominent on the table, Elizabeth still hadn't reversed her opinion. Lydia was behaving with decorum in every way, the state so unnatural Elizabeth nearly wanted to shake her. Elizabeth's only clue she was correct and her father and Charlotte wrong was the unaccountably smug look that would pass across Kitty's face whenever their father or Charlotte praised Lydia's behavior.

"My parents are holding a party for the officers," Charlotte said. She didn't look at anyone in particular as she said it.

Silence returned in the wake of that pronouncement. Elizabeth hated how quiet their dinners were. Mama would never have stood for it, and Kitty and Lydia wouldn't have managed it. This silence, though, was of a different sort than usual. Elizabeth knew Charlotte was testing Lydia's reaction. Lydia must know as well, for she continued to eat, not looking up or speaking.

"You are all invited," Charlotte finally said.

"May we attend?" Mary asked, obviously realizing being invited and being permitted to go were not of the same ilk.

"You may."

"All of us?" Lydia asked, looking up.

"Yes. As you have behaved so decorously the past several days, and assuming you continue in this vein, you are permitted to attend as well, Lydia."

"Thank you."

In spite of her lack of belief in Lydia's contrition, Elizabeth was pleased her youngest sister would be allowed to attend. She didn't think it was fair to completely stifle Lydia's personality. Yes, their mother had encouraged Kitty and Lydia to run too wild, but Charlotte seemed likely to take all youthful exuberance from them. It wasn't fair for a woman of eight and twenty to rob Lydia and Kitty of the joy of their young years.

Yet they were in mourning, and it was important for Kitty and Lydia to behave accordingly. Charlotte had said they could dance and wear bright colors after six months had passed. Many families would have insisted on a full year. Mr. Darcy was right in a way. Charlotte was making Lydia and Kitty behave better than they normally would have.

Elizabeth frowned down at her plate. Why did she keep thinking of Mr. Darcy? His opinions shouldn't matter to her.

When the eve of the party arrived, Lydia seemed a bit more her usual self. This somewhat buoyed Elizabeth as well. Though they all wore the black of mourning still, it was pleasant to be going out. Elizabeth could, if she studiously ignored several things, pretend her life was somewhat as it had once been.

They hadn't been at Lucas Lodge for long when Elizabeth noted Mr. Wickham approaching her. Though the revelations at Pemberley had robbed him of much of his charm in her eyes, she made no effort to avoid him. If nothing else, she'd had so little conversation with anyone not in her family or Charlotte's for so many weeks, she shouldn't wish to turn a soul away.

"Miss Bennet." Mr. Wickham bowed, coming up with a charming smile on his boyish face. "How good it is to see you once again. It seems like an age."

"I daresay it has been," she said. "I've been away, as you likely know."

"Yes. I understand you recently spent some time at Pemberley."

"I did. It's a beautiful manor, and so aptly situated as to be quite enviable."

"Truly spoken." His face took on a sad cast. "I often regret I can't return there. It was my home."

"Perhaps if you had made the effort to be on good terms with Mr.

Darcy, you might not have lost your right to visit." Rather, Elizabeth thought, perhaps if Mr. Wickham had made less of an effort to be on especially good terms with Miss Darcy, Mr. Darcy wouldn't despise him as he did, but this she would not speak aloud.

"I stopped being on good terms with Darcy when we were at Cambridge."

"Was that Mr. Darcy's fault?" she asked sweetly, wondering what lies he would opt to tell that day.

He looked at her with a speculative expression. "No," he said slowly. "It was mine. I sowed some wild oats, which I regret, but that is very normal."

"And you've behaved very well ever since." She made her response not quite a question.

"No," he said with a grimace. "I started behaving well at the ball at Netherfield."

"Why with the fire?" She was impressed with his honesty. It seemed he was still endeavoring to maintain the good image he'd spoken of when last they met, though she knew he'd misled her about the living then and was resolved to be wary of such half-truths now.

Mr. Wickham shrugged. "I've been admired before, but never because I'd earned it. I've always been obliged to scheme to find ways to make people think well of me. Having achieved deserved admiration, I don't want to lose it. It seems the only way I can keep it is to actually behave well."

"Most people do that as a matter of course," she felt obligated to point out.

"Most people don't crave respect."

"I believe I must contradict you. Everyone wishes to be respected." Elizabeth was aware she did, which was much of the reason she'd so adamantly rejected Mr. Darcy's proposal.

"Perhaps then, I mean most people don't grow up in the shadow of someone who commands respect without effort."

"You mean Mr. Darcy?" she guessed. "Did he then, always?"

Mr. Wickham nodded, looking a bit somber. "Always. It comes along with his inherited wealth. He's commanded respect since we were boys, always without having to do a thing to earn it."

"Yet, at Pemberley he is respected by those who have known him for many years. They say no man is a hero to his valet. I haven't spoken with Mr. Darcy's valet, but it's clear his servants and tenants respect him." She paused, considering Wickham's charge, and shook her head. "I do not know if I can agree he does nothing to earn that respect, or that the respect he holds is simply a product of his station. He is a man of sense and education, and who has lived in the world." As Elizabeth said this, she realized, for all his highhandedness, she did respect Mr. Darcy. Why couldn't he respect her?

"It would be easy with his wealth, education and background to behave well."

"Do you believe so? For you cannot say all of his station do. Society is rife with examples of wealthy men exploiting their standing." Elizabeth recalled how a titled man had taken the horses reserved for Mr. Darcy, and Mr. Darcy's restrained reaction. She gentled her tone. "Why don't you accept what you are and behave well?"

Mr. Wickham's handsome face took on a sullen cast, emphasizing that his charms were of a boyish leaning. "Because I don't wish to behave well. I've spent months being a model soldier. People are starting to forget my heroism and treat me like anyone else. No one gives me credit for how hard I work to keep from behaving badly. Being virtuous is boring and unrewarding."

Elizabeth was forced to laugh. He reminded her of a child, his petulance in keeping with what she'd come to understand of his nature. "You sound like my sister Lydia. She is tired of behaving well."

Mr. Wickham's eyes brightened with interest, he looked around the room until he saw Lydia. "I should go and commiserate with her. We can compare sorrows. This is my last chance before the regiment leaves." He bowed. "Miss Bennet."

She nodded in acknowledgment of the courtesy. "Mr. Wickham."

Leaving Elizabeth's side, Mr. Wickham wove his way between Sir William's guests until he reached Lydia. From that point onward, the two spent most of the evening conversing. Elizabeth didn't mind in the slightest, no longer craving Mr. Wickham's company as she once might have.

Later, as the sisters regrouped to depart Lucas Lodge, Lydia was more cheerful than she'd been since Elizabeth's return from Pemberley, making her glad she'd pointed Mr. Wickham in the direction of her youngest sister. In the morning he would be on his way to Brighton, so their exchange would become a distant memory for both, but Elizabeth liked to think it had done Lydia good.

At least, it seemed to have done, for Lydia remained in good spirits the entire walk back to Longbourn. When they reached home, she slipped away from the others and into the parlor. Elizabeth likewise remained below as her other sisters went upstairs to check that all candles were extinguished and coals raked back. As she finished that task, she was drawn to the parlor by a flickering light. She saw Lydia still there, standing before the open door to the large glass-fronted china cabinet at the back of the room.

Elizabeth crossed to her, finding her holding, one in each hand, the ceramic shepherdess and shepherd. Lydia looked over to her as she approached. "Mama loved these."

"She did," Elizabeth replied. "There was a shepherdess like this at Pemberley."

"No shepherd?"

"No shepherd." Elizabeth reached out to touch a white ceramic ewe. "No sheep, either. Only a lonely shepherdess."

Lydia placed them back on the shelf with care. "I wanted to look at these once again. Charlotte has them all put away where they won't gather dust and they are cramped together so you can hardly see them."

Elizabeth looked at the room again. She'd admired Pemberley's simplicity, but this room wasn't only simple, but severe. Looking at the shepherdess through the glass door wasn't the same as seeing her in a place of honor on the mantel. "I've become used to the room as it is now and hardly notice what it looks like."

"I notice their absence." Closing the door, Lydia picked up her candle. "Good night, Lizzy," she said, heading from the room.

"Good night," Elizabeth called after, her voice hushed as one keeps it in a nearly dark house.

Lydia took after their mother in more ways than temperament. Both of them noticed beauty, or its absence. As Elizabeth cast a last look about the parlor before following Lydia upstairs, she realized she would notice the absence of the regiment. They added variety to the gatherings. There had never been so many young men in Meryton. She supposed, with the regiment gone, life would soon be quite uninteresting.

Chapter Eight

~ Marriages ~

Darcy

Darcy was slightly relieved when Bingley finally received a letter from his attorney saying his problems were solved. The owner of Netherfield Park was not going to hold Bingley responsible for the destruction wrought by the fire. Darcy knew it was uncharitable of him to wish for Mr. and Mrs. Bingley's departure from Pemberley, but Mrs. Bingley was a constant reminder of Elizabeth, a nagging discontent Darcy could do without.

Therefore, it was with good humor he agreed to accompany them when Bingley's investigations of an appropriate estate to purchase led him to a candidate. With Darcy's servants in tow, they investigated the house from cellar to attic. They analyzed the practicality of the kitchen and the number and size of the bedrooms, investigating the suitability of all areas both for private use and for entertaining. Darcy had his people look at the tenants' cottages and the crops. They traveled to the nearest two towns to assess the businesses available as well as to judge the quality of the roads. Darcy walked some of the forest to estimate if the timber would sustain the estate. They even attended a service in the local church.

Being so much in the presence of Bingley and his wife, Darcy couldn't help but know how happy Bingley was. Mrs. Bingley was as well, as she should be at marrying a man so above her station. It wasn't the happiness of triumph, though. Both of them seemed to hold genuine affection for each other. Constantly exposed to their contentment and to Mrs. Bingley's grace and excellent manners, Darcy was beginning to think perhaps a lady's breeding and connections mattered less than her appeal, her comportment and the happiness she could bring into a man's life.

Not that it mattered in the case of Elizabeth, of course. She'd made her feelings for Darcy quite clear. Rather, he felt it was a good lesson to keep in mind in the future.

When all was deemed satisfactory with Bingley's planned home, negotiations began with the owner's representative. When a price was found that was acceptable to both sides, Darcy and Mr. and Mrs. Bingley journeyed back to Pemberley. Darcy was almost reluctant to return, for being away from Pemberley, even in the company of Mrs. Bingley, had somewhat alleviated his turmoil in the face of memories of Elizabeth. It hadn't put her from his mind in any way, for he continuously wondered what she would make of her sister's new home, but it at least kept at bay recollections of Elizabeth as part of his daily life.

Once they'd returned, recuperated from the journey and reconvened in a sunny parlor, Mrs. Bingley was presented by Darcy's staff with a sizable stack of correspondences. Bemusement clear on her face, she accepted them, moving to a desk.

Bingley took a seat in a nearby chair, paper in hand, but watched her curiously. He claimed the single piece of mail he was offered, setting it on a nearby table. "That's a great many letters, my love," he said.

Darcy, concealing his dismay at being privy to endearments, sat on a nearby sofa, accepting his modest stack of envelopes. Of course, they would only be ones deemed personal in nature. His staff would have placed any missives seeming related to business on his desk in his study.

"Yes, it is a rather daunting number," Mrs. Bingley said. She opened the first one, scanning it. "Charlotte is pregnant. She expects the baby to come in the autumn."

"Perhaps that explains your bounty of letters," Bingley said.

"Maybe it's because I write letters," she replied.

"You're with me. Why do I need to write anyone?"

They exchanged smiles that gave Darcy a pang of jealousy, even while forcing him to contain a grimace. After so many days of traveling together, their closeness was wearing on him, yet he couldn't deny his envy. Perhaps if he'd made a more agreeable effort at proposing, he would have someone to be cloying with.

He shook his head slightly. No, he'd been over it all in his mind many times. Elizabeth Bennet couldn't have expected, nor wanted, him to lie. Pretending she and her family were anything more than they were would have been false, and no basis for a union. Darcy was morally bound to uphold his values even in proposing, and even if being honorable denied him the woman he loved.

Loved? Had loved, rather. Once.

Darcy tore open his first letter, not even looking at the address. Besides, if Elizabeth was too great a fool to understand the excessive favor he'd done her by proposing, she wasn't the woman he thought her to be. She was correct. They were both better off this way.

Mrs. Bingley gasped. Darcy turned, taking in the slightly diminished pile of sealed letters and neat stack of opened ones. Mrs. Bingley's eyes were wide as she read.

"What's the matter?" Bingley asked.

Mrs. Bingley turned in her chair, handing him the letter. As soon as he took it, she turned back and began sorting through the rest of the unopened pile with quick movements.

Bingley pursued the letter for a moment, then looked up at Darcy. "You'd better hear this, Darcy. It's from Miss Elizabeth." He cleared his throat. "Dear Jane. Something has occurred of a most unexpected and serious nature; but I am afraid of alarming you—be assured that we are all well. What I have to say relates to poor Lydia. The regiment left Meryton this morning, for which reason the Lucases had a party last night. By Kitty's report, when Lydia reached their room last night, she said she was going to sort through her clothes to see what she could wear, because we are coming out of mourning. Kitty fell asleep before Lydia was done. When she woke to find Lydia gone, Kitty assumed she'd risen early." Bingley looked up, his expression grim.

Bracing for what was to come, Darcy gestured toward the letter. "What else does it say?"

"It says Miss Lydia left a note advising she was eloping with Mr. Wickham. The regiment had already left when the family found the note. Mr. Bennet is trying to find them. It also goes on about how Miss Elizabeth considers herself responsible, as she encouraged Mr. Wickham to speak with Miss Lydia." Bingley shook his head. "I can't imagine why she would do such a thing, although I'm sure she felt there was little harm even he could do in a few short hours."

Mrs. Bingley held up another letter. "This one is from Elizabeth as well. It says they didn't go north to Scotland but south, possibly to London. My father has no idea of where they are. Elizabeth wrote again about how guilty she feels." Crumpling the letter to her chest, Mrs. Bingley burst into tears. "Oh dear, whatever will become of her."

Bingley stood and hurried to her side.

Darcy wasn't certain if Mrs. Bingley meant Elizabeth or Miss Lydia. He didn't care a whit what happened to Miss Lydia, whom he'd always felt was bound for ruin. He did care what happened to Elizabeth, though. As much as he resented her refusal of him, he didn't want her alone or married to someone unworthy of her. Elizabeth, and the other two sisters, would never make good matches now, if any at all. Mrs. Bingley's connections were not elevated enough to lift them from the depths Miss Lydia had sunk them into.

Agitated by the thought of Elizabeth wed to someone undeserving of her, Darcy excused himself, knowing they wouldn't hear, and left Bingley to comfort his wife. Strolling through Pemberley without a clear notion where he went, Darcy soon found himself outside, following one of Elizabeth's favored paths.

He felt restlessly ineffective, as if he should be taking steps to right this wrong, but he had no right to intervene. On top of that, he also had no reason to intervene. Certainly, he didn't have any obligation toward the Bennets. Elizabeth had rejected his proposal. He owed her nothing and her future prospects should not trouble him.

Yet they did.

Darcy couldn't help but ponder Mrs. Bingley's distress and assume it on Elizabeth. He attempted to imagine her state of mind. She'd written about her guilt, but that wasn't rational. Even knowing Mr. Wickham's character and past actions as she did, suggesting he speak with Miss Lydia at a gathering was hardly encouraging them to run away together.

He didn't want Elizabeth to be distressed. Maybe it would be less troubling if she'd someone to comfort her, a husband or fiancé, but the way things stood, she seemed alone and vulnerable to society's censure and whims. Those whims, Darcy had observed, could be quite cruel and could cause a young woman irreparable harm.

He stomped down a path, aware that, no matter how much he wanted Elizabeth safe and cared for, it roused a deep anger in him to think of her married or affianced to another man. He couldn't help but be secretly pleased no news to that affect had appeared in any of Mrs. Bingley's letter, and not because of any petty desire to see her regret not accepting him. No, for an even worse reason; jealousy.

Somehow, Darcy found himself in the spot where he'd proposed. He hadn't meant to come that way. Had, in truth, studiously avoided the location since. He looked about, finding the forest floor empty now of crocuses, though violets peeked through.

No, it wasn't rational for Elizabeth to blame herself for Miss Lydia's and Wickham's behavior, but then Elizabeth wasn't as rational as she ought to be. She'd refused him, after all, and blamed him for harboring concerns about her family, which had turned out to be founded. Was that the behavior of a rational woman?

Darcy rubbed his temples, trying to see the world through Elizabeth's eyes. What would he do, he wondered, should someone judge him based on a low opinion of company he'd kept? Once, he'd been a comrade to Mr. Wickham. Should he be valued based on that association?

Wickham aside, Darcy had relatives he wasn't proud of. What would his reaction be to people who had a low opinion of him because of those relatives? In the silence of the forest, the words he'd spoken when proposing to Elizabeth rang in his own head.

He'd done worse, he realized, than judge Elizabeth based on her relatives. He'd implied she was better off with her mother dead. That would have been inexcusable at any time, but was even more so because he'd said it within half a year of the event.

What, truly, had the first Mrs. Bennet been aside from aggravating and crass? Social crimes, perhaps, but nothing more. She'd been a silly fool, but she'd worked to secure her daughters' futures. Darcy knew many society women who put their own interests ahead of their children's. Did their seemlier behavior, coupled with that neglect, make them better people than Elizabeth's mother?

Darcy paced the path, his concern for Elizabeth growing the more he thought on her. It was distressing enough to have lost her mother a scant six months passed, but now to face ruin on top of that? He wondered if she'd overcome her unreasonable guilt at not rescuing her mother. Even if she had, a new weight was upon her, her letters making it clear she blamed herself for this fresh trauma.

If Miss Lydia didn't marry Mr. Wickham, she would drag her family down. All of the remaining sisters would have trouble marrying, if they managed to wed at all. The first Mrs. Bennet's concern was reasonable. They had to marry well or live in poverty. Well, not poverty. Bingley would see they were fed and clothed.

Darcy found he didn't want Bingley to be the one to do that. He wanted to be responsible for Elizabeth and whichever of her family needed help, not because he respected Elizabeth's family, but because he respected her emotions. She had the right and obligation to love her family. Had he really ever thought he could regard her better for not doing so? What sort of woman would that make her?

One like Caroline Bingley or Mrs. Hurst, he realized. The exact opposite of the kind of woman he wished to have in his life, and Georgiana's. How could he expect a woman to hold all of the virtues and characteristics he lauded, as Elizabeth did, and then turn from her own kin? Only a charlatan would have done so. Elizabeth, unlike most every other marriage minded miss Darcy had encountered, was not a charlatan. She would not say and do whatever was needed to secure him as a husband. Was his pride truly so fragile he wanted a simpering sycophant more than a woman like Elizabeth Bennet?

Not like Elizabeth Bennet, he realized. Similar would not do, and not simply because there was no one else like her. Only one woman could fill the void in both Pemberley and his heart. The very one he'd issued such a degrading and detestable proposal to right there on the path he paced.

Having admitted as much, Darcy realized he hadn't ever stopped loving her. Had done so since he and Bingley first journeyed to Hertfordshire. He didn't know if he'd ever be able to make amends for his foolish, reprehensible opinions of her and her family, but he did know he didn't want her hurt, even if she was never again part of his life.

Decided, he returned to the Bingleys, finding Mrs. Bingley still teary eyed, though they sat together on a sofa now. "I will go look for them," Darcy said without preamble.

"It's my concern, not yours," Bingley said.

"No. It's Wickham. If I'd told people about him, he would not have been in a position to run off with Miss Lydia. My silence allowed him to act."

"You can't hold yourself responsible for him," Bingley said. "Besides, Miss Elizabeth knew about him. She could have warned her family."

"Lizzy wouldn't do that," Mrs. Bingley said, looking startled.

"I agree," Darcy said. "Nor did I expect her to. You know her well enough to realize she wouldn't air my doings or Georgiana's secret before others. Not without express permission."

Bingley glanced at his wife, who looked hopeful. For some reason, her expression only dimmed his. "It is not for you to fix, Darcy," Bingley said in aggrieved tones. "You have no attachment or obligation to the Bennet family. This is my responsibility, not yours."

"Practically, no, I'm not responsible. Perhaps morally I'm not responsible, either, but I feel accountable and am in a position to do something about it. You are not."

"Of course I can do something," Bingley said with surprising anger.

"You've just committed yourself to a huge expense. You will be taking possession of your new home in days. You need to be there to see everything is handled smoothly. A year from now you may have someone else running the estate to your satisfaction, but you can't delegate the responsibility now. Certainly, you can't expect Mrs. Bingley to supervise taking over the estate on her own?"

Bingley looked at his wife, and his anger diminished. He turned back to Darcy. "You will let me bear the expense."

"No. You know I don't take lightly what I deem to be my duty."

They continued to argue, but Darcy was adamant. The more Bingley attempted to dissuade him, the more Darcy realized he was resolved to be the one to aid Elizabeth and her family. Standing in the clearing, reviewing his words the day he'd proposed, he'd come to realize two things. One was that he'd meant it when he told Elizabeth he loved her, meant it to the bottom of his soul. The other was that, in view of his words, she very well might despise him. In Miss Lydia's disgrace, Darcy began to see a hope of repairing what pride had falsely bid him shatter.

In spite of his argument with Bingley, Darcy was on the road to London within an hour, but his haste went unrewarded. Even after several days of searching, he couldn't find Mr. Wickham. Darcy had even run to ground his sister's former governess, the one who'd allowed Mr. Wickham access to Georgiana, but she wasted his time and provided no information.

Finally, desperate, he thought to visit Miss Bingley. She'd talked about providing Wickham with money. He often returned to anyone who'd been foolish enough to do that, hoping for more.

He handed his card to the butler, who disappeared only to return almost immediately. Darcy was escorted into the parlor, as he'd expected to be. Unexpected, however, was the other occupant of the room aside from Miss Bingley, a gentleman about a decade Darcy's senior.

The gentleman and Miss Bingley stood when Darcy entered. He bowed. "Miss Bingley."

"Mr. Darcy," she said. "How pleasant to see you. Do come in."

Darcy entered, turning slightly toward the older gentleman.

"May I introduce Lord Hays?" Miss Bingley asked.

"Lord Hays," Darcy greeted, bowing again. Darcy had heard of Baron Hays, though they'd not met before. He was a widower and noted for his charities.

"Lord Hays, this is Mr. Darcy," Miss Bingley said. "I'm sure I've mentioned him."

"Darcy, a pleasure," Hays said with cool condescension.

"Do sit down, Mr. Darcy, and tell us to what we owe the honor," Miss Bingley said.

They all seated themselves, Lord Hays sitting in the chair nearest Miss Bingley, casting a possessive look her way. Darcy did not consider himself overly aware of women's fashions, but Miss Bingley's attire wasn't fashionable. Her neckline was unusually high and her gown plainer than the clothes she usually wore.

"Miss Bingley," Darcy said. "I don't wish to presume, but perhaps we could speak in private?"

She smiled slightly, a malicious gleam in her eyes. "We may not speak in private. I have no secrets from Lord Hays."

Darcy contained a grimace, aware of the fairness of her words after his recent treatment of her. Casting a glance at Lord Hays, Darcy decided he should tread carefully, not implying more than there was. "Very well. When we last spoke, you told me about a man who was bothering you, Mr. Wickham. I am trying to get in touch with him."

"Why?" Lord Hays asked.

Darcy was surprised by the question. He glanced at Miss Bingley, trying to ascertain if Lord Hays had the right to question her guests.

She raised her eyebrows slightly, her expression bland, yet the still-present gleam in her eyes mocking.

Darcy didn't allow his annoyance to show as he turned to Hays. "He appears to have run off with the sister of the wife of a close friend of mine. My father brought Wickham up in such a way as to permit him to pass himself off as a gentleman. I hold my family somewhat responsible for him using that education to seduce a gentleman's daughter."

"It is unusual for someone in your class to claim that level of responsibility," Lord Hays said.

His class? Weren't they essentially in the same class? Hays was reputed to be wealthier than Bingley, but not as wealthy as Darcy. Did he weigh his title so heavily? Darcy shrugged. "I am not responsible for everything he will do in the future, but in this case, I would like to get her to return to her family or persuade them to marry."

The baron and Miss Bingley exchanged a glance. She smiled sweetly at him.

Hays turned back to Darcy. "I can give you his current address. We are dealing with him and are troubled about Miss Bennet."

Darcy knew it wasn't his place to pry, but he couldn't imagine why Lord Hays would deal with Mr. Wickham. "If I may ask, what is your interest in Mr. Wickham?"

"Miss Bingley has consented to be my wife, which makes Mr. Wickham my concern."

Darcy glanced at Miss Bingley, surprised this was the first he'd heard of the news. Turning to Lord Hays, he said, "I offer my congratulations to you and my best wishes to Miss Bingley."

"Thank you," she said, her smile a touch smug.

"Yes, well, thank you, Darcy," Hays added. "The crux of the matter is, Miss Bingley, given her charitable nature, now understands she owes a debt to Mr. Wickham for saving her life, but we do not wish to encourage immorality. We've been looking into Mr. Wickham's past very carefully and are trying to see what is best for him."

"I suspect if you pay a substantial amount of money to Mr. Wickham, he will be happy to send Miss Bennet home," Darcy said, trying to ascertain if that was Hays intent. The upper class often solved such issues in this way. Darcy didn't care for that outcome, however, as it would still leave the Bennet family disgraced. He would rather encourage Wickham to wed Miss Lydia, now that he'd ruined her.

"That was the impression I received from him, but that is not the goal I wish to achieve. Miss Bingley had come to accept she must sell her jewelry and have the proceeds go to Mr. Wickham. After investigating him, I am concerned the money would be spent frivolously and do him more harm than good. I feel, instead of handing a man of his nature a large sum, we should arrange a pension for him.

It would come to about ten pounds a quarter. Mr. Wickham does not seem to feel that is generous enough for him to take on a wife."

Ten pounds a quarter was enough to keep Wickham from starvation, but barely. "Would you mind if I try my hand at achieving a marriage?"

"Not at all. I shall get you the address." Lord Hays stepped from the room, ironically leaving Darcy alone with Miss Bingley when there was no longer any reason for him to wish to be alone with her.

"I'm surprised you hadn't heard of my engagement," Miss Bingley said as Hay's footsteps dwindled down the hall. "I've written of it to Charles."

Darcy wondered if the news had been contained in Bingley's solitary letter and missed in the fuss before his departure. "I'm sure you'll both be quite happy," he said, though he wasn't.

"Thank you," Miss Bingley said.

She turned toward the door, and Darcy realized he could already hear Hays returning. In moments, Lord Hays entered the room again, a piece of paper in hand.

"This is not what I'd planned for my life, but Lord Hays has persuaded me my previous goals were shallow," Miss Bingley continued. She smiled at her fiancé. "I'll be forever grateful for his opening my eyes to a better way of life."

Hays smiled down at her in a way Darcy found unbearably condescending and self-satisfied. He didn't know how even Caroline Bingley could look back with such an appearance of calm acceptance. Turning from her, Hays proffered the paper he held.

"Thank you." Darcy stood, accepting the folded sheet. "And thank you both for your time. Again, my congratulations." He bowed to them both, accepting their farewells before making his exit.

On his way to the address Lord Hays had provided him, Darcy permitted himself to muse over Miss Bingley's sincerity. Was she truly grateful for the changes Lord Hays demanded, or had she simply found a way of getting the wealth she craved, with a title thrown in? Darcy distracted himself by pondering the meeting for much of the journey across town, but Miss Bingley was too accomplished an actress. He couldn't decide.

The address Hays sent Darcy to was a lodging house. It wasn't a residence a gentleman of any worth would take, but was better than Wickham would be able to afford if he took Lord Hays' offer of forty pounds a year. To Darcy's surprise, the wayward couple was coming down the front steps as he arrived. He alighted, waiting for them, wondering why Wickham was burdened by a cloth bag. Were they being turned out?

Lydia Bennet spotted Darcy, her eyes going wide. "Mr. Darcy," she said with obvious surprise.

Wickham looked up, saw him, and stopped walking. He eyed Darcy with suspicion, but Miss Lydia hurried down to him, a broad smile on her face. Shrugging, Wickham followed her.

"Miss Lydia, Mr. Wickham." Darcy nodded politely to each. "I would like to speak with you both."

"We don't have time," Miss Lydia said. "We're late as it is."

Darcy glanced to Wickham, who nodded confirmation. "Perhaps I can offer you a ride to your destination?" Darcy suggested.

"La, that would be helpful," Miss Lydia said. "George, can you direct the driver?"

"Certainly, my dear," Wickham said, quickly climbing up to sit beside Darcy's coachman.

Realizing he'd been neatly stuck entertaining Miss Lydia, Darcy handed her into his carriage, resolved to put this time with her to good use. Once they were settled, he knocked on the roof and they began moving.

"It's ever so surprising to see you here, Mr. Darcy," Miss Lydia said. "Why, I didn't think anyone would discover us. Not that we're hiding, but George said my family would make me leave him."

"It's on their behalf I've come."

"Well, you can't make me leave him. I won't do it."

"Don't you wish to return home? Don't you miss Longbourn, and your father and sisters?"

Miss Lydia shook her head, sending her curls bouncing. "No. It's too dreadful a place to miss. Longbourn is no fun anymore. Charlotte has made it ugly."

"Ugly?" That wasn't the complaint he'd expected.

"Yes. Mama had everything arranged just so, like the sheep."

"Sheep?" Darcy was trying to follow the girl's inane prattling, but he was having difficulty understanding what sheep had to do with Longbourn's ugliness or the new Mrs. Bennet.

"Well, not only the sheep. Mama had china figures of a shepherd, shepherdess, and sheep and they were kept in a pretty pattern on the mantel. Charlotte said they weren't worth the time it took to dust them. She put them in a cabinet with glass doors. It's all the way to the back of the parlor, and they're clumped together. They don't add to the room. You can hardly notice them."

"So you would wish to return home if Mrs. Bennet placed the flock back on the mantel?" Darcy asked, recalling Elizabeth had mentioned a shepherdess, and how beguilingly intelligent she'd looked while pondering the formation of the piece. He hadn't noticed the ornaments the time he'd been in the Bennet's parlor. All he'd seen was Elizabeth.

"La, you're funny, Mr. Darcy. Who would have guessed?" Miss Lydia giggled. "It isn't only the sheep, of course. That would be silly."

Like you, he thought, but contained the words.

"It's so many things," Miss Lydia said, sighing, her laughter momentarily subdued. "Charlotte opens the curtains during the day, to help heat the house. Mama would use more firewood to keep warm, to make sure the furniture didn't fade. Charlotte says faded furniture works as well as furniture that isn't faded, but I don't agree. Isn't part of the reason for furniture to make the room look inviting?"

"I suppose it is," Darcy said, somewhat surprised he and Lydia Bennet had a point of agreement.

She nodded. "Of course it is, or all furniture would look the same. Then there's the food. When Mama was alive, food was placed artfully on serving dishes. Now it's dumped on them. In the garden, instead of growing flowers for the house, Charlotte planted vegetables. Mama wanted us to spend time embroidering, but Charlotte has us sewing undergarments."

Darcy blinked, manfully battling down imaginings of Elizabeth and undergarments. He wondered if Miss Lydia thought money could be saved without sacrificing anything, but decided it wasn't worth attempting to make the point. Likely, she didn't agree with the new Mrs. Bennet's attempts to save, though they'd almost certainly been implemented at least partially to benefit the Bennet girls. Miss Lydia was the type to want what she wanted in the now, and assume tomorrow would take care of itself, as her mother had. "You are aware your sojourn in London will make it difficult for you to be accepted by your neighbors," he said, attempting to bring the conversation around to where he wished it to go.

"That's all the more reason to stay here," she said triumphantly.

"It would be better if you married." He tried to keep censure from his tone, aware that would alienate her.

"That's what that boring baron said. He talked about me being a fallen woman and said I should devote the rest of my life to prayer and good works. What a windbag he is." She flounced her curls again, her grimace revealing how she felt about Baron Hays and his ideas.

Darcy partially agreed with Miss Lydia, thinking less of Hays. Such words were hardly the way to entice a young lady back home. "Would you like to marry Mr. Wickham?" he pressed, channeling her flighty thoughts back to the topic he wished to speak on.

"I would love to, but he hasn't asked me."

"What did he say that made you go with him?" Darcy was surprised. Hadn't Elizabeth's letter said Wickham and Miss Lydia had eloped? He frowned, attempting to recall Bingley's reading of it. If Wickham hadn't offered marriage, Darcy was at a loss to understand why Miss Lydia had run off with him.

"He said he was tired of being good." She grinned, looking completely unrepentant. "He said he'd spent six months being a good person and this was the first time he'd left a town without debts, but he needed to do something crazy. I said I was in the same predicament, except for the bit about debts. He suggested we run away to London together and said he would show me how to really have fun." If possible, her grin grew wider. "He has."

Fortunately for Darcy, for he had no notion of how to respond to that improper statement, the carriage pulled to a stop. Wickham opened the door, offering Miss Lydia his hand. She disembarked, Darcy following. To his bewilderment, the two of them walked into a millinery shop. Darcy followed, baffled. As he entered, an eager looking salesgirl hurried toward him, ignoring Miss Lydia and Mr. Wickham.

Glancing over his shoulder, Wickham made a shooing gesture. "He is with us, more or less," Wickham said. "He'll wait for a few minutes."

The salesgirl looked to Darcy expectantly.

He nodded, though he was annoyed at both Wickham's dragging him about London and by what was in essence an order for Darcy to wait. "I'm not buying."

The shop girl dropped a quick curtsy and returned to her work. Darcy stood near the door and watched as Miss Lydia looked over the hats. Not taking as long as most women he knew did to shop, and not trying any on, she selected five of them. In view of her previous comments about ugliness, Darcy was forced to wondered at her selections, and her taste. From where he stood, it appeared as if she'd selected what were easily the most unbecoming hats in the store.

Miss Lydia brought the hats to the counter. There was a little bit of haggling and Wickham handed over some money. Lydia took the hats and the cloth bag Wickham carried and disappeared through a doorway in the back of the store, increasing Darcy's feeling he had no notion what the two were about, especially as they couldn't have much money to spend frivolously on hideous apparel.

Wickham thanked the clerk and came back across the shop to Darcy. "Lydia will be a while."

"Meaning you have time to speak with me now?" Darcy asked.

Wickham smiled slightly, likely noting the displeasure in Darcy's tone. "I'll find out where the nearest place a person can get a drink is. You're buying, I assume?"

Darcy nodded.

Wickham returned to the clerk, inquiring, and they ended up at a nearby tavern. After paying for their drinks, Darcy took out a shiny ha'penny he'd saved for the occasion. He placed it on the table and slid it toward Wickham.

"What's this?"

"Payment on our bet. You bet me a ha'penny I would get in trouble with my pride before you got in trouble over your… well, before you got in trouble."

"Yes. I remember. I'm simply surprised. Am I not in trouble?"

"I believe I fell long before you," Darcy said, his proposal to Elizabeth having taken place unequivocally before Wickham's recent scandal.

"May I have the details?" Wickham picked up the coin, turning it slowly in his fingers.

"That wasn't a part of our agreement."

Across the table from Darcy, Wickham flashed a grin. "From your tone, I gather you let your Fitzwilliam pride get the better of you in a devastating way. I never would have known, you realize? Why pay me the ha'penny?"

Darcy stiffened. "I believe in paying my debts, even if only a ha'penny." He scowled, but Wickham didn't seem daunted. Feeling he owed some slight explanation, Darcy offered, "If you must know, I permitted my pride to cost me the respect of someone I care about. You were right about my behavior. I've always known I offend some people, but thought if they were offended by my belief in my superiority then I wasn't interested in their respect."

Wickham looked at him for a long moment. "You still believe you are superior to most people."

Darcy was briefly surprised Wickham didn't press him for a name. Then, Wickham was good at assessing people and knew when probing would be unproductive. Wickham's observation sunk in and Darcy shook his head. "If I were superior, I wouldn't offend those I care about. It has been a humbling experience."

Wickham's smile wasn't pleasant as he pocketed the ha'penny. "Well, as you said, details were not part of our agreement, and none of my affair." Wickham's expression turned serious. "For what it's worth, I hope you can mend whatever fence your pride broke."

"I may be able to, but I doubt you can fix the mess you've put yourself in," Darcy said, firmly changing the subject. "You can't go back to your regiment and you have no means of support. You are unlikely to be welcomed by any other militia and you don't have the money to join the regulars. Without owning land, and without being able to join the military, you've lost the right to be called a gentleman. This fall came from a whim, apparently. What was it Miss Bennet said? You were tired of being good."

"It was a foolish thing to do," Mr. Wickham admitted, eyes on his as of yet untouched drink. "I know that. I knew it then, too. I just couldn't . . ." He pursed his lips. "Rather, I would not stop myself."

"So what happens now? Are you going to marry her?" Darcy wanted to shake the man and remind him he was ruining more lives than his and Miss Lydia's, but he didn't believe Wickham would care. He also didn't want Wickham to guess the truth, that Darcy was here because he couldn't disentangle himself from caring what happened to Elizabeth.

"What would marrying her get me? I suspect I could persuade Mr. Bennet to give me a thousand pounds, but he can't afford any more than that. Let's be honest, Darcy, she's a pretty enough thing but she's thick as a rock and I've already had about all the fun I care to with her." Wickham shrugged. "Besides, if I don't marry her, I leave myself open to the opportunity of winning a wealthier woman."

"And you might have the opportunity to land yourself in debtor's prison if you borrow enough to attract the kind of woman you want to marry."

Wickham grimaced, but the expression seemed more one of distaste than surprise at the idea. Darcy was pleased to hope Wickham had considered that consequence.

Wickham took a long pull from his glass, emptying half of it in one sip. "Down to business, then. I can't imagine you hunted me down only to give me a ha'penny, or to discuss whether or not I wish to wed Miss Lydia. So the real question is, what are you willing to pay me to marry her?"

Darcy loosed a bark of laughter at the other man's directness. "You may have made some stupid choices, but you aren't stupid. It will probably end up being less than you want and more than I would like."

Wickham nodded. "Quite right."

"What amount were you thinking?"

Wickham opened his mouth, but shut it again. "Are you in a great hurry?"

Darcy shook his head.

"In that case, before we start on the negotiations, I would like to see how Lydia does at the millinery." He eyed Darcy, the amusement back. "Let's pretend we're friends and talk of other things."

Darcy wanted to declare they could never be friends, but realized there was no advantage in saying it, especially as Wickham must already realize as much. Instead, he merely nodded. Smiling, Wickham put himself out to be charming, and in spite of himself, Darcy felt the charm. He knew Wickham had the advantage of knowing his audience well, but not a syllable escaped his lips that was offensive. He told stories of his time in Meryton and led Darcy to describe Bingley's problems with Netherfield Park. Darcy suspected Wickham must have heard some of the story from the gossips in Meryton, but Wickham played the part of the uninformed listener very well. The one topic Wickham refused to touch was what Miss Lydia was doing at the millinery shop, saying he wished it to be a surprise. After what must have been about two hours and three rounds of ale, they returned to the shop.

Miss Lydia was sitting in a chair but jumped up when she saw them. She rushed over to Wickham, a broad smile on her face. "One hat sold already," she said. She handed Wickham some money, which he counted.

"Wonderful, my sweet. You are very clever."

"It was fun to see their faces when I told them how much they had to pay to get their hats back," Miss Lydia said, giggling. "When she refused at first, I told her I would sell them to Madame Belanger for that price. Then people would buy the hats there, not here."

Darcy looked between Miss Lydia and Wickham, taking in the triumph on both faces, and wondered how much he was going to have to pay.

Elizabeth

In a fit of guilt, Elizabeth quietly took over Lydia's tasks about the house. The tasks weren't very onerous and it eased her conscience a bit. She daily lamented the moment she'd suggested Mr. Wickham speak to her sister, wondering what she could possibly have been thinking, and remained diligent in her self-imposed duties. Slightly onerous or not, she didn't mind having a useful occupation during the long days that followed, without word of Lydia or Wickham.

Elizabeth's father returned from London after an unproductive search. Longbourn remained tense and quiet. There seemed nothing to be done but wait for word from Lydia.

Finally, awash in remorse, Elizabeth told her father and Charlotte what she'd done. They both tried to absolve her of blame. Charlotte pointed out it was hardly as if Elizabeth had suggested to either they run away. Her father said he'd had the raising of Lydia and permitted her to grow into such a silly creature, which could hardly be construed as Elizabeth's fault. They were both unflagging in not assigning blame to her, and diligently kind. It only made Elizabeth feel worse.

Elizabeth was weeding the garden, a task she rather preferred and had envied Lydia, when a shadow fell across her. Looking up, she saw Charlotte, not yet noticeably round in the middle, standing at the end of the row. Elizabeth sat back on her heels, taking out a handkerchief to blot her brow.

"Lizzy, could you come to the parlor for a moment? You can finish later, though you've weeded so many times of late, I daresay you don't need to worry any more about it today."

"Yes, of course," Elizabeth said.

She followed Charlotte inside, pausing to remove her heavy

outdoor apron, hat and gloves. Charlotte continued on, apparently not disposed to wait. Elizabeth dusted off her hands and performed a brief inspection of her hem. When she reached the parlor, she found the rest of the family gathered there. She sat on the sofa between Mary and Kitty.

Her father cleared his throat and they all looked to him expectantly. "Lydia's been found," he said, holding up a letter. "She went to your uncle in London and said she wants to marry Mr. Wickham. Wickham will agree to the marriage if his financial terms are met. The terms are very reasonable. I've written to agree. Lydia will be staying with the Gardiners until the wedding."

"Lydia's to be married?" Kitty said. "That's not fair."

"This is wonderful news, Papa," Mary said.

Mr. Bennet handed the letter to Elizabeth, who read it to herself with her sisters reading over her shoulders. "They aren't asking for much," she finally said, looking up.

"One thousand pounds, to be invested so they only have access to the interest. I didn't think Mr. Wickham had any money, and I can't see them living on fifty pounds a year, but who are we to question such good fortune?" Mr. Bennet said.

Elizabeth didn't know what was going on. Not only was she in agreement with her father in not thinking Mr. Wickham had any money, she would also wager he hadn't any restraint, which the investment of the one thousand pounds seemed to show. She looked to her father, who appeared as confused as she felt.

Could the Gardiners have paid Mr. Wickham to marry Lydia? Elizabeth was sure her aunt and uncle would do such a thing for them if they could, but it hardly seemed likely they would be able to afford to. They had children of their own to think of.

Elizabeth knew now quite well how expensive children were. She'd not only been keeping the family books, but going back over past entries. Due to Charlotte's economy, they were spending much less money than when Elizabeth's mother was alive. Yet there was another child on the way, meaning more money would be needed. They would not be kicked out of Longbourn if it was a boy, but it could easily be a girl. Troubled, she left the parlor along with the others and returned to her chores.

It wasn't long before news of Lydia's elopement and subsequent marriage spread through the neighborhood. Elizabeth suspected Kitty accounted for the initial tale, for she overheard her younger sister discussing it with Charlotte's little sister, Maria. Elizabeth knew it didn't signify who first told, as the news would hardly be contained.

What did signify was that Elizabeth's father told her Lydia and Mr. Wickham would not be visiting Longbourn. He declared he wouldn't permit it, surprising both her and Charlotte. Elizabeth felt it would be better for the married couple if they were seen to be recognized by their family, but her father wouldn't be moved on the subject. Ultimately, it seemed not to matter, for Lydia wrote they wouldn't be stirred from London, regardless. She said they were too busy to travel. They were opening a shop to sell hats and would live above it.

In the weeks that followed Lydia's wedding, Jane wrote to invite Mary and Kitty to spend a month with her in her new home. Elizabeth felt a pang of jealousy. Uncharitably, she wondered if she was being punished for requesting to return from Pemberley early, for she'd never admitted to Jane the impetus for her rapid flight. Jane had known there was one, able to detect as much, and Elizabeth knew her refusal to confide the details hurt Jane's feelings.

Her uncharitable thoughts about Jane's motivation in inviting Mary and Kitty to stay in her new home were what finally returned Elizabeth to her natural humor. Jane, after all, was completely incapable of maliciousness or guile, so the suspicion was confined exclusively to Elizabeth's head. The more obvious, and likely correct, supposition was that Jane realized Mary and Kitty had been confined in Longbourn while their sisters had been afforded opportunities to see more of England.

Elizabeth realized she'd been out of sorts ever since refusing Mr. Darcy. It wasn't, she was sure, out of any lingering doubt as to the correctness of her reply. It had more to do with having misjudged his behavior concerning Mr. Wickham, her chief complaints against Mr. Darcy, and for the harsh nature of her refusal. In refusing him, though, she was sure she'd been correct, for she couldn't possibly come to love Mr. Darcy, no matter how often she found him in her thoughts.

That established and her temper restored, Elizabeth settled into a happy, quiet life at Longbourn. They visited neighbors and had neighbors in, but not frequently. She corresponded with Jane weekly, and her other sisters routinely though not as often. She worked in the house and garden alongside Charlotte, always an agreeable companion. Evenings were spent practicing the piano or in pleasant, learned conversation with Charlotte and her father, who rarely seemed to feel the need to hide in his library any longer.

It was a happy time, with but two shadows. One was Elizabeth's inability to banish Mr. Darcy from her thoughts, where his intent visage as he'd declared his love haunted her. The other was an ongoing argument between Charlotte and Mr. Bennet. The one thing able to drive Elizabeth's father back to his library was Charlotte's insistence he reforge a connection with Lydia.

"Mr. Bennet," Charlotte said one evening. She'd ordered one of Elizabeth's father's favorite meals served for dinner, which he'd complimented, and now the three of them sat companionably in the parlor. "I believe the time has come to remember Lydia is your daughter."

"She is not, nor ever has been, a good child to me, my dear. I do not understand your insistence on this."

"It will quiet talk if we're seen to accept her. It will be better for Elizabeth, Mary and Kitty. They still must find husbands."

Elizabeth agreed with Charlotte, but kept her peace, her eyes on the book she held.

"Jane's connections will afford them husbands now that Lydia is wed," Mr. Bennet said. "There is no reason to subject ourselves to her, or that man."

"That man is Mr. Wickham. Most men would consider him a son."

"After what she did, I almost don't consider Lydia a daughter."

"Mr. Bennet, I believe that may be going too far," Charlotte said, her tone mirroring Elizabeth's shock at her father's words.

"My dear, you're with child. You shouldn't travel," Elizabeth's father said in a switch of tactics.

"I am still perfectly capable of travel, but soon will not be. That is why we must go now."

"Us going is another stumbling block, as I see it," Elizabeth's father said. "Why should we go? We are the injured party. They should come to us, hats in hand."

Which would be easy enough, Elizabeth supposed, since they now reputedly owned a hat shop. She kept that comment to herself, turning a page for effect, though she wasn't reading.

"They cannot leave their new shop at this juncture," Charlotte said, her tone one of patience. "They're just starting out. It's an important time for a business."

"We aren't squandering all of the money your economy has saved us on a stay in London."

"Of course we are not. We shall stay with your relations, the Gardiners. Mrs. Gardiner has already extended the offer to me, on more than one occasion."

"She has?" Elizabeth asked, lowering her book. "That is kind of her." Elizabeth wouldn't have faulted her aunt and uncle for not offering, as they were her late mother's relations and Charlotte was her mother's replacement. Of course, her aunt and uncle were exceedingly fair minded and kind people.

"Yes, she has," Charlotte said, casting Elizabeth a smile. "And you're to come too, Lizzy."

"Thank you. I should very much like to," Elizabeth said. "Kitty will be sorry to miss seeing Lydia."

"That can't be helped. As your father so thoughtfully pointed out, I won't be able to travel for much longer. If we're to go, it must be soon." She turned back to Elizabeth's father, a determined glint in her eyes.

"I take it you are quite resolved to this?" Mr. Bennet asked.

"I am," Charlotte said.

"It truly is the right thing to do, Papa," Elizabeth added.

"Well, if it is the right thing to do, then I suppose we must do it."

They made the trip a few short days later. The Gardiners made them as welcome as Elizabeth had always felt in their home, and she was pleased to find any lingering worry over their reception of Charlotte unfounded. The day following their arrival they waited until the shops of London were near to closing, the better for visiting with store owners after hours, and then went to see the Wickhams.

Their shop was on the edge of a fashionable neighborhood, freshly painted and with a fine sign over the door declaring their trade. Elizabeth, her father and Charlotte entered to find Mr. Wickham engaged with a customer, a woman in her forties. Under the guise of scrutinizing hats, Elizabeth watched with fascination as he flirted and flattered the woman into buying three hats at what Elizabeth considered outrageous prices. In fairness, the hats were lovely, and did make the customer look prettier, but they hardly seemed worth the cost. Looking about, Elizabeth decided their shop contained many beautiful hats, although there was a small section that were very plain, though still attractive.

After taking her money and packaging up her hats, Mr. Wickham walked the woman to the door, stepping outside to hand the hats to her footman. He came back in, smiling at them, and paused to turn the sign in the window to 'closed' and lock the door. When the lock clicked home, his expression turned from pleasure to relief. "I never thought selling hats would be so much work. Let's go back and tell Lydia you're here. She'll be delighted."

They followed Mr. Wickham behind the counter and through a door, to find Lydia working in back. Elizabeth knew Lydia could turn an ugly hat into a pretty one, but she'd been having trouble imagining her doing it regularly. The workshop surprised Elizabeth. There were two worktables, Lydia appearing to be hard at work at one, a girl working at the other.

"Papa! Lizzy!" Lydia exclaimed, jumping up from the table. She didn't run to them as Elizabeth expected, but turned instead to the girl. "Go ahead and leave early, Nancy. My family is visiting."

"Yes, missus," the girl said. Setting down her work, she stood from a table cluttered with numerous cloth flowers, including one partially made. "Have a pleasant evening, missus," Nancy said, taking a cloak from a peg and disappearing out the back.

As soon as she was gone, Lydia rushed around the table. She hugged Elizabeth first, exclaiming, "Lizzy, I've missed you ever so," before turning to embrace Charlotte. "Look at you! You're showing," was added, with a giggle. She then turned to their father. "Papa."

Elizabeth's father frowned at her for a long moment.

"Oh Papa," Lydia exclaimed, flinging her arms about him. "Don't be angry. Look, I'm married, and we have a shop, and it all turned out ever so well."

Elizabeth could see the mixture of weariness and resignation on her father's face. He closed his arms about Lydia. "Yes, my girl, it turned out well enough."

"I knew you wouldn't stay angry with me, Papa, or with George." As she spoke, Lydia released their father and hurried over to stand beside Mr. Wickham.

"Yes, well," Elizabeth's father said, leveling a hard look on Mr. Wickham.

"Who was that girl?" Elizabeth asked at the same time as Charlotte said, "What a lovely shop."

Lydia looked back and forth between them, smiling, seeming unaware that her father was still displeased with both her and Mr. Wickham. She turned to Charlotte. "Thank you. It is a lovely shop, isn't it? And so well placed. I never did think we could afford such a grand location."

"And the girl, Nancy?" Elizabeth prodded, not because she cared, but to keep the conversation on safe ground.

"Nancy was an apprentice to a seamstress who treated her badly. Uncle Gardiner knows the family. She's afraid to live anywhere but at home. It saves us the expense of feeding her, except we give her some food around noon."

"If she doesn't live in, don't you have to pay her more?" Charlotte asked, sounding genuinely curious to Elizabeth's ear.

"Yes, but Uncle Gardiner explained we shouldn't be concerned about how much we pay her but how much she costs us," Lydia said. She gestured toward the worktables. "Did you ever think we'd be doing so well? Look at how many hats I must finish!"

"Do you make everything here yourself?" Charlotte asked.

"No," Lydia shook her head. "We buy basic straw hats and trim them. We make the cloth hats, though. Nancy is very good at sewing. Often I just pin things on and she sews them. Most of the time, we work for several hours after the shop closes. Sometimes I help George sell hats, but he's so much better than I am at selling." She gave her husband a loving look.

Elizabeth took in her father's deepening frown. "I noticed some very plain hats," she said. "Do they sell?"

Lydia giggled. "Surprisingly well. You remember Miss Bingley?"

Elizabeth nodded. How couldn't she?

"She married a baron and is now Lady Hays. Since George saved her life, she buys hats here. Only, Lord Hays wants her to wear very stern hats. Come, let me show you."

They went back out into the shop and Lydia took a hat. It was trimmed conservatively in two shades of brown. Lydia handed it to her and Elizabeth realized it was really a very attractive hat in spite of, or perhaps because of, its simplicity. It was well made and of very fine material.

"Lady Hays' sister, Mrs. Hurst, came and bought three hats here. One was from this section. She isn't a setter of fashion, but I keep hoping. Every Sunday, Wickham and I go to a church where some of the members of high society go. I wear one of my hats," Lydia said, not pausing once for breath, her face glowing. "If the weather is nice, we stroll through parks where the rich people go. Some of them know we sell hats and some of them come here and buy them. Sometimes I wear one of the conservative hats. It's so much fun when they come to buy from us."

Elizabeth couldn't help but smile at Lydia's enthusiasm. A glance showed her indulgent tolerance on Mr. Wickham's face, and a contemplative look on her father's. Charlotte, Elizabeth noticed, appeared pleased. Elizabeth was as well, but couldn't help wondering over one thing. Where could Mr. Wickham and Lydia possibly have come by the money to start their shop?

Chapter Nine

~ Pursuit ~

Darcy

The next time Darcy was in London, he made a point of visiting the millinery shop. Though he'd assisted in establishing it, he had misgivings about the enterprise. He feared, between them, Mr. and Mrs. Wickham had little notion on how to work diligently or manage a business, though mention had been made of seeking the advice of Mr. Gardiner. Gardiner had struck Darcy as quite competent when they'd met before Bingley's wedding. Successful as the man was in trade, Darcy was sure any advice Mr. Gardiner gave the couple would be good.

Darcy decided to visit during business hours, to ascertain how the shop was functioning. He entered to find the millinery occupied by a patron, a pleasant surprise. That surprise was tripled when Darcy realized Wickham himself was waiting on the woman, who seemed to be endlessly trying on hats. Looking toward the door, Wickham spotted Darcy and gave a nod of greeting, before returning his attention to his customer.

The door opened again and another woman entered. She eyed Darcy appraisingly before moving deeper into the shop. Spotting her, Wickham excused himself from his client for a moment and moved to the counter, pulling a cord. He returned to the woman he'd been helping and Mrs. Wickham appeared to work with the second customer. She wasn't nearly as skillful as her husband, but succeeded in selling a hat. She returned to the back of the shop when the customer left, giving Darcy a jaunty wave.

Wickham's customer also departed, having purchased several hats. The shop momentarily empty, Wickham gestured Darcy over, where he'd taken up a position behind the counter while accepting payment.

"Darcy, how good of you to come by."

"I was curious how the shop is doing."

"Don't worry, we'll be able to pay the rent, plus," Mr. Wickham said, sounding satisfied.

Darcy raised his eyebrows, surprised a third time. He didn't require or expect the higher payment. After buying the property, he'd given them two amounts they could pay. The lower amount was rent. The higher was rent plus a sum Darcy would put toward them purchasing the property from him, although it would take years. "You are doing well, then, I take it."

"I've never worked so hard in my life," Mr. Wickham said. "But I hate the idea of you being able to turn us out on a whim. If I correctly read the contract your attorney sent me, if I keep making the higher payments, you can't turn us out."

"True." Darcy eyed him for a moment, trying to decide how candid he should be. "I did that to motivate you toward more responsible behavior. I didn't think it would work."

Mr. Wickham smiled slightly. "I've made many bad choices in my life, but I've finally realized I live with the consequences of my actions." He glanced toward the back, then leaned across the counter. "This isn't the life I imagined for myself," he said in a low voice. "It's more work than I ever thought I would do. I have to flatter and cajole customers into buying hats and I have to do the same thing with Lydia to keep her working. Fortunately, the work she does is worth it. Lydia isn't very bright, but she has a feel for beauty. I think she finally realizes if we don't succeed here, we may end up trying to live on ninety pounds a year."

"I'm pleased she's learning restraint."

"You know, Darcy," Mr. Wickham said, his eyes taking on a bemused cast. "Sometimes, after I close the shop, I stand in the doorway to the workroom and watch her. When she works hard, and makes things people truly want to buy and possibly even treasure, it's the oddest feeling. I think I'm actually proud of her."

"And well you should be," Darcy said, taken aback by Mr. Wickham's expression and tone. He supposed, in a way, he was proud of both of them as well. Or at least pleased and, looking about the shop, growing in respect for them.

Mr. Wickham shook his head, seeming to come back to the moment. He shrugged, giving Darcy a quick grin. "And glad I am for her stepmother. Without the half year Lydia spent under her tutelage, there is no way I could persuade her to work."

"Are you on good terms with her family?" Darcy asked, feigning indifference even as he found himself suddenly doubly invested in the conversation.

"Yes, we are now, again thanks to the new Mrs. Bennet, I gather. Mr. and Mrs. Bennet and Miss Elizabeth visited us a couple of weeks ago. They were impressed with our industry." Mr. Wickham made a face. "I'm impressed with our industry."

"So am I," Darcy said sincerely. He'd thought Mr. Wickham would never change.

Mr. Wickham insisted on showing Darcy around. He also showed Darcy the books, and though his mind wished only to dwell on Mr. Wickham's mention of Elizabeth, Darcy reigned in his imagination and paid Mr. Wickham the compliment of looking at the figures closely. He was pleased to see the Wickhams truly were making a profit. They were even putting a small amount of money away for emergencies. Their present income would not make them rich, but it would make them comfortable.

Darcy left with a growing respect for the Wickhams, and satisfied in what he'd done for them. He'd actually done it for Elizabeth, of course, but no one would ever know that. Though Elizabeth's happiness was what had been paramount in Darcy's decision, it was an indisputable boon that Mr. Wickham had learned to live with the mistake of running off with Lydia Bennet, and now seemed to be learning to live within his means as well. His months pretending to be a good man in Meryton must have benefited him more than Darcy would have imagined.

Darcy climbed into his carriage, signaling for his driver to go. He leaned back, sighing, aware of a continued disquiet within. It seemed unfair Wickham's fall from good behavior had led to learning, growth and what seemed to be greater contentment, when Darcy's outburst of pride had lead only to heartache.

Or had it, he wondered. The heartache was indisputable, any pretense at contentment laughable, but perhaps he had grown, or at least learned? In his months of mourning his relationship with Elizabeth, he'd come to fully realize and regret how badly he'd behaved. The more he'd thought on his words, the more he'd comprehended that even if Elizabeth had been in love with him, she couldn't have accepted such an insulting proposal.

Now she'd been in London, a scant few weeks past. He hadn't seen her. Hadn't known she was so near. That he'd missed seeing Elizabeth in London reopened the never-healed wound to his heart. Yet, much as Mr. Wickham had finally learned, Darcy knew he had to accept the consequences of his actions.

Or inactions.

He sat bolt upright in his seat, nearly toppling his hat from his head. Was there a difference? Was Darcy not intelligently accepting a fate of his own making, but rather failing to take what actions he should?

He had grown. He had changed. Why shouldn't he therefore find at least the acceptance and contentment Mr. Wickham now knew? Could the fates conspire to be so unkind?

Elizabeth hadn't married. Not if she was traveling with her father and stepmother. She was still free. Maybe, if he saw her again, they could start over. He could show her he was contrite. He could show her he was genuinely learning to respect her family, starting with Lydia Wickham. He'd long felt Mrs. Wickham was the worst of the lot, which meant that if he gave the rest of the family a chance, he might learn to respect them too. He might be able to court Elizabeth and win her.

All he needed was an excuse to go to Meryton. Darcy racked his brain, but couldn't come up with a single person he was close with there. Yet, he'd bought one investment property for Elizabeth. Maybe he could consider another.

Elizabeth

Not long after their return to Longbourn, Elizabeth's father called her into his library. She was unsurprised to find Charlotte already seated across from him. She took the other chair, noticing her father had three letters lined up before him on his desk. She couldn't read the letters from where she sat, but she recognized Jane's hand, and Mary's. The third was written with strong, unfamiliar strokes. The unknown hand was decidedly masculine, and she had the brief, unaccountable idea it might belong to Mr. Darcy, which she immediately rejected, having seen his writing, both at Pemberley and at Netherfield Park. Elizabeth frowned, annoyed he must be forever intruding into her thoughts.

"How did you find the journey back from London, Elizabeth?" her father asked.

"Pleasant, as I had agreeable company and the ride was smooth," she said, containing her curiosity.

"Then you shouldn't mind another journey, in the same company, in the near future?" Mr. Bennet asked.

"I should not, if Charlotte is sure she's still able."

"Charlotte deems herself quite capable of another journey, so long as it is taken immediately, which should please all parties involved," Mr. Bennet said.

"That is welcome news," Elizabeth replied, refusing to be baited into cajoling.

She leaned back in her chair, effecting nonchalance. She recognized the pleased gleam in her father's eyes. He had good news. He was amusing himself by drawing it out. Perhaps, she thought, Jane was with child. She'd been surprised to find no letter for her from her sister when they'd reached Longbourn, a clear indication Jane had news she didn't wish to spoil. Bless her, Jane couldn't even write without giving the whole truth, feeling not to was to lie. Elizabeth had no notion how her sister had managed to hide her engagement with Mr. Bingley so very well, but was sure Jane's success was owed to true love.

After several long moments of silence, Charlotte shook her head, sighing. "The pair of you," she said. She turned to Elizabeth. "Your father received three similar letters while we were in London, Lizzy. One from Jane, reporting Mary has met a fine gentleman, a Mr. Housley, while staying with her. One from Mary, reporting she has received a proposal of marriage from this Mr. Housley. The third is from Mr. Housley himself, asking for Mary's hand in marriage and inviting your father and me to visit."

"That's wonderful news," Elizabeth said. "Papa, you were cruel to keep it from me."

"Jane also wrote to invite you to stay with her and Mr. Bingley while we visit, Elizabeth," Mr. Bennet said, shooting Charlotte a quelling look, the effect ruined by the amusement in his eyes. "Mr. Bingley added a postscript saying that Mr. Housley has an estate worth about eight hundred pounds a year."

"Why, what a pleasing turn of events," Elizabeth said. "Mary, to be wed, and to what sounds like a fine gentleman. Papa, you'll have three daughters out of the house." And I shall get to see my dearest sister's new home, she added to herself.

She wondered if Mr. Darcy would be visiting. It would be like the Bingleys to invite him, to repay his kindness to them. Not that she wished to see him again, except to apologize for her treatment and for misjudging him. Both weighed on her conscience. Maybe a proper apology would permit her to put thoughts of Mr. Darcy from her mind.

Imposing on Charlotte's parents and Mrs. Hill's diligence once again, arrangements were made for them to leave Longbourn a second time in as many weeks. Charlotte, who did seem up to traveling, fretted about their home much more than her condition. Elizabeth knew, in her mind and on paper, Charlotte had a list of steps to be taken to continue Longbourn's improvement, and a timeframe for those steps. Her step-mother was laudably dedicated to the estate. Elizabeth very much hoped Charlotte's baby would be a son.

When they reached the Bingleys, Elizabeth was pleased to see

Jane's home was as splendid as her favorite sister deserved. Mr. Bingley and Jane were obviously still very much in love, and treated each other with every kindness. The grounds, though not extensive, were pleasant and the house stately but comfortable.

Mr. Housley turned out to be a good-natured man who was clearly in love with Mary. Mary, who Elizabeth was amused to see still wore dark dresses and styled her hair as Lydia had recommended, seemed quite happy. Elizabeth wasn't able to determine if it was the happiness of love or of being loved by a pleasant, eligible man, but doubted the difference mattered to her sister.

If there was any shadow on the couple, it was that Mr. Housley had lost his mother as well, several months before theirs had died. He was still in mourning, necessitating a longer engagement than many young couples wished, for he deemed it improper for him to marry within a year of losing his mother. That nuance aside, it appeared providence, for once, was smiling on Mary.

Only Kitty seemed unaffected by the Bingleys', Mary's and Mr. Housley's contagious happiness. When the time came for the Bennets to return to Longbourn, Mary and Kitty accompanying them back, Kitty spent the entire journey in near silence. She seemed so troubled, Elizabeth began to worry for her. As soon as they arrived at home, Kitty headed to the room she once shared with Lydia, saying she wished to put away her things. Elizabeth exchanged a worried look with Charlotte, who made to go after Kitty.

"Let me," Elizabeth said, staying Charlotte before she ascended the steps.

"Of course. I'll be in the library with your father should you require me," Charlotte replied.

"I'm going to practice. I've hardly had time to touch a piano in weeks," Mary said, a broad smile on her face.

Mary hummed as she left them, obviously too wrapped up in her engagement to notice Kitty's odd behavior. Elizabeth met Charlotte's amused glance. They shared a smile before going their separate ways.

Elizabeth headed up the steps, walking the short way down the hall to Kitty's room. She knocked softly. "Kitty, it's Elizabeth. May I come in?"

"Yes," came Kitty's reply, muffled by the wood.

Elizabeth pushed the door open to find Kitty sitting at her dressing table. She toyed with a brush, but obviously hadn't applied it to her hair. Her eyes met Elizabeth's in the mirror and slid away again.

Stepping in and closing the door behind her, Elizabeth crossed to stand behind Kitty. She placed gentle hands on Kitty's shoulders, watching her in the small mirror. "Kitty, whatever is the matter?"

"I don't know. Something. Maybe I'm hideous?"

Elizabeth blinked in surprise. "Hideous? You? You know you're lovely."

"I'm skinny, and I cough too much, and my hair isn't bright enough, or light enough, or dark enough."

"Kitty, wherever is all this coming from?"

Kitty set the brush down, crossing her arms over her chest. "Something must be wrong with me. I suppose I always understood when I was passed over for Jane, or Lydia, or even you," she said, obviously unconscious of the insult. "But Mary? Mary isn't pretty. Everyone knows she isn't. So how could someone pass me over for her?"

"Oh, dearest, don't tell me you have feelings for Mr. Housley?"

"Feelings for Mr. Housley?" Kitty repeated, her eyes going wide. Foregoing their reflections, she looked over her shoulder at Elizabeth. "No, not at all." She turned back to the mirror, frowning. "Well, that is, he's nice enough, for a brother. He's a kind person and all those things. I don't have affections for him, though. He's not even an officer, and he's practically ancient."

Elizabeth didn't think that was true. He couldn't be any older than Mr. Darcy, who was definitely not ancient. She relaxed, allowing herself to smile slightly. "So you aren't jealous of Mary?"

"I am, but not because I wanted Mr. Housley to marry me."

"Because you want someone to marry you?" Elizabeth guessed.

"Do you know, he wasn't even looking for someone to marry," Kitty said, scowling at her reflection. "He was looking for a housekeeper. He came to ask Mr. Bingley's and Jane's advice, and met Mary and I there. He met us both, and he spoke to us both, and he chose her. Mary!"

"I see," Elizabeth said, schooling the smile from her face.

"How could someone look at me and Mary, side by side, and pick her? It's those stupid black ribbons Lydia told her to wear."

"Kitty, you are very pretty. Everyone says so." Elizabeth squeezed her shoulders in gentle reassurance. "Even Mama said you were pretty, and you know she never spared anyone's feelings."

"Mama didn't think Mary was pretty. She would be horrified to learn Mary is to have a husband before I do. Perhaps I should run off with an officer too, like Lydia did. She seems happy now. She lives in London and has a shop and Mr. Wickham."

"Don't be silly," Elizabeth said, her tone sharp, feeling fortunate the officers were long gone. She took a deep breath, forcing a smile onto her face. "Why didn't Mr. Housley have a housekeeper?" she asked to change the subject.

"His sister kept house after their mother died, but then she got married. He was angry with her, you know, because she insisted on getting married when their mother hadn't even been dead ten months. He thinks that's terribly improper, and won't permit himself to marry yet because it still hadn't been a year, but he doesn't seem to mind that Mary is planning to marry him when our mama still won't have been gone that long. That's how much he loves her. He doesn't even care about Mary observing proper mourning, even after being so angry with his sister and while observing it himself."

Elizabeth found she wasn't surprised by Mr. Housley's inconsistency. There were plenty of inconsistencies in the people in her life. One more made little difference. "Well, if our family is anything to go by, his sister should be commended for observing deep mourning for so long. Ten months appears to be a lengthy wait," Elizabeth said, determined to lighten Kitty's mood now that she knew how silly her pique was. "You and I simply aren't keeping up."

"How am I to keep up when men are proposing to Mary and not me?" Kitty met Elizabeth's eyes in the mirror. "Doesn't it trouble you that no one has asked for your hand, Lizzy, yet someone is so in love with Mary?"

"Certainly not. I'm happy Mary has found someone. You know Mama always worried she would not." Elizabeth hoped her calm reply, which was fully truthful, hid the flutter in her chest. Kitty's words conjured up that particular look on Mr. Darcy's face, the intent one he had right before he proposed. The one she'd banished with her anger.

"I suppose you're right," Kitty said, looking down. "I don't want someone like Mr. Housley, anyhow. I want an officer, like Lydia."

"Well, we are neither of us fortune tellers, so I can't promise you an officer," Elizabeth said, doubly glad there were none about any longer. "You'll find a husband, though, Kitty. It's impossible you shouldn't. After all, if there's one man willing to wed Mary in this world, think how many there must be who would wish to have you?" she added, realizing she could turn Kitty's own argument back on her, though it felt unjust to Mary.

"That's true," Kitty said, brightening. She finally smiled, picking back up her brush.

Elizabeth stepped back, happy to see her sister looking like herself again. "So you no longer begrudge Mary her Mr. Housley?"

"I'm happy for Mary," Kitty said, starting to tug the brush through her curls. "She's proven it possible for any of us to wed well."

"Yes, I suppose she has. I'm going to go unpack my things. I shall see you at tea."

Kitty nodded, smiling as she brushed her hair, her eyes on her reflection. Shaking her head, Elizabeth left the room. She felt a bit guilty for demeaning Mary, but hopefully no harm would come of it. Mary was likely too happy to care about a few poorly chosen sentiments, and soon she would be off to live with her Mr. Housley, near Jane.

Elizabeth grimaced. Now it was her turn to be jealous, but only for the dream of living nearer her sister. She supposed that would be a good fortune for the woman Mr. Darcy did finally marry, and a point of continued envy for Elizabeth. Whomever his future bride was, as Darcy's wife, she would likely be afforded considerable time with Jane and Mr. Bingley.

The banns for Mary's nuptials would be read in both parishes so that the marriage could take place in either one, as Mr. Housley and their father were still corresponding on the details of the event. Mary threw herself into housework with a new enthusiasm, with the expressed desire to know as much about running a household as possible before she married. Kitty spoke often of her letters from Lydia and of how hard their youngest sister was working. Always a follower, Kitty was now surrounded by people who did their tasks cheerfully, and she copied this attitude.

Soon, all fell back into a normal seeming routine. As part of that, they dined with Charlotte's family on a regular basis, something Elizabeth always looked forward to. Though she enjoyed her life at Longbourn, it was nice to sometimes have people outside her family to speak with. Not only the Lucases, but Sir William was as likely to invite additional guests as not, something Charlotte rarely permitted at home.

Even knowing that propensity of Sir William's, when they next arrived at Lucas Lodge for dinner, Elizabeth was surprised to see Mr. Darcy. She hung back while her family greeted their hosts. Mr. Darcy waited for that ritual to conclude before coming forward.

Elizabeth's first instinct was to excuse herself, but rationality disparaged the idea. It had been months, after all, since his proposal. He must have realized he would see her that evening, as Sir William was unlikely not to mention who his other guests were. If Mr. Darcy was willing to put the incident fully behind them, so must she be. After all, by some estimates, he was the injured party.

"You see we have a special guest come to stay with us, Bennet," Sir William said to Elizabeth's father. "One of the heroes of Netherfield Park."

Even from where she stood, Elizabeth caught Mr. Darcy's slight grimace at being referred to as a hero, though she doubted Sir William had noticed.

"Mr. Darcy," her father said. "A pleasant surprise, sir."

"Mr. Bennet, Mrs. Bennet, Miss Mary, Miss Kitty," he greeted, bowing with each name. His eyes moved past them and, when they met hers, he offered a politely blank expression. "Miss Bennet."

"Mr. Darcy," she murmured, along with Charlotte and her sisters.

"What brings you to Hertfordshire?" Mr. Bennet asked. "I am almost aggravated with you for not staying with us, rather than the Lucases. After housing my daughter, or should I say my daughters, for so long, you really should stay at Longbourn."

"I'm actually staying at the inn in Meryton," Mr. Darcy said.

"I had just invited him to stay with us," Lady Lucas put in. "Only moments before you arrived."

"Well, uninvite him, Mama," Charlotte said. "We owe Mr. Darcy our hospitality for allowing the Bingleys to stay with him for so long."

"My dear child, I have already offered. I can't uninvite him. It would be rude."

"I am not a child, Mama," Charlotte said. "I demand you uninvite him this instant."

Elizabeth suppressed a laugh, for in that moment Charlotte sounded more like a child than Elizabeth had ever heard her. Elizabeth had noticed, however, that Charlotte's usually imperturbable temper was deteriorating as her middle expanded. She glanced at Mr. Darcy, who of course had the final say, hoping he wouldn't allow the argument to escalate. He nodded, as if understanding her silent wish.

"I am honored by your invitations, but you should hear why I'm here before you are so free with them," Mr. Darcy said. "I'm thinking of purchasing Netherfield Park."

"You wouldn't want to give up Pemberley," Elizabeth said, shocked into speaking.

"I'm not thinking of it as a residence, but as an investment. There are several possible ways the property could be profitable. One would be to build a magnificent house and lease it. But I think it would be more profitable to build a small house for a steward and turn the parkland into farmland. It's called Netherfield *Park* for a reason: It has extensive parks. This made it a desirable gentleman's residence, but its farms barely supported it. Those parks could very easily be used to raise sheep and less easily be turned to crops."

There was a shocked silence. Elizabeth was horrified at the thought. Turn a local treasure into grazing ground for sheep? The arrogance of the man.

"One thing I would like to consider would be the reaction of the community," Mr. Darcy said, a slight smile turning up the corners of his mouth. "I don't want hostility, and I could see that occurring whatever was done with the property."

"How would hostility occur if you rebuilt the manor?" Mr. Bennet asked.

"For a period of time there would be jobs for local workers. Although the workers would be happy, the people competing for those workers would not. For such an extensive project, additional workers would need to be brought in. They would impact the community in a variety of ways, and all would be left with much less employment once the new manor was complete. Some would be migrant and simply leave, some wouldn't."

"Mr. Darcy is correct," Charlotte said, her tone thoughtful and once more of its typical level nature. "I don't think there is anything that could be done to the property which would not aggravate at least some people."

"Even leaving it as is, a burnt out shell," Mr. Bennet said. "You are welcome to stay at Longbourn, whatever you do or don't do at Netherfield. Give us a chance to pay back some of what we owe you."

Elizabeth thought that slight smile touched Mr. Darcy's lips again, but he answered seriously enough. "It would be my pleasure."

It wasn't Elizabeth's pleasure. She'd resolved to behave

accordingly here at dinner, but having him in their house seemed doubly awkward. She tried to convey her disagreement with his acceptance in her expression, but for what seemed like the first time since she'd entered, he wasn't looking at her. How could he read so well her desire not to aggravate Charlotte only moments ago, and now seem oblivious?

Dinner passed with all cordiality, alleviating much of Elizabeth's worry. Mr. Darcy seemed not only determined to behave genially toward her, but also to everyone else. He was not gregarious, something she assumed him incapable of and didn't think would suit him regardless, but he was polite, droll and engaged. Often as they dined, she found herself amused by something he said, or undertaking small bouts of verbal sparring. Reluctantly, she had to admit it was the most pleasant evening she'd passed in ages.

They parted ways with him after dinner, him to collect his possessions and them to ready a room for his arrival. As she and Mary made up the bed, Elizabeth couldn't help but look about the austere room and think of Mr. Darcy in it. It didn't seem fine enough, yet it was nicely kept and neat. He would fit well in it, though he was likely too tall for the bed. That thought caused her to blush, something she hoped Mary couldn't see in the candlelight they worked by.

She came back downstairs to find Mr. Darcy standing in the parlor. Not knowing where the rest of the family had gone to and still not sure they should be alone together, Elizabeth paused in the doorway. Mary had gone to her room for a book, an errand Elizabeth assumed wouldn't take long. Elizabeth knew she ought to wait for Mary in the hall, but instead found herself watching Mr. Darcy.

He was impeccably dressed, though in a more casual jacket than he'd worn for dinner. It amused her slightly that he'd made the change. He was standing near the mantel, and lightly ran a hand over its barren surface. Elizabeth felt he must be contemplating the absence of ornaments, seeing anew through his eyes how severe the room was. Her supposition seemed to be confirmed as he turned slowly toward the back of the room, stopping when his eyes reached the china cabinet there.

Mr. Darcy's long legs brought him to the piece in a moment. As he came to stand unerringly before the ceramic shepherd, shepherdess and sheep, Elizabeth realized they'd been his goal, not the cabinet itself. His keen eyes must have spotted them from his place by the mantel. He bent near to scrutinize them and she realized he couldn't see inside without doing so. The front of the cabinet was glass, the contents all but invisible in candlelight.

Elizabeth found herself frowning. To her knowledge, Mr. Darcy had only been in their parlor once before, when he'd come to claim his coat. She doubted he'd spent much time looking at the decorations on the mantel, especially as she recalled he hadn't been seated facing it. Had he been looking for the shepherdess after their conversation about it at Pemberley? As there was little possibility he could have seen the collection from his place at the mantel, she wondered how he'd known where to seek the flock and its tenders.

He suddenly straightened, turning on his heels. Elizabeth blinked in surprise, embarrassed to be caught staring at him. He regarded her with raised brows, obviously curious about her scrutiny. To her relief, footsteps sounded behind her. Mary appeared, along with Kitty. Elizabeth smiled at them and they all joined Mr. Darcy in the parlor.

Chapter Ten

~ Reconciliation ~

Darcy

Arriving downstairs to find only Mr. and Mrs. Bennet at breakfast, Darcy noted they weren't standing on ceremony as far as seating went, nor did he see a buffet set out yet. Waving them down when they would have stood, he claimed a chair at the end of the table opposite them. He calculated his choice as most likely to result in sitting beside or across from Elizabeth.

"Mr. Darcy," Mr. Bennet said, nodding.

"Good morning, Mr. Darcy," Mrs. Bennet said. "I see you keep an early schedule."

He detected approval in her voice. "Good Morning, Mrs. Bennet, Mr. Bennet."

Elizabeth and her sisters chose that moment to arrive. Darcy stood as a matter of reflex. Elizabeth smiled, though he didn't know if it was in appreciation of his manners or amusement with them.

"Good morning, Mr. Darcy," she said, taking the seat opposite him.

Her sisters mimicked her, and he nodded to each in turn as he reseated himself. He was pleased with the success of his strategy, for now he would be able to look at Elizabeth all through the meal.

Breakfast wasn't what Darcy was accustomed to. Instead of a buffet of enough food to feed five times the number of those who ate, they sat at a table with limited choices. There was sufficient food, to be sure. It was also quite good. Darcy concluded it wasn't fancy, but the cook was excellent.

"You'll be going out to Netherfield today, Mr. Darcy?" Mrs. Bennet inquired as dishes were passed.

Darcy, feeling Elizabeth's eyes on him, made sure to give no outward remark on the style of dining. "That is my plan, yes."

"Will you return for lunch, or shall I ask Cook to pack something for you?"

"A packed lunch would be very considerate of you," he said, meaning it. He'd planned a long day of reconnaissance at Netherfield to validate his being in Hertfordshire. He'd considered perhaps skipping a meal or riding into town. "Your cook is excellent."

"That is thanks in large part to Charlotte," Elizabeth said.

"It's her skill that creates the dishes," Mrs. Bennet demurred.

"You found the recipes for her. She only knew such heavy, extravagant dishes," Elizabeth said. She shook her head in mock dismay. "But you shall never get Charlotte to own up to all she's to be credited for, Mr. Darcy. She's dismayingly modest."

"It is true I taught her all of the recipes my mother uses," Mrs. Bennet said. "However, it is a testament to her skill she is able to copy what I showed her, and oftentimes improve it."

Elizabeth cast her stepmother an indulgent look.

Darcy felt it was also a testament to how much the cook wished to keep her position. He wondered if he should ask for some of the recipes, though he felt the cook at Pemberley might misconstrue it as criticism if he attempted to introduce them. "I'm unsure if you're aware that my aunt is Lady Catherine de Bourgh?" he asked the table at large.

Mr. Bennet looked up sharply, frowning. "No, I was unaware of the connection. I assume you mean the same Lady Catherine who is patroness to Mr. Collins."

"Calm yourself, Papa," Elizabeth said. "I am quite certain Mr. Darcy wouldn't refer to Mr. Collins while sitting at breakfast with us unless he wished to impart good news." She cast Darcy a look that made it clear she'd best be right.

"Yes, well, you are better acquainted with Mr. Darcy than I, but I hope you are correct, my dear," Mr. Bennet replied.

"She is," Darcy hastened to assure, sorry he hadn't thought to blunt the shock of bring up the man responsible for the first Mrs. Bennet's death. "Lady Catherine learned of the fire and of Mr. Collins' behavior. She can't rescind the living she's given him, but she's withdrawn all support from him. She used to invite him to her house often, but has ceased the practice. She cuts him at church services. As he was never popular, everyone is willing to follow her example in this. Most of the congregation gets up and leaves when he begins his sermons. No one in the neighborhood will speak to him at church, and local businesses charge him more to buy from them."

Darcy watched Elizabeth push food about on her plate, taking in her expression. He'd expected, perhaps, smugness or triumph, but she looked more relieved than anything else.

"Yes, that is good news," Mr. Bennet said. His voice was a bit gruff about the edges.

"It's the least of what he deserves," Miss Kitty said. In contrast to Elizabeth, Miss Kitty's tone was vindictive.

"I agree," Miss Mary put in.

"Yes," Elizabeth said, drawing the word out. "Yes, it is good news. Thank you for sharing it, Mr. Darcy. I can't in good conscience agree Mr. Collins should go to the gallows for what he did, but it has weighed on me his sole punishment was to be removed from this house and made to take an uncomfortable carriage ride or two. I feel relief at knowing he must come to regret his actions."

She sounded so sad, Darcy wished he were allowed to go to her. He realized, for all of her liveliness, Elizabeth was nearly as kind hearted as Mrs. Bingley. He was enchanted to have a new fragment of information about her, though sorry to have caused her unhappiness.

"I'm surprised he doesn't hire a curate and live elsewhere," Mrs. Bennet said.

"It will probably come to that, but he is remarkably stubborn," Darcy said. "It appears to be taking him a long time to realize that would be the best thing to do."

"Oh, he can't be stubborn enough to wait them out, can he?" Miss Kitty cried.

"How long has this been going on?" Mr. Bennet asked.

"I believe three or four months," Darcy said. He cast a reassuring look around the table. "You do not know my aunt. No one is more stubborn than Lady Catherine. You may be assured she will not relent until he leaves."

The rest of the meal was passed on less distressing topics. Darcy found the general discourse much improved over what he'd expected. His only true complaint was he found no opening to invite Elizabeth to accompany him to Netherfield Park. Reluctantly, he accepted his lunch and went out for the day.

Later that day, when he returned for dinner, Darcy found himself seated between Mrs. Bennet and Miss Mary, Elizabeth and Miss Kitty across the table from him. With what was at first considerable effort, he managed not to direct all of his attention to Elizabeth, but spoke instead to Mrs. Bennet and Miss Mary. He endeavored to appear interested and polite, knowing Elizabeth's eyes were on him.

In short order, speaking with the two became less of a chore. In fact, not a chore at all. Miss Mary was not a stimulating conversationalist, but she had recently read some of the books he'd read at Cambridge. For all he'd never considered her quite bright, she was remarkably proficient at retaining what she'd read, and so able to converse quite fluently on it. Mrs. Bennet, in turn, seemed well educated on many practical topics. She was possessed of surprisingly modern views, especially for a woman, and understood what she conversed about.

Darcy was at first surprised with how easy she was to talk with, but later found himself reflecting that Elizabeth's father was an intelligent man. No matter how much he wished a male heir, he'd obviously learned from his first marriage and endeavored to make a more suitable match in his second. Mr. Darcy could see Mr. Bennet hadn't in truth selected the nearest woman at hand, as one might think, but the correct woman to enjoy his years with.

The following morning, still unable to work any pretext for a journey with Elizabeth into the conversation, Darcy settled for having Mr. Bennet ride over with him. They spent an agreeable day looking over Netherfield. Mr. Bennet, like his wife, turned out to be easy to converse with. On the journey back, he praised Darcy for his agricultural knowledge, a compliment Darcy couldn't help but sincerely return.

"It isn't me you should compliment, but my wife," Mr. Bennet said, his tone one of pride.

"Mrs. Bennet? I did notice her interest in the subject last night at dinner," Darcy said.

"Take the sheep you praised so highly, for example. It was at Charlotte's suggestion I bought sheep from Mr. Coke of Norfolk. He's crossed the Norfolk Horn with the English Leicester and had excellent results. They say his sheep have the best features of both, and thus far I'm inclined to believe it. We purchased six lambs, four ewes and two rams. The lambs are maturing faster than the Leicester, which we were raising before, and have a more even fleece than the Norfolk Horn."

"We've been using Coke's sheep for several years at Pemberley,"

Darcy said. "That is why I recognized the stock. They live up to their reputation."

"That's good to hear. I was leery of the investment at first, but Charlotte insisted. I suppose there's something to be said for assured women." He smiled slightly as he said it.

"I suppose there is," Darcy said, keeping his tone neutral. He knew what Mr. Bennet was hinting toward, but refused to show his hand. As much as he liked to think he'd become less arrogant, Darcy still had too much pride to wish to risk public humiliation being added to private if Elizabeth rebuffed him a second time.

The conversation returned to sheep for the remainder of the journey back to Longbourn. Darcy thought they'd nearly exhausted the topic, but it began again at dinner, with Mrs. Bennet adding her thoughts. The three of them branched out from comparing breeds into a discussion of feeding, specifically the trend to augment a flock's diet with Scottish turnips.

Darcy was engaged enough he didn't need to remind himself not to dance attendance on Elizabeth. In truth, as the meal drew to a close and he paused to take in her conversation with Miss Mary and Miss Kitty, concerning Shakespeare, Darcy realized he'd all but ignored her. He could only hope, in his efforts to prove he considered her family members his equals and was pleased to converse with them, he hadn't overstepped and insulted her.

Yet, it seemed he must be doing something right, for each time he looked Elizabeth's way, he found her eyes on him.

Elizabeth

Elizabeth could admit to herself, though with difficulty, that she felt a growing pique. Upon finding Mr. Darcy at Lucas Lodge, it had been all she could do not to flee. She'd been worried he was there to pursue her, or punish her decision by flaunting his wealth, or otherwise make her uncomfortable and force her to bear his attention. Her only solace had been knowing seeing him in Hertfordshire, proud and condescending toward nearly everyone and everything important to her, would bolster the rightness of her rejection. Not that her decision needed bolstering, for she was quite sure she held no love for him, but learning how she'd misjudged him still cast a shadow on the way she'd resolved to feel toward him.

Instead of living up to her expectations or fears, Mr. Darcy was cordial to everyone else and all but ignoring her. He spoke often and freely, more so than she'd ever witnessed before, but not with her. While her father, Charlotte, Mary, and Kitty received engaging and respectful conversation, Elizabeth was the recipient of only the occasional remark, other than polite good mornings or other similar social niceties.

Sometimes, as she watched him converse with the other members of her family day after day, his handsome face mobile, she began to feel a bewildering annoyance at his lack of interest in her. When he spoke on particularly arresting topics, but not with her, she almost resented his fellow conversationalists. Worst was when he laughed. It didn't happen often, but she found he had a rich, warm, engaging laugh. When he employed it, never with her, Elizabeth felt what she despised to admit to herself was jealousy.

To her further dismay, she couldn't shake the feeling. As his stay lengthened, she began to suffer from it with greater frequency. She also suffered a mounting invasion of her thoughts. Mr. Darcy seemed to fill more and more of her mind. To her even greater horror, it came to the point where, while she wished him gone, she dreaded that he should leave.

Ignoring her seemed to provide him with extensive amounts of time. Aside from engaging her family members regularly, Mr. Darcy spent his days visiting Netherfield or talking to people in the neighborhood. It seemed he was willing to spend his time with any and everyone who wasn't her, though his politeness toward her never wavered.

Unable to help herself, Elizabeth at last resorted to speaking with others about Mr. Darcy. She was careful to begin these conversations with the pretext of Netherfield, of course. What soon came to baffle her was the prevalent feeling about Mr. Darcy's project, from all corners. Though everyone spoke highly of him, most thought it unlikely Mr. Darcy could make a profit, and more likely he would lose money, whether he farmed Netherfield or rebuilt it to rent.

Finally, after he'd resided in Longbourn for well over a week, Mr. Darcy looked across the table at her one morning. "Miss Bennet, would you care to view Netherfield with me? I should like your opinion on the project."

Elizabeth could have pointed out her opinion was ready without seeing the property again, but found herself too happy he was finally attending to her to refuse. "I would be pleased to, Mr. Darcy."

He turned and looked at Charlotte. "I have both a carriage and a curricle at my disposal, Mrs. Bennet. Shall Miss Mary and Miss Kitty accompany us?"

Chagrinned, it was all Elizabeth could do not to rescind her agreement. She didn't fancy a day spent watching Mr. Darcy converse agreeably with her younger sisters, while all three forgot she was there. Was it too much to ask, after all the time he'd now spent in Longbourn, for a few moments alone with him? She longed to recapture the easy comradery they'd had on their walks at Pemberley. Looking back, their walks had formed some of the most pleasant afternoons she could recall.

"I'm afraid I can't spare all three, Mr. Darcy," Charlotte said. "I'm sure if you take your curricle, open as it is, all propriety will be met. Will a packed lunch be in order?"

Elizabeth composed her expression as Mr. Darcy turned to her. He looked almost contrite, and she wondered if he'd noticed her brief displeasure.

"Miss Bennet?" He made her name into a question.

"I should like to take a proper look, if that's acceptable," she said, turning to Charlotte. "So I believe lunch would be amiable." Elizabeth caught the glint of amusement in Charlotte's eyes, but couldn't fathom the source.

"Of course. I shall let Cook know it will be two lunches today," Charlotte said.

"If you will excuse me, I will order my curricle readied." Mr. Darcy rose from the table as he spoke.

They set out about an hour later, Mr. Darcy seeing to the stowing of their lunches himself before handing Elizabeth up. He took his place beside her, gathering the reins, and set out in silence. It was a lovely morning for a drive, but in spite of the fresh air and sunshine, Elizabeth was aware of an ongoing feeling of peevishness. It must stem, she felt, from being mostly ignored. Invisible was a highly disagreeable state of existence to her.

"I was wondering if you would ever seek my feelings," Elizabeth said after permitting the quiet of the ride for a time.

"Your opinion is of the utmost importance to me."

He said it with every appearance of sincerity, though he was facing the road, making him more difficult to judge.

"Truly?" she asked. "For it seems to me you've sought the feelings of every other being in Hertfordshire before mine."

"Not Miss Mary's or Miss Kitty's, nor those of the sheep."

She couldn't help but laugh. "Well, I am rebuked."

Though he didn't turn to look at her, Elizabeth could see his answering smile. They fell into another stretch of silence, but it seemed less awkward than the first.

"Have you been back?" he asked after a time, his tone quiet.

Elizabeth looked down at her gloved hands. "No, I have not." She'd been so caught up in her conflicting emotions over Mr. Darcy, she hadn't paused to give consideration to what it would be like to see Netherfield Park again.

In truth, she'd been deliberately avoiding seeing it. She'd heard stories and descriptions enough, but somehow in her mind it remained as it had been before the fire, or, in her darker dreams, as it was during the fire. She was suddenly concerned what effect the reality of it may have on her. She pondered this in silence for some time until, with mounting distress, she realized they were near to turning down the drive.

She held up a hand, not sure if she was intent on shielding herself from the upcoming view or gesturing for Mr. Darcy to stop the curricle. Warm fingers wrapped about hers, pressing them in reassurance, before releasing her. Elizabeth let her hand fall as Mr. Darcy recaptured the rein he'd transferred to his left hand. She didn't know if she was more comforted or shocked, but she made no additional protest as he turned up the drive.

Elizabeth took in the scorched and burnt out shell. Portions of the walls were toppled, and much of the stone blackened with soot. Skeletal fingers reached into the air, and tumbled chimneys splayed across the ground. The stable still stood, but the roof was dark with charcoal and falling in. All about, the grounds were unkempt and overgrown.

Yet, it wasn't as terrible as she'd feared. Time had already softened the violence of the damage. What had once been a well-groomed lawn was awash in wild flowers. Oddly, some of the stone looked as if it was being systematically removed.

Fixating on that as a safe topic, she glanced at Mr. Darcy. "Has the owner asked for the house to be taken down?"

He shook his head, bringing the curricle to a halt before the collapsed manor. "People have been taking the stone. It's easier than quarrying it and I can imagine they don't think of it as stealing."

"Probably not, but they should. If you purchase Netherfield, you could use the stone to rebuild." Her eyes moved restlessly, resisting attempts to identify landmarks, such as the front door. They fixed instead on a dense swath of flowers. She realized they weren't all wild. Or, rather, some of the blooms were the gardens gone wild with neglect. "Would it be stealing to pick some flowers?"

"Less so than the stone, since the flowers will be long gone by the time anyone who owns them sees them."

"You are seeing them," she said.

"If I do buy Netherfield Park, it will take longer than the life of those blossoms." He turned fully to her now, his expression warm enough to cause her to blush. "Before you gather any, I have something for you." Turning away, he reached behind him, coming back with a paper wrapped package.

"I can't accept a gift," she said, the heat in her face growing. The curricle seemed immediately smaller, Mr. Darcy's impressive frame taking up more than his fair share of the space, leaving her nerve rackingly close.

"It's not for you." The caring, soft tone had returned, reaching into her heart. "I know you put flowers on your mother's grave, but I thought you might like to put flowers where she died."

Elizabeth stared at him for a long moment, attempting to keep her emotions in check. She was stunned by his thoughtfulness, and nearly overwrought with fresh sorrow.

"Open it," he ordered with gentle insistence, carefully placing the package in her hands.

With slightly shaking hands, Elizabeth unwound the paper, exposing a stunning bouquet. They were hothouse flowers, not in season. "You didn't pick these," she said, swallowing down emotion.

"No. I sent to London for them. I didn't know her well, but I believe your mother would not have liked wild flowers as much as these."

"You are right," she said, her voice catching. "That was very thoughtful."

"Your mother appreciated beauty."

"She did." How considerate of him to have observed that. "It would have been more economical to pick some flowers here," she said, letting her gaze wander back over the plethora of blooms before them.

"I think your mother would have wanted hothouse flowers."

"She would have." Elizabeth blinked rapidly, holding back tears.

Mr. Darcy alighted, coming around to help her down. As soon as her feet touched the earth, he stepped back. "This way," he said, but he didn't move. After a moment of hesitation, he offered his arm. "The footing is uneven."

"Thank you," she said, accepting the offer.

Together, Elizabeth gripping the beautiful bouquet he'd sent for tightly in one hand, they negotiated the rubble leading up to the front entrance. Unable to concentrate on her footing, her mind in the clutches of sorrow, Elizabeth's steps were awkward. After a moment, Mr. Darcy halted, dropping her arm to face her.

"Here," he said. He took up the hand in which she held the

flowers, carefully loosening her fingers. Taking the bouquet, he tucked it into the crook of one arm. He then took her other hand, the one he'd briefly held in the curricle, and placed it firmly back on his arm, covering it with his own. "Now you will be better able to manage your skirt."

"Thank you," she murmured, too full of sorrow to muster more words.

They avoided the few still standing front steps, circling them to stand before the tumbled down inner staircase. Elizabeth knew, for she'd been told, her mother had died there. Her remains had been found in that spot, confirming Lydia's and Kitty's tale.

Elizabeth looked about, her eyes anywhere but on the ground at her feet. Everywhere was ash and charred remains. She realized she was making a disaster of her hem. Her mother would never approve of that. Perhaps, she thought idly, walking about the grounds would rub the ash off. If only other things could be mended so easily by a walk, like the hole in her life where her mother should be.

Drawing in a deep breath, she took her arm from Mr. Darcy's. Resolutely, Elizabeth turned her gaze on the marble steps before her, easily visible in the rubble. She followed the few that still stood down until her eyes rested on the place where her mother had died.

It looked like any other place in the burnt out manor. Charred and ruined. "I believe she died here." Her voice came out squeezed sounding, from a throat closing with tears.

Mr. Darcy handed her the flowers.

Gathering her up skirt, for her mother truly wouldn't approve of her ruining it, Elizabeth leaned over and placed the flowers. She closed her eyes, uttering a brief prayer. Then she opened them, taking in the beautiful blooms, which her mother would have swooned for, their soft petals like bright jewels in the ashes and dust.

Drawing in a steadying breath, she spoke from the heart. "Mama, I don't know if you can hear me, but we are all fine. I know you'll be pleased to know Jane married Mr. Bingley and they are very happy. Lydia is married to a handsome and charming man. You remember Mr. Wickham? He's her husband. Mary will be marrying soon to a nice gentleman with some property. Kitty is doing so well, really, they all are doing well, and so is Papa, although I think he misses you more than he shows. He moved your portrait, the one Jane did, into his library to replace the one of you when you were young. I think he likes you to keep him company there." She took another breath, but it was short and shuddering. "I miss you, Mama. I hope you are in a place where you are happy."

Tears filled her eyes, welling over and down her cheeks. "I remember being so frustrated when I was learning to embroider, and you sat down next to me and helped me. I remember you brushing my hair and teaching me how to put it up. I remember you helping me arrange flowers. You taught me to read and to figure. So much of me comes from you. Sometimes I forgot what you gave me and was annoyed with you." She drew in a shuddering sob. "I hate that it wasn't until you died that I realized how much I owe you and how much I love you. I hate that I didn't do anything to save you."

She wanted to tell her mother Mr. Collins was being punished for what he'd done. She wanted to ask her why she hadn't left, as Mr. Darcy ordered. How could a cloak, no matter how fine, have been worth her mother's life? Tears flowed freely down Elizabeth's face, hot and angry.

A handkerchief was placed gently into her hand. Elizabeth pressed it to her eyes, sobbing. An arm slid about her shoulders, the pressure of it light and comforting, and her tears lost their vehemence. She knew she could no more have carried her mother than Mrs. Goulding could have. If she'd been there, though, maybe she and Lydia together . . . Yet, Lydia hadn't even realized their mother needed help until it was already too late.

Elizabeth shook her head, letting anger seep away, and stood there, crying. A part of her wished to turn to Mr. Darcy, who stood so patiently, offering what comfort he could. Somehow, she was sure if she permitted him, he would wrap both arms about her and hold her near, a true balm to her sorrow.

Elizabeth stepped slightly away knowing, in view of the feelings he may still harbor for her, how unfair it would be to take any more advantage of his presence. He immediately let his arm drop, breaking all contact, and she felt the absence keenly. She blotted her face, hoping it wasn't too unsightly in the wake of her crying.

Finally, she cleared her throat, tucking his handkerchief away, as she should wash it before returning it. "Thank you. I'm sorry I became so emotional." Grasping her skirt in both hands, in indication he needn't offer his arm again, she hurried back through the rubble toward the curricle.

Mr. Darcy fell in beside her. "You are welcome," he replied, his voice tinged with feeling as well. "Sometimes it is appropriate to be emotional."

Reaching the curricle, Elizabeth shook most of the ash out of her skirt, keeping her face averted from him. He stood for a moment, then began doing something with the horses. Picking a direction at random, so long as her back was to Mr. Darcy, Elizabeth started walking. Not caring where she was going, she soon found herself strolling through the overgrown garden. A short time later, she could hear Mr. Darcy's long strides coming closer, but he remained a slight distance behind her.

Finally, feeling more herself, Elizabeth stopped. She looked about, taking in the grounds. Netherfield Park was lovely in spite of being unkempt. Or perhaps, in some ways, the more so for it. She drew in a last calming breath, mustered a pleasant smile, and turned to face Mr. Darcy. He'd asked her there for her opinion, not for the company of a weepy companion. "I'd forgotten how beautiful it is here."

"It is. It wouldn't take much work to bring the park back." His eyes were dark with concern.

"It would be a shame to turn it into pasture," she said, feeling the best way to allay his worry was to behave normally. "I think you could easily persuade some local people to clear it in exchange for the lumber, though, if you decide on that route. The wood would be valuable."

"It would, but to cut the woods down would likely be to relegate this land to pasture for generations to come." He looked about. "I'm not sure if I have the heart for it."

She readily recalled how lovely the grounds were about Pemberley, and how plentiful and ancient the trees. It was a singularly beautiful place, and Mr. Darcy's home. His forefathers were all to be congratulated, but she knew Mr. Darcy well enough to see it was his love for and appreciation of that beauty which caused it to remain so. "Then you will rebuild the manor?"

"Building another house like the one that burned down would probably not be profitable. The Netherfield Park manor was the largest residence in the neighborhood. Wealthy people who buy country estates usually don't want to be without other wealthy people to socialize with."

Elizabeth wondered if he'd really brought her there for her

opinion on what to do, or for her thoughts on what his conscience would bear. She considered pointing out Mr. Bingley had been willing to rent there, and he was a wealthy person, but she knew Mr. Bingley was unusual in that he liked everyone. Mr. Darcy was undoubtedly correct about most wealthy people. "So build two smaller houses. Something on the scale of Longbourn. Make the division somewhere in the middle of the parkland. Give both houses tenant farmers for income. Those who rented them would be more in tune with the neighborhood."

He turned to her, looking surprised. "I hadn't thought of that. It could work," he said, his tone revealing excitement. "Let's look for locations."

They walked through the property for some time, finding two potential sites for houses. At one point, they stumbled upon a flock of sheep, grazing contentedly. The boy watching them offered a jaunty wave, but whistled to his dog. Together, they started moving the sheep away.

"Stones and flowers aren't the only things being taken from here," Elizabeth said. She watched the retreating forms in mild amusement. "I suppose being caught gives him scruples?"

"It's well known I'm considering buying this place. I don't mind the poaching or the grazing, but I did chase away some people who were cutting down trees."

"Shall we go after him and bring his flock back?"

"Not minding and encouraging are not one in the same," Mr. Darcy said.

His tone was light, but Elizabeth wondered if the comment was applied to her, something his glance her way seemed to confirm. As they walked on, Elizabeth wondered which Mr. Darcy thought she was doing with him, not minding or encouraging? She realized the more pressing question was, which did she intend to be doing? Perturbed, she found herself unsure. Remembering his arm about her, his hand briefly taking hers, she realized she wasn't leaning in the direction she would have been not a scant two weeks ago, before he appeared in Hertfordshire and conducted himself so amiably.

They located two more sites, entering into a discussion on which two would be most desirable, or if two was in fact the correct number when four such amiable locations existed. On their way back to the curricle, Elizabeth spotted men in the distance. As she and Mr. Darcy drew near, she could see the men were laying out an oddly shaped chain with long links. They acknowledged Mr. Darcy as if they knew him. He walked over to them with Elizabeth, but didn't introduce her. He asked them to pay particular attention to sites he and Elizabeth had looked at as possible places for houses.

"Surveyors," he explained as he and Elizabeth walked away. "They use a compass for direction and a chain to measure. I wanted a good map of the estate so I could see how much of the land was farmland, how much park, and how much woodland."

"If you build two houses, the park could be extended I think, at least near the site we first looked at," she said.

He smiled slightly. "That location is your favorite."

"It is. It will offer the most pleasant views. I think a person with the amount of wealth you would wish to attract to the location would place a premium on that."

"Why is that?"

"They would be wealthy enough to make the move. They wouldn't be leaving London, or wherever they reside, because they must, but because they wish to." Her unspoken thought was that much of what wealthy people routinely bought was cheaper in London.

"You can't know that. What of a formerly wealthy family forced to take a new home more in their means?"

"They won't consider it if they can't afford it," she said. "If they are of enough wealth that this will be, in essence, the affordable choice, they'll likely be accustomed to great beauty and seek it out."

He nodded, looking thoughtful.

Elizabeth studied him for a moment. He was so tall, and undoubtedly handsome. He walked with his hands clasped behind his back. She felt a flush of pleasure at how seriously he was taking her thoughts and opinions. She realized that, in remaining slightly aloof, he made his good opinion seem all the more valuable.

She knew Mr. Bingley often sought Mr. Darcy's advice. Jane had written of how they couldn't purchase a home without it. Mr. Bingley had obviously won Mr. Darcy's respect at some point, and valued what he'd achieved.

"Besides, you will want to attract a family that appreciates beauty, will you not?" she said, returning to their discussion and hoping he hadn't caught her staring. "Perhaps one willing to pay more for it? A family who appreciates beauty enough to pay for it will be better renters, I believe."

"You make excellent points. I say, as well, that your argument brings us back to two properties, both built to be on par with the finest in the area, but not above."

"Or did I argue against myself? I worry now that will attract someone slightly finer than the area warrants, and the company here will soon send them away again."

His smile broadened, as if at some inner amusement. "You do not know how petty people can be. The perfect renters of whom we speak will be pleased to have the company of each other, and to feel themselves to be slightly above the rest of the community. They will find Hertfordshire good enough for them, but be permitted to assure themselves they are gracing the neighborhood with their presence."

"You paint them to be quite the snobs, these renters of yours."

"Oh, I should hope they will be. Snobs are always willing to pay extra to maintain their perceived station."

Elizabeth smiled at that. "There you have it, then, the perfect plan for the property."

They walked on in easy silence. Soon, the way steepened as they started uphill toward a large oak. In unspoken accord, neither moved to take the easier path around the base of the hill.

"Yes," Mr. Darcy said, his surprised voice low as if he spoke more to himself than her. "I think Netherfield would make a profitable purchase after all."

They crested the hilltop on which the single, pristinely beautiful oak stood. One more hill lay between them and the shell of the house, the curricle, their waiting lunch, and the ride home. Elizabeth stopped, turning slowly to take in the beauty of the day. The sky above was a seamless blue. Atop the windswept hill on which they stood, wildflowers danced in the breeze, the leaves of the oak swishing above. Mr. Darcy halted as well, mimicking her movement of looking about them.

Elizabeth realized she didn't want to walk on yet. She wasn't ready to return home. Although she'd begun with tears, their day together seemed perfect. She wasn't sure she wished for it to end, to go back to Longbourn where Mr. Darcy would have time for everyone but her.

She looked up at the huge limbs of the oak, wondering if it was like the tree she and Miss Darcy had seen from the carriage, beautiful only because it stood alone. This tree, in a different season, had a different kind of beauty than that stark apparition, since it was clothed in green and surrounded by flowers. Taking in its symmetry, its near perfection, Elizabeth decided this oak would be stunning anywhere, in any season. Lowering her gaze, she found Mr. Darcy's eyes on her, oddly intent.

Elizabeth contemplated him, her mind turning over his last statement. Why had he sounded surprised Netherfield would be profitable? Not surprised she'd come up with a way to make it so, to her relief, but surprised the idea of purchasing it had merit. "You didn't think Netherfield was actually worth buying before?" she said with deceptive calm.

He met her gaze directly. "No. I didn't."

She supposed it was to his credit he didn't try to lie to her. "Why have you been working so hard then?"

"Because of you." One long stride closed the distance between them.

Elizabeth tilted her head back to look up at him. Again she saw the warmth in his eyes, but it was joined by a deeper emotion. She told herself she should step away. She was encouraging him by not, and that wasn't fair. Yet somehow, her feet wouldn't move.

"I've tried to do as you wished, to persuade myself I should be happy you refused me," he said.

Elizabeth recalled her words, regret sweeping through her. How could she have ordered him to do any such thing? She'd been angry, she knew. She sometimes let her temper get the best of her. She'd had cause, though, she reminded herself. She shook her head slightly to clear it. "What are you accomplishing by pretending you want to buy Netherfield Park?"

"It gives me an excuse to be here," he said. "To be near you."

A shiver of delight ran through her. She resisted the urge to shake her head again. "You haven't been courting me." Not until today, she added silently.

"No. Not directly." He reached up, as if he would stroke her cheek, but hesitated, returning his hand to his side.

Elizabeth was aware of a sharp disappointment, and slightly embarrassed by how her breath quickened at the thought of his touch. "Not directly?" she repeated, encouraging him to continue.

"I was ensuring I could learn to respect your family by coming to know them better, as I now comprehend the futility of offering for you if I don't care for those you love."

"And?" she asked, aware of an almost painful hope. He was right, it was his disdain for her family which had stood between them, even more so than his lack of respect for her.

"I have succeeded in that, and easily. Each member of your family has at least one strength, some of them many, though your mother was difficult to learn to respect."

"Because you held her in contempt," she said, taking a half step back. She folded her arms across her chest, not trying to conceal her own contempt, aware of disappointment pooling in the pit of her stomach.

"Because she is dead," he said gently. "I'm not going to lie to you. Your mother had characteristics I disdained. There is no point in listing them."

Elizabeth squeezed her lips into a tight line, the confusion of emotions swirling within her not overpowering the anger and disillusionment she felt. He hadn't changed. She'd thought he had, as she watched him with her family, but he was the same overly proud man who couldn't respect those she loved. The man she'd refused. Despairing, she felt almost near to tears again.

"I have learned some things about her I do respect," Mr. Darcy said.

"What are they?" she whispered, wanting to believe him. Although her mother had sometimes embarrassed her, she couldn't love a man who felt only disdain for her parent.

"She cared for her daughters' futures. She was hospitable. She had a great appreciation for beauty." He held out a hand. "And she raised two very remarkable daughters, and didn't do badly with the other three."

Thinking of Lydia's elopement, Elizabeth couldn't agree with him, and knew he was being kind. Yet, Lydia was apparently working hard now, and making a good living for herself. Mary and Kitty were much more reasonable than they had been. That hadn't been her mother, though. It was Charlotte who'd accomplished that. Mr. Darcy was being too kind. To her. For her. Reaching out, she took his hand, hopeful once more.

"Elizabeth, please permit me to extend an apology," he said. "I was wrong to propose the way I did. I know that now. I was wrong because I offended you, but more importantly, because I didn't respect your family. They do deserve respect. I want you to know I understand that."

"Thank you," she said.

He tugged gently on her hand, bringing her close once more. His fingers loosely intertwined with hers and she imagined she felt the warmth of his body, mere inches away. His height should have been intimidating so close, yet instead she felt the sureness of the strength in him. This was a man to be counted on, who would protect those he cared for.

"I told you once that I love you," he said, angling his head down nearer her own. "That hasn't changed."

Elizabeth searched his eyes, taking in the fervor and warm regard there. She opened her mouth, but could find no words to speak.

"Marry me, Elizabeth," he whispered, bringing his lips closer still.

"Yes."

He pulled her into his arms, kissing her, and all else fell away.

Darcy

Darcy held the reins loosely, pleased his horses were well trained because his driving was distracted. On the way to Netherfield Park, Elizabeth had sat on the edge of her seat, noticeably distant from him. Now, on the way back to Longbourn, she sat nearer, though they weren't quite touching. He wanted to stop the curricle and take her in his arms. He wanted to drive straight to London and see they were wed immediately. He wanted to make her his, forever, as soon as possible.

A bump in the road brought her closer. Counting on his horses' continued good behavior, he turned to her and smiled. He was rewarded by a radiant smile in return. Suddenly, her eyes shifted to something behind him. She frowned. Darcy swiveled his gaze, wondering what could merit the expression.

Over his shoulder, he spied the young shepherd and his flock. He turned back to her, confused. "You have altered your opinion on his theft of grazing ground? He has incurred your ire?"

"You went from the mantel right to the shepherd and shepherdess in the cabinet. You couldn't have seen them in the cabinet before, could hardly have noticed them on the mantel behind you when you came for your coat." She leveled a piercing gaze on him. "Did you help Lydia?"

Darcy grimaced before he could stop himself. He hadn't meant for Elizabeth to know. At least she hadn't found out until after she'd accepted him. "I . . ." He trailed off, unsure what to say.

Her eyes went wide, her lips twitching. Then, to his surprise, she began to laugh.

She laughed so freely, he couldn't help but smile. "I'm pleased to bring you such amusement."

"You," she gasped out, still laughing. She shook her head, swiping tears of joy from the corners of her eyes, obviously wishing to say more.

Darcy was delighted again, not having known his Elizabeth could laugh with such ease. He inwardly vowed he would make it a regular occurrence when they were alone together. "Yes, me," he offered, unsure what she wished to say.

She calmed herself, once again composed, but still smiled.

"I what?" he prompted, glancing back at the flock dwindling behind them.

"I can't tell you. It's too silly."

"We're to be wed. You may tell me anything of any persuasion of silliness."

"You'll think less of me," she said, but her happy expression didn't falter.

"Impossible," he stated, all the more intrigued.

She looked at him, her eyes merry. "When I accused you about the shepherd and shepherdess, you looked so . . . sheepish." She dissolved into mirth once more.

It was Darcy's turn to shake his head. "I was wrong. My opinion of you is forever altered. Miss Elizabeth Bennet, I had no notion you were one for puns."

"I know, it's very low of me," she said with a tilt of her chin and a glint of challenge in her eyes.

"I also, though I've often applauded your intelligence, didn't realize what a keen observer you are. Had I, I wouldn't have wandered over by those sheep."

Her look grew contemplative. "I assume my family doesn't know."

"The Gardiners do. Your uncle helped them find their first employee. Bingley as well, so you may assume your elder sister does. Some of Bingley's family is still in trade. He introduced them to a supplier and the man who recommended the building to them."

"And your role?"

"I bought the building. They're paying rent. I might even make a profit."

"Like with Netherfield Park?" she asked, looking a bit awed.

Her expression embarrassed him slightly. It was only money, after all. "Yes, much like Netherfield Park." He felt he had to be honest with her. "Except in the case of the Wickhams, I only did it partly for you. It was also partly for Mr. Wickham. My family made him what he is. I inherited my wealth, but I also inherited the consequences of that. I don't plan on bailing him out again, but in view of his heroic behavior during the fire, I felt it reasonable to try to give him another chance."

"You should have told me."

"I didn't want it to influence you."

"Why shouldn't it influence me to know I was being offered marriage by such a wonderful man?" she asked, compounding his embarrassment. "Isn't that precisely the sort of thing one should consider?"

He shrugged, turning his gaze back to the road and hoping his embarrassment didn't show.

"There's one other thing," she said. "I think you must pull to the side to hear it."

Slightly alarmed, he did so, resolving whatever it was, he would not be swayed from Elizabeth again. He turned to her, trying to hide his worry, which soon dissipated. The mischief was back in her eyes.

"What must I know so urgently?" he asked.

"You should know, Mr. Darcy, that you are a terrible man for all but ignoring me for the past two weeks."

"It wasn't quite two," he protested.

She held up a hand. "You should also know it taught me a valuable lesson." She slid across the seat until she was quite close. "I don't want to be ignored by you. I can't abide it. I won't. I love you, Mr. Darcy."

He couldn't help himself. Right there, in an open curricle on the side of the road for any passerby to see, he took Elizabeth in his arms and kissed her. He kept kissing her, uncaring and unaware if anyone saw, until the bleating of sheep brought him to his senses. The flock had caught up with them.

Reluctantly, he set her slightly away from him. "I need to speak with your father."

"I should hope so."

"And Elizabeth."

"Yes, Mr. Darcy?"

"I believe it would be appropriate for you to address me as Fitzwilliam."

She laughed, and Darcy drove them slowly back to Longbourn. They returned to a house filled with accusing looks, much to Darcy's dismay. Those were alleviated in mere moments by Elizabeth's radiant smile. All, that was, save for the one on Mr. Bennet's face.

"Mr. Darcy," he said. "I believe you would like to see me in my library."

"Yes, Mr. Bennet, I would," Darcy replied, calling on years of composure.

Mr. Bennet led the way into his library. Darcy hadn't yet been in, having kept himself quite occupied with Netherfield Park. He immediately noticed, among all the books and shelves, a well done and fairly recent drawing of the former Mrs. Bennet hanging on the wall beside Mr. Bennet's desk. Elizabeth's father took his chair, gesturing for Darcy to sit across from him. Darcy did, having the oddest feeling the image of the first Mrs. Bennet was smiling as she looked down on him, though inspection showed her expression to be inscrutable.

"So you want to marry Elizabeth?" Mr. Bennet asked.

Darcy turned from the portrait. "I do, sir, if I may have your permission."

"I gather from her expression and the rumor that preceded you home she has consented."

Again, Darcy called on his composure, not able to regret kissing Elizabeth, but sorry for any worry he may have caused. "She has."

"Does this mean you'll no longer pursue purchasing Netherfield Park?"

"I believe I will purchase Netherfield."

"You will?" Mr. Bennet seemed surprised.

"Yes, but why should my asking to wed Miss Elizabeth suggest to you I would no longer be interested in the property?"

"Charlotte thought you were here because of Elizabeth. She said neither of your ideas for Netherfield would be profitable enough for you to purchase it, once you'd gained my daughter's hand." Mr. Bennet appeared amused. "I'm not used to being married to someone who is smarter than I am, but she is. She doesn't read Greek or Latin, but she reads people."

"Your wife was correct, on all points, but today I decided I will still attempt to purchase Netherfield Park."

Mr. Bennet nodded. "Well, I'd best call them in." He stood up and went to the door of the library. "Lizzy, Charlotte. Come in here."

Darcy assumed they'd been waiting for the summons, as they appeared almost instantly. They came in, Darcy standing, and closed the door behind them. Both were smiling. Elizabeth mouthed something that looked suspiciously like, "Sir William Lucas saw us." Darcy winced, picturing Charlotte's father hurrying over with the news. They were all seated.

"Charlotte, my dear, you were right," Mr. Bennet said without preamble. "You correctly guessed why Mr. Darcy is here, but I'm wondering if I should give my permission for him to marry my daughter. I'm not certain Elizabeth should spend her life with someone who thinks it wise to spend his money either rebuilding a manor at Netherfield Park or turning it into farmland, especially after admitting he realizes neither idea will be profitable."

Mrs. Bennet tilted her head slightly, regarding her husband with an indulgent smile. "I think he can afford the loss. Perhaps it will teach him to invest more profitably in the future. At least he's intelligent enough to know the venture won't be profitable. We wouldn't want Elizabeth to wed a foolish man."

Darcy raised his eyebrows, aware he was being teased and not accustomed to the sensation. He was even less repentant for kissing Elizabeth on the roadside, though perhaps this was payment in kind.

"Charlotte, Papa, you are too cruel," Elizabeth said. "You know Mr. Darcy is not a foolish man."

"On the contrary," Mr. Bennet said. "I believe he may have behaved foolishly at least once already today, in view of the fact we are only now having this conversation."

Elizabeth blushed. "Papa."

Yes, Darcy thought, the teasing was definitely payment. It was also done in a kind fashion. He didn't want to be prideful, knowing where that had landed him in the past, but he felt Mr. Bennet planned to acquiesce. "May I defend myself by conveying it wouldn't be foolish in the slightest to purchase Netherfield Park?"

"You may attempt it, certainly," Mrs. Bennet said.

"Miss Bennet has suggested we divide the property in two, creating on each resulting portion a moderate sized estate more in keeping with the area," Darcy said. "The park is beautiful and if maintained, could be very attractive to both tenants. I feel the strength of this suggestion, when added to the overwhelming support I've found in the community for me to make the purchase, brings the project to validity."

Mr. Bennet appeared thoughtful, casting Elizabeth a pleased look.

"Why only two? Why not four or seven houses?" Mrs. Bennet asked.

"I think three would work," Elizabeth said, glancing at him. "Mr. Darcy, I know your surveyors are going to give you a proper map, but do you have a rough one?"

"I do. I'll retrieve it," Darcy said, standing. At that moment, he would prefer an answer from Mr. Bennet over a discussion of the property, but he would continue to play out their game of testing him. It was the least he could do to atone for his improper behavior on the roadside. He crossed the room and opened the door.

"Mr. Darcy," Mr. Bennet said.

Darcy paused in the doorway, turning back.

"In answer to your question, yes, of course, you have my permission to marry Elizabeth." Mr. Bennet smiled. "But get the map."

***

Later, Darcy was pleased that everyone else in the household mysteriously had business elsewhere and he and Elizabeth were given the parlor alone. He longed to pick back up where they'd left off in the curricle, but in view of his already questionable behavior, restrained himself to sitting beside her on the sofa with his arm around her and his free hand holding hers. He thought it was a good idea to have both of his hands occupied, as there were things he was tempted to do.

"I'm glad you get along with my father and Charlotte," she said.

"Now that I know them better, they are both remarkable people," he replied, toying with her elegant fingers. It was the first time they'd held hands without gloves on. He was enjoying the softness of her skin.

"Mmm," she said, snuggling closer to him.

"I've never been in this position before, but your father certainly has unconventional ways of giving permission for his daughters to marry."

Elizabeth smiled up at him, her lips enticingly near. "Jane's husband was told to tell no one of their engagement and allowed secret meetings."

"Mr. Wickham got a cold letter confirming the financial arrangements," he said.

"And you got four people in a room poring over a map."

"Instead of a financial discussion, which I believe is normal."

"You have to admit, Charlotte's ideas about Netherfield Park were good," she said with an impish smile.

"So were yours." Unable to resist, he kissed her, long and delightfully. "Everything about you is good."

Epilogue

~ Thirty Years Later ~

Elizabeth

Elizabeth Darcy walked into 'Wickham's Hats' to find Mr. Wickham occupied with a customer. She was mildly amused at how he flirted with the elderly woman, undoubtedly a wealthy dowager from her bearing and dress. Wickham was still handsome, in spite of the lines on his face and the gray in his hair. He glanced toward the door, where Elizabeth stood, and cast her a quick smile. Not breaking off conversation, he reached over and pulled a cord.

Familiar with this routine, Elizabeth turned to greet her sister Lydia as she came out of the back. Lydia hadn't aged as well as Wickham had. There was more white in her hair and her face bore an excess of creases, both from laughter and sorrow. Elizabeth hugged her and the two of them went into the workroom in the back of the shop.

She made these visits to Lydia on a monthly basis when she was in London. Elizabeth had been expressly forbidden by her husband from giving the Wickhams money unless there was an unusual need, which there never had been. This was the only time Darcy had ever been insistent with her. So instead, she visited, as a form of penance for not helping her sister, even when she watched them spend some of their savings when Wickham's Hats briefly went out of fashion. Elizabeth did buy her hats from Lydia, but that wasn't a penance, since Darcy understood Lydia's hats were flattering. Sometimes, when she was expected, Lydia would bring out a hat she had made for Elizabeth.

After admiring and buying a creation, which Elizabeth knew was well worth the price, they settled down to talk. Normally, they spoke of customers, who bought what hat for what engagement. Today, Elizabeth had family news and was hoping for a change in conversational pace.

"You don't have to tell me the news," Lydia said as soon as they reached the back of the shop. "I know Edward's wife had a second son. Kitty wrote me."

"Yes. He was named William Charles Bennet," Elizabeth said, taking in the industry of the three women working at tables about the room. A fourth table, presumably Lydia's, stood unoccupied but cluttered.

"I suppose the Charles is in honor of his grandmother, Charlotte," Lydia said.

Elizabeth nodded. "But it's also a nod to Mr. Bingley."

"And the William is after Charlotte's father, Sir William Lucas, not after William Collins."

"I'd almost forgotten about him," Elizabeth said, not having thought of their cousin Mr. Collins in years. "I have no idea what happened to him or if he's even alive."

"It hardly matters with three male heirs to Longbourn ahead of him."

"No, it doesn't." Elizabeth was glad she and her sister could speak of Mr. Collins without anger. It had taken time for the sorrow and resentment to fade, but thirty years had passed since their mother's death. Elizabeth still missed her, but in a mild way, less now for herself than for her mother. Mama would have enjoyed seeing how their lives had turned out.

"William is another relative I haven't seen," Lydia said with a trace of bitterness, her thoughts obviously not in parallel with Elizabeth's. "Edward is my brother, but I see him less than once a year."

"Can't you take time off? He's quite busy with his family and managing Longbourn," Elizabeth said, realizing Lydia was in one of her less cheerful moods.

"No. I thought with running our own business we could, but it doesn't work that way. No matter how many hours a week we're open, our customers want us to be open more, even those who buy only two hats a year. Besides, even when we aren't open, I have to make hats. Even with my helpers here and a woman who makes cloth flowers at home, I'm working longer hours than the store is open." Lydia sighed, casting a look at the women working nearby. "Let's go upstairs."

Elizabeth nodded. She appreciated that it soothed Lydia to complain of her circumstances, and that it was likely best not to do so in front of those they employed.

Lydia gave instructions to the three women before leading the way to the upper floor, where she and Wickham lived. Elizabeth looked about the plain, now familiar parlor. The only ornaments were the ceramic shepherd, shepherdess, and sheep. Charlotte had given them to Lydia some years ago. Lydia moved to the sitting area, Elizabeth following. The furniture was worn, and hadn't been of good quality when it was new.

"George gets time off when the shop is closed, but I keep working," Lydia said in an aggrieved tone as they sat down. She stared at nothing for a short time before sighing again. "I'm being unfair. He does do much of the heavy work around here. It's too expensive to hire a manservant." Lydia rubbed at her hands, more coarse and bent than her age warranted. "I can't visit Longbourn. I'm working whenever I can. We're trying to save enough so we can live on it if people stop liking our hats again, but it seems whenever we put away more money, prices go up."

"But you go out, don't you?"

"Every Sunday, if it isn't raining. If we miss Sunday, we go out on an evening during the week. We stroll outside the opera or at other fashionable places. I have to see stylish people, to know what's in style, and wear hats, to attract business. We're lucky we live close enough to walk to enough places."

"You don't enjoy it?" Elizabeth asked, distressed for her sister. She'd always had the impression Lydia loved London.

"I do. For years, George didn't enjoy it. I think it used to seem to him he was being taunted by what he couldn't have. Now, he seems pleased to go out. I think he's become what he at first only pretended to be with customers. Every woman is beautiful if she's wearing the right hat. He's respectful to all their male companions, be they father, husband, son, brother or lover." She shook her head. "He's not pretending any more. Sometimes I miss the old George, the one who thought he was better than everyone."

"And the old Lydia?" Elizabeth suggested, thinking her sister must miss being naïve and free of care.

"She was a fool. I'm much better the way I am now. I have no regrets."

Elizabeth tried to hide her skepticism, but Lydia's eyes narrowed.

"I don't, Lizzy," she said. She smiled slightly, still rubbing her hands. "Oh, I would have liked to have had children, but not everyone is blessed." Her eyes took on a distant look. "There is an advantage to hiring helpers. When they don't work out, they go. If I'd trained my own children, they might not have met my standards and I would still have had to keep them. So, perhaps it's better we didn't manage any. They'd be grown and gone by now, either way, so I'm content enough."

"But you are happy, Lydia? Really?"

"Yes. I am happy to be my own person, even if I must work hard for it."

Elizabeth wanted to believe her. She looked down at her own hands, encased in fine gloves, but still smooth and elegant beneath. Still able to play the pianoforte with Georgiana when she visited, or alone in the evenings for Darcy, now that their children were rarely home. Could Lydia truly be happy with the life she'd made for herself?

"I can see you don't believe me," Lydia said. She shrugged. "I'm not saying there aren't things I miss."

"Like what?" Elizabeth said, offering a smile.

"Longbourn partridges. Our cook did a wonderful job with them." Her eyes took on a dreamy cast, and Elizabeth could see the old Lydia for a moment before her gaze refocused. "I suppose the recipe has been lost."

"It hasn't been. You remember Sally Smith?"

"Sally Smith?"

"The girl Charlotte hired right after Netherfield Park burned down. Longbourn's cook taught her all she knew." Elizabeth smiled, thinking of little Sally Smith now, grown and a wonderful cook. So wonderful, multiple attempts had been made to secure her services elsewhere, but Sally was loyal to Longbourn.

"Yes, now I remember," Lydia said. "I thought Char-little didn't allow fancy dishes."

Elizabeth smiled slightly at the old nickname. "One dish, every now and then. Sally learned them all."

"And she's still cooking at Longbourn?"

Elizabeth nodded. "She never married and is saving for her old age. Edward has to pay her well because several families have tried to lure her away. Even Darcy has threatened to hire her."

Lydia smiled politely, but Elizabeth could tell she didn't enjoy references to Darcy's wealth and quickly changed the subject. They returned to the safer topics of who had been in to buy hats, and what they'd selected. Lydia had developed an uncanny ability to discern what was going on in people's lives simply based on what hats they chose.

After an hour, Elizabeth rose to leave. She hugged Lydia, who still seemed sadder than usual. "You're sure you're well?"

Lydia smiled slightly. "Miss Bingley was in again yesterday. You know how sour she's become, especially since she was widowed. I daresay it's mostly her son's fault. He holds the purse strings tight, ungrateful wretch, and requires she wear only black at all times, even in private." Lydia shook her head at that. "I think she'd like to be fashionable again, but she can't offend her son, as the late Lord Hays left him most everything. When she comes here, she tries on almost every hat in the place, looking in the mirror for hours, but only buys the ones with black crepe. She once told Wickham she longs to wear prettier things, but doesn't dare."

"Yes, you told me," Elizabeth said gently.

Lydia nodded. "The truth is, Lizzy, I do work hard, and maybe I did make mistakes, but my life is a good one. Who's to say how it would have turned out if I'd made other decisions? I'm happy where I am now. At least I can be what I want in my own home and not follow society's rules." She smiled once more, and this time the expression carried greater sincerity.

They embraced again and returned to the shop, where Elizabeth selected a lovely hat. She left reassured, promising to come back soon. She returned to Darcy House, looking forward to an evening with her husband. She knew he would even enjoy her showing him the hat she'd bought.

Later, seated on a sofa leaning against Darcy, who had his arm around her, she detailed the visit, knowing he liked to be aware of how the Wickhams were getting along. "They are saving," she said in conclusion. "Lydia told me once, about a year ago, if they had to stop working, they would still have an income of four or five hundred pounds a year. She also told me Wickham's goal is to earn enough to match the income from the living your father willed him."

"It was six hundred pounds a year. The land attached to the living brings in more."

Elizabeth nodded, smiling, knowing why. Without telling her, something he seemed apt to do when being generous, Darcy had helped both Mary's husband and the holder of the living Wickham was once to have, when he'd married Kitty. Darcy had asked them to be part of an experiment on sheep breeding, saying he would cover their losses. Far from losing money, the project was successful, and the sheep on their properties, as well as on the Bingleys', brought in more money than other sheep in the area. Elizabeth reached for Darcy's free hand, wondering how she'd been so lucky in her husband. "Who would have thought Wickham would be such a hard worker," she mused.

"Not I," Darcy said. "I'd given up on him, even when I helped him start the business."

Elizabeth snuggled against him. They'd discussed these things before, but she didn't mind hearing again. Especially when he told the stories of how he had, in his way, moved heaven and earth to win her.

"At the time I thought it was worth it, for your sake, even if he failed in business." He leaned over and kissed her.

"At the time?" she asked when he pulled away, arching an eyebrow.

He smiled down at her, still heart-flutteringly handsome, especially to her eyes. "Yes, at the time I did." He kissed her again. "And I still do."

~ The End ~

About the Authors

Renata McMann

Renata McMann is the pen name of Teresa McCullough, someone who likes to rewrite public domain works. She is fond of thinking "What if?" To learn more about Renata's work and collaborations, visit **www.renatamcmann.com**.

Summer Hanford

Starting in 2014, Summer was offered the privilege of partnering with fan fiction author Renata McMann on her well-loved *Pride and Prejudice* variations. More information on these works is available at **www.renatamcmann.com**.

Summer is currently partnering with McMann as well as writing solo works in Regency Romance and Fantasy. She lives in New York with her husband and compulsory, deliberately spoiled, cats. The newest addition to their household is an energetic setter-shepherd mix…not yet appreciated by any of the three cats. For more about Summer, visit **www.summerhanford.com**.

Get Your Thank You Gift! Sign Up for Our Mailing List Today!

Visit: **www.renatamcmann.com/news/**

Made in the USA
Monee, IL
23 November 2020

49289003R00132